The Guru of Love

Books by Samrat Upadhyay

ARRESTING GOD IN KATHMANDU

THE GURU OF LOVE

The Guru of Love

Samrat Upadhyay

HOUGHTON MIFFLIN COMPANY

BOSTON • NEW YORK 2003

Copyright © 2003 by Samrat Upadhyay
All rights reserved

For information about permission to reproduce selections from
this book, write to Permissions, Houghton Mifflin Company,
215 Park Avenue South, New York, New York 10003.

Visit our Web site: www.houghtonmifflinbooks.com.

Library of Congress Cataloging-in-Publication Data
Upadhyay, Samrat, date.
The guru of love / Samrat Upadhyay.
p.   cm.
ISBN 0-618-24727-0
1. Triangles (Interpersonal relations) — Fiction. 2. Mathematics
teachers — Fiction. 3. Tutors and tutoring — Fiction. 4. Married
people — Fiction. 5. Adultery — Fiction. 6. Nepal — Fiction.
I. Title.
PR9570.N43 G8 2003
823'.92 — dc21   2002032234

Printed in the United States of America

Book design by Robert Overholtzer

QUM 10 9 8 7 6 5 4 3 2 1

Excerpt from "Try to Praise the Mutilated World" from *Without
End: New and Selected Poems* by Adam Zagajewski, translated
by Clare Cavanagh. Copyright © 2002 by Adam Zagajewski.
Translation copyright © 2002 by FSG, LLC. Reprinted by
permission of Farrar, Straus and Giroux, LLC.

TO BABITA

Praise the mutilated world
and the gray feather a thrush lost,
and the gentle light that strays and vanishes
and returns.

—ADAM ZAGAJEWSKI,
"Try to Praise the Mutilated World"

ACKNOWLEDGMENTS

The energy to write this book came from
the birth of my daughter, Shahzadi. I am also
blessed to have an editor like Heidi Pitlor,
whose enthusiasm for my work has made me,
in the words of the poet Rumi, "like someone
suddenly born into color." Thanks to my
agent, Eric Simonoff, and Janklow & Nesbit.
I am grateful for the support of the English
department at Baldwin-Wallace College,
and especially thankful to my student Stacey
Clemence for combing through the first
drafts. Finally, I am heartened to belong to
a family that believes in my writing without
having to read it: Ammi, Buwa, Sangeeta,
Arup, Babu, Chotu, Mummy, and Hajur.

The Guru of Love

1

. . . .

THIN AS A WAIF, she wore a faded kurta suruwal. She stood in the doorway of Ramchandra's bedroom, where he tutored his students. "I am very weak in math, sir," she said as he gestured for her to sit next to him on a cushion on the floor.

To ward off the chill, unusual for late September, she also wore the traditional khasto shawl. She had long eyelashes and a slim nose; fine fur dotted her upper lip. Her hair, glistening with oil, was pulled back in a prim style. Malati, she said, was her name, and she appeared slightly older, past her teens, than the students he normally tutored.

"I charge five hundred rupees a month," he said. "Three sessions a week, one hour each."

A shadow came over her face.

"Can't you afford that?" Ramchandra drew the electric heater close to him, even though he had a blanket wrapped around him and was wearing the thick socks that Goma had sewed for him. The walls of this old house, where Ramchandra rented his flat, were thin, and on a chilly day like this, harbinger of the cold that would soon envelop the city, the entire house became almost unbearable. One of the coils of the heater had come loose, and it protruded dangerously, still glowing red. He'd have to fix it soon, before the children burned themselves on it, before the coming months of winter, when "even the fish feel cold," as Ramchandra's mother used to say.

"I come from a poor family," she said.

Ramchandra glanced out the small window. From his seated position, he could see the electric and telephone wires zigzagging outside his window. A kite swooped in the tiny blue patch of sky. Dashain festival was here, which meant more expenses.

His tutees had often cited their poverty, even those who came from well-to-do families, as their reason for defaulting on their payments. Well, he wasn't rolling in money either. He and Goma and the children were living on the top floor of this old house, with its rickety stairs and cracked ceilings, its cramped, dank rooms that never got enough sunlight, this house controlled by a landlord who came rapping on the door if the rent wasn't paid on time, where deafening traffic from the street penetrated the thin walls, shook the rooms, and made reasonable thinking impossible. For years he'd been harboring the dream of buying some land and building a house in the city, if only to silence his in-laws. For the past three years, he and Goma had been putting away five hundred rupees a month. Or at least trying to; some months, especially during the festivals, not only could they not save, but they had to dip into their savings, which troubled Ramchandra constantly. "This way we'll never build a house," he'd said to Goma dejectedly the other day after he'd checked his bankbook and discovered that the balance was not even a lakh rupee. A few months ago, he'd even looked at some plots of land, but most of them had been exorbitantly priced. There was one plot, near Dillibazaar, that was nice—close to the vegetable market and to the bus station—but the seller wanted five lakh rupees. Ramchandra had told him that no reasonable fool would buy the plot at that price, but as he walked away, he knew that the land would be sold within a few months. Many people were getting rich in Kathmandu. The country was poor, but in the capital, wealth was multiplying in the hands of those who'd opened new businesses or those with government jobs who didn't turn away from hefty bribes.

With her worn-out clothes, Malati indeed looked poor, unlike his only other tutee, Ashok, a merchant's son who arrived every morning in a shiny black car, with loud music thumping from the speakers.

"I don't have a father," Malati told him. "And my mother raises chickens to support the family."

"Then perhaps you should be working," Ramchandra said. "Help your family."

"Right now I am not in a position to work, sir," she said solemnly. "Besides, I want to go to college." And for that, she needed to pass the School Leaving Certificate exam. She admitted that she'd barely passed the preliminary Sent-Up exams, administered by her school, and was worried about the actual exams.

"What's the point of going to college when you need some income right now?"

She pursed her lips and glanced out the window.

She is pretty, he thought. But it was her determination that moved him. If he could help her, then it was his duty as a teacher to take her on. In the afternoons he taught at the rundown Kantipur School, with its crumbling walls and dark, crowded classrooms. It was a government school, which meant that it had a meager budget and disgruntled teachers. Most of them, like Ramchandra, tutored students on the side for extra income. These days, he was tutoring only Ashok, and he could have Malati join their sessions. "Okay, how much can you afford?"

"Two hundred rupees, sir."

"That's too little," he said, thinking of his bank account. "I can tutor you for only two sessions a week for that."

"That's fine, sir," she said. "I can do the rest on my own."

"I'll need the money first."

"I'll bring it tomorrow morning."

There was an awkward silence. He expected her to leave, and when she didn't, he was about to say, "Okay, then." But she asked, "Sir, are you from Kathmandu itself?"

He studied her a bit more closely. People from Kathmandu rarely asked each other that question. Only outsiders probed one another, searching for something that bonded them in the city.

"Originally from Lamjung," he said. After his father died, he and his mother had sold their land and house in Lamjung to pay off creditors and had come to Kathmandu, with his mother's jewelry in a plastic bag and with the address of a distant relative. Mother, God bless her. He hoped her soul was at peace in heaven.

"I knew," Malati said. "I knew you were not from here. Your face tells it."

"Is it really that obvious?"

"Well, couldn't you say the same about me? Where do you think I'm from, sir?"

He had no idea, but he was amused by her excitement. "Jumla?"

His mention of this remote, barren area in the northwest part of the country made her laugh. "You like to joke, don't you, sir. No, I'm from Dharan."

"When did you move here?"

"A few years ago. But I still miss it. People in this city are so . . ."—she seemed to be searching for the appropriate word —"unfeeling."

Ramchandra's own memories of Lamjung remained clear: the general store in a mud house perched dangerously on top of a hill; the biting cold in the morning; the haze that hung over the hills, and the clouds that rolled in and made the house in front of you disappear; the smell of sweet rice cooked in the mud oven, the smoke stinging his mother's eyes and making water run down her nose. But it was the memories of his early years in Kathmandu, the hardships he and his mother had endured, that were imprinted on his mind like a religious text. For a long time he had been angry at the city for making their lives difficult. But he'd grown to love the city, and although he understood what Malati was saying, he didn't want to identify with her sense of helplessness. "It's been so many years," he told her, "that I consider myself a local of Kathmandu."

"Of course, sir. Still, this city can really make you suffer."

Tears started to well up in her eyes and, strangely, he was moved. He asked, "Do you want to sit down? Have some tea?"

She composed herself. "No, sir, I have something to attend to." As she was leaving, she smiled at him, revealing small white teeth. "I've heard you're very good, sir."

Ramchandra waved his hand in the air.

Malati turned out to be very poor in math. She'd mull over a problem for a long time, often missing the most obvious connections. When he'd explain a problem and hint at a possible solution, she'd nod slowly and chew her lower lip, as if everything were sinking in, but when it was time to solve the problem, she'd scratch her head and tighten her eyebrows, unable to move beyond the most rudimentary step. In contrast, Ashok, whose math skills Ramchandra had previously considered weak, now appeared bright. "Addition," Ramchandra would gently say to Malati. "You need to add the interest to the principal, not subtract it. Don't you see?" And slowly recognition appeared on her face, as if to say, "Why didn't I see that before?" Then she would nod, her head bobbing up and down. But that understanding soon proved false, and the next moment she would frown and chew her pencil's eraser.

One morning, two weeks after she'd started, Malati was stumped on a particular problem that they'd gone over repeatedly. Ramchandra slammed down his pencil on her notebook with the neatly written numbers. "Even a monkey from the Pashupatinath Temple would be able to solve such a simple problem." He jabbed a finger at the air in front of her. "You're not a monkey, are you?" Malati looked down at her toes, her face red. Ashok smiled at him in disbelief, and Ramchandra's wife, Goma, who had come in to collect empty tea glasses, shot him a glance.

He was about to say something conciliatory to Malati when she, still looking down, said in a strong voice, "I told you my math is poor. That's why I'm here. That's why I need help."

"Okay," he said slowly. "Let's look at this from another angle."

Ashok was still smiling, watching Ramchandra closely.

"Is my face going to get you a pass in the S.L.C.?" Ramchandra asked him.

For the rest of the session, Malati remained quiet. Mechanically, she did what Ramchandra asked her to do, her lips pursed, and when it came time for her to solve a compound interest problem on her own, she said, "I have a headache. I'll go home now."

"Still fifteen minutes left, Malati."

"Didn't I just tell you I have a headache?" she said, and quickly got up and went down the stairs.

A sense of remorse plagued Ramchandra throughout the afternoon, when he was teaching at school; throughout the evening, when he came home, tired, and tutored a student and, later, played snakes and ladders with his son; and into the night, when he tried to sleep. This lingering guilt surprised him. Ramchandra rarely scolded his students, and he never hit them, as many of his colleagues did. But he also knew that it was necessary to protect his dignity as a teacher, so at times he would verbally discipline students for being unruly, as the older ones were likely to be. The issue of discipline had never arisen with those he tutored at home; this was the first time he'd scolded anyone. But Malati's reaction to his disparaging her went beyond the shame a student might feel at being scolded. Somehow he'd wounded her deeply.

Ramchandra also regretted that he'd wasted the rest of her session, during which more could have been accomplished. He prided himself on the number of his tutees who went on to pass the S.L.C. exam. Sometimes it took only minutes for a student to move from one level to another. That's why Ramchandra, no matter how tired he was, insisted that his students stay the full time they were scheduled for. This was especially important in the case of Ashok, who often came up with all kinds of excuses to leave early. With Malati, it was even more crucial, because it was difficult for her to pay her fee.

In the dark of night, Ramchandra pulled his sirak closer around himself and stared at the ceiling, unable to sleep. Lately, he'd been having a repeated nightmare, in which he couldn't solve a simple algebra equation in front of his students. He attributed the dream to his heavy load of tutoring and teaching.

Ramchandra had discovered his skills in math early. When he was in the dangerously situated general store in Lamjung with his mother, he'd quickly deduct the cost of the kilo of lentils from the five- or ten-rupee note that she'd just handed to the vendor, and announce, loudly, "Need to return two rupees and twenty paisa." He'd solve math problems so fast on the small slate his father had given him that his father would say, "Wait, wait, before you erase it; let me see if you did that correctly." And Ramchandra would hand over the slate and grab a pencil and a notebook to scribble something else.

Later, after he and his mother had moved to Kathmandu, he would see a storekeeper in a spice shop laboriously scrawl the items and the prices. But the numbers would zoom inside Ramchandra's head, and he'd announce, in his sullen voice, "Total, seven rupees and fifty paisa." Often the shopkeeper would squint at him and, in jest, offer him a job as his assistant. He'd want to take the offer, but his mother would always say no, that she wouldn't dream of putting her son to work until he'd finished school. "I want you to be an engineer," she said. She seemed particularly bent on engineering, either because she liked the foreign-sounding word or she associated it with mathematics. "Engineer, yes," she would say. "You'll build things."

Once he started attending school, in a crowded little classroom in Kathmandu, not too far from where he was now teaching, his hand would shoot up every time a math problem was put on the board. Eventually, the teacher started eyeing him with resentment. His friends gave him the nickname Hisabey Hanuman, because his prowess in math equaled the strength of the monkey god Hanuman, who uprooted an entire mountain, held it up on his palm, and flew.

How odd, thought Ramchandra, that he'd called Malati a monkey when he himself had been called a monkey in his youth. In college, when Ramchandra was called to the board to solve a calculus problem that gave the professor a headache, he knew that teaching would be the natural profession for him. And it was, for the most part, but the tutoring sessions wore him out. These days before falling asleep, he'd try to ward off nightmares by visualizing pleasant scenes, like a walk by a blue pond, a bountiful garden, cool mountain air. But Malati's voice, saying, "That's why I'm here. That's why I need help," kept ringing in his ears.

Tonight, his tossing and turning awoke Goma, who asked, "What's the matter?"

He said maybe he'd had too much tea that day.

She turned on the light. "That girl is bothering you. You should think before you speak. Serves you right."

"I'm tired," he said. "It's hard enough, teaching full time at that hellhole, and then tutoring these students day and night."

"Still," Goma said, "she's a young girl, and very sensitive. Treat her gently. Think of her as your own daughter."

"And who'll treat me gently?" he asked. "Who can I turn to for comfort?" He took her hand.

She placed her other palm on his forehead and said, "Why don't I rub your head for a while? You'll feel better."

He put his head in her lap, and she massaged his face, her smooth fingers gliding across his temples lulling him into a drowsy state. Through half-open eyes he looked at her face. Goma was a small, chubby woman, only a few months younger than he, and he was reaching forty-two. On her forehead was the small red tika she got every morning at the Ganeshthan Temple in the neighborhood. Before the sun's rays fell upon the streets, she would go to the temple with a plate of rice and with flowers she'd picked in the courtyard garden. She'd return home just as the sun's rays lit the window of the house on the opposite side of the courtyard. A large mole sat right below the bridge of her nose, her "beauty spot," Ramchandra called it.

"You don't need to keep taking on tutees, you know," Goma said.

"If I don't, how will we pay for the expenses of Dashain and Tihar?" Dashain was only a week away, with Tihar chasing at its heels. It meant that Ramchandra had to dip into his savings to get new clothes for the family, plus at least a hen, if not a goat, for sacrifice to the goddess. In fact, this year he was going to argue against buying a goat, which would cost several hundred rupees. He'd thought of suggesting to Goma and Rakesh and Sanu that they satisfy themselves with a hen, but of course everyone would be disappointed, and neighbors and relatives would talk, especially his in-laws. What else could he do, though? Right now he had only Goma to convince. The children tended to absorb Goma's feelings and mirror them, so if she felt the family couldn't afford more than a hen, they'd reconcile themselves.

"Without the tutees, how will we get out of this hellhole?" Ramchandra asked. "How will we ever build a house of our own?"

Goma put her index finger to her lips. Sanu, thirteen, and her brother, Rakesh, nine, were sleeping in the next room. But as if to support his argument, a horn blared outside, tires screeched, followed by a bang and the revving of an engine. Both Goma and Ramchandra instinctively closed their eyes.

"You can't seem to utter a sentence without using the word *hellhole* these days," Goma said.

"Well, what do you call this?" He waved a hand.

"I'm not unhappy here," she said.

"Your parents are unhappy that you're here."

Over the years, he'd become more bold when speaking of her parents, even though he knew that his complaints made Goma uncomfortable. They had never taken a liking to Ramchandra, even though they had chosen him as their son-in-law. When Ramchandra and Goma got married, he was still living with his mother, in an even smaller flat in Thamel. At that time he was attending Tri Chandra College and, on the side, tutoring students, one of whom was Goma's sister, Nalini.

The marriage proposal had come as a surprise, a few months after Nalini took the S.L.C. exam.

"The proposal is not for Nalini?" he'd asked his mother.

"No, it's for her older sister."

He'd seen Goma at her parents' house only a few times, when she passed by the room where he was tutoring Nalini, but now he couldn't recall her face clearly. He did remember noting that she was prettier than Nalini, who had a sad, deprived look.

"Why would they want to give their daughter to someone like me?" he asked his mother. Usually, he tutored his students in his small apartment, but the Pandeys had asked him to come to their house, and since they offered him a hundred rupees more than he usually got, he'd gone. He'd been intimidated by the grandeur of the house, by the stern look on Mr. Pandey's face. But he needed the money, and he found Nalini an easy student to tutor.

His mother suggested that maybe his reputation as a bright student had led Goma's parents to give their daughter to him, knowing that he was poor. Perhaps they believed that, with his intelligence, he'd soon occupy a position that was lucrative and that their daughter would live in luxury. Perhaps they were impressed by his behavior when he tutored their younger daughter. "This is a great honor for our family," his mother had said. "Perhaps our hard days are over."

At the time he married her, Ramchandra didn't even know that Goma was his age. When his mother showed him her picture, he recalled her face more clearly, and a sweetness entered his heart, and he said yes. The age factor had never bothered him, and it didn't bother him now, although he was annoyed whenever relatives referred to it, as if it were fundamentally wrong for the wife to be the same age as the husband. One relative had said, "Seven years' difference; that's the best. Our ancient texts say that a difference of seven years helps the harmony between the husband and wife." The man had looked affectionately at his wife, who, exactly seven years younger, was chewing pan, which made the inside of her mouth bright red. She had established herself as a petty gossipmonger, belittling those who had less than she did. Ramchandra didn't know which ancient texts the relative was referring to, but Hindu texts were often sprinkled with such petty advice. "I don't believe in those rules and myths," Ramchandra had replied, and the relative, still smiling at his wife, had said, "This is our culture."

In moments of quiet Ramchandra did wonder why Goma hadn't married earlier, when she was in her early twenties, when she could have been easily negotiated into a well-to-do family. Had she done something scandalous when she was young? he wondered. Although when he looked at his wife—the devotional tika on her forehead, her straightforward, sweet manner with him and their children—he knew that he was sinful in even thinking such things about her.

Ramchandra was in a classroom in the basement of a dark building, wearing his dirty dark-blue shorts and stained sky-blue shirt. Suddenly the teacher's whip came slashing through the air and struck him across the face, where it became numbers, problems, and he couldn't, no matter how hard he tried, solve them. The other students, in their recently laundered uniforms and ties, mocked him, and Ramchandra called for his mother, "Ama, ama," and woke to discover that Rakesh was crying out for his mother from the next room. Goma, who usually awoke at the slightest noise, was fast asleep. Ramchandra hurried to the children's room, but he didn't turn on the light lest it disturb Sanu. She was awake, though, and said, "Ba, I think he had a nightmare." Ramchandra sat beside Rakesh, who was whimpering, and stroked his hair, trying to calm him. Gradually, the boy became quiet and then asked, "Ba, what am I going to get for Dashain?"

"What do you want, my son?"

"A bicycle."

"Bicycle is too expensive. How about a toy bicycle?"

Rakesh made a face. "All of my friends have bicycles."

Ramchandra turned to Sanu. "And what do you want?"

"Nothing," she said. Every day Sanu seemed to be growing more aware of the financial restrictions of her family. "And he doesn't need a bicycle either."

Rakesh started arguing with her, and, fearing that they'd wake Goma, Ramchandra raised his hand and said, "I can give you a nice story right now. Free of cost."

"If he gets a bicycle, then I too need something big," Sanu said.

"We'll deal with that later," Ramchandra said. "Now the story. In a distant land a long time ago there was a poor girl," Ramchandra began. He spoke softly so that Goma wouldn't wake up. The naked bulb hanging from the ceiling in the corridor revealed the outlines of his children.

This girl, Ramchandra continued, was seventeen years old and lived with her mother in a hut. The roof of the hut leaked in the monsoon rains, and the entire mud floor became flooded.

They were so poor that they ate only one meal each day, usually in the evening by the fire, and the girl's stomach rumbled during the night.

"Will this be a sad story?" Sanu asked.

"Maybe. Just listen."

"What was her name? The girl?"

Ramchandra was stumped. Then he said, "Malati."

"But Malati is your student," Rakesh said.

"Do you want to hear the story or not?"

Rakesh became quiet, and Ramchandra continued. The girl always thought about her father, who had left the village a few years ago in search of a job in the city and had never returned. When she went to cut grass for their cow, whose milk they sold for money to get by, she stared out at the horizon, hoping to see her father return, his pockets filled with money and gifts of jewelry for her and her mother. Each night, as she lay on the mat on the floor where they slept, she listened for the knock on the door that would signal his arrival. In her dreams he would appear, well-fed and prosperous, in the city, missing his daughter.

One day, the richest merchant in the village came to their hut and asked the mother for her daughter's hand in marriage. "Your daughter is very beautiful," said the merchant, who had a long mustache, which trickled down his chin. "She is also a hard worker, so she will make a good wife." The mother was delighted. In her mind she saw herself in a bright, gold-studded sari, wearing a diamond necklace, with five servants ready at her command. The girl was not happy. The merchant was her father's age, and she didn't like the way his eyes glinted when he looked at her.

Ramchandra didn't know where to go from here, so he stopped, but the children pestered him to continue. "And they lived happily ever after," he said.

"Who lived happily ever after?" Sanu asked. "The merchant and the girl? But she doesn't like him! That's no story."

"Shhh, you'll wake up Mother," Ramchandra said. "We'll continue tomorrow." And despite their protests, he tucked them under the blanket and left.

In the next room, Goma was awake and bleary-eyed. "I was so tired I didn't even hear. Did Rakesh have a nightmare?"

"Yes, and I told him a story."

"Which one?"

"I made one up."

"About what?"

"Nothing." He snuggled close to her. "It was a nonsense children's story."

2

· · · · · · ·

MALATI DIDN'T APPEAR at the next session,
and Ramchandra couldn't focus on Ashok,
who smiled and kept repeating, "I wonder what happened to
that girl." After he left, Ramchandra changed from his suruwal
to his cotton pants, the ones he'd had tailored two years ago.
They were already beginning to fray at the bottom, and Goma
had been pestering him to have a new pair made, but he'd re-
sisted, immediately calculating the cost: at least fifty rupees for
the cloth, another fifty for the tailor. The shirt he wore had a
hole in the chest, but Goma had darned it a few months ago,
and people would have to look closely before they'd notice it.
The ready-made, fine nylon shirt he had received from his in-
laws during last year's Dashain festival hung in the closet, un-
worn. He had fingered the fine cloth a few times, but had never
put it on; this was the only way he could strike back at their
criticism of his poverty. Just the other day, Mrs. Pandey had

mentioned a schoolteacher, a relative, who had moved from a crummy school to a more prestigious one run by the wife of a well-known businessman. "When's that going to happen to our son-in-law?" she said, not looking at Ramchandra but at Goma. And Mr. Pandey had said, as if Ramchandra weren't present, "Keep dreaming, wife. It's been so many years, and still nothing."

He called to Goma in the kitchen that he was going for a walk, and before she could respond, he headed down the stairs, noticing that one wooden board creaked dangerously under his weight.

Malati had told him that she lived in the neighborhood of Tangal, right behind the Sunrise Boarding School, and Ramchandra began to walk in that direction. But it was already eight-thirty, and if he wanted to see her, get back home for lunch, and make it to school on time, he'd have to take a three-wheeler. He contemplated turning back. What was the point of spending his hard-earned money on this girl? But he needed to see her, say something to her. He hailed a three-wheeler, in his head deducting the nearly seven rupees' fare from his savings account, and gave the driver directions.

The wind whipped inside the small cab, and Ramchandra tightened the muffler around his face. The driver drove at breakneck speed, often missing bicycles and pedestrians by inches. Ramchandra leaned forward and shouted into the driver's ear, "Slow down. What's the hurry?"

"You think you're the only passenger I'll have today?" the driver said.

It was impossible to talk reasonably to anyone nowadays, thought Ramchandra. It wasn't like this even ten years ago, when civility existed among the Kathmandu people. Within the last few years, the city had swollen to such a point that it was ready to explode. People from the hills and mountains to the north and the plains to the south were migrating here daily, trying to survive. The land in their villages didn't yield good crops, and the rising inflation made it impossible for them to feed their families.

Because of the steady influx of migrants, the city's skyline had become dotted with satellite dishes, and one couldn't walk anywhere without inhaling fumes from three-wheelers and old, rickety buses. Ramchandra understood the suffering of these poor people, who'd had to abandon their villages and towns, but the result was that too many hands prodded, probed, and fed on the innards of Kathmandu. Soon only its carcass would remain. The other day he'd seen small huts that had sprouted up on the shore of the Bishnumati River, a sight he'd previously thought was limited to cities in India, like Bombay.

But — Ramchandra was bitter when he thought of it — the city was not his. He didn't own a house; he didn't even own a piece of land. He was no different from the driver of this three-wheeler, who probably had to rush passengers to various destinations all day and then go to the small room in a squalid part of the city where his wife and kids waited for him.

In Putlisadak, the three-wheeler got tangled in traffic, and they had to wait for several minutes. Nearby, outside a shop, stood a long line of people, plastic containers in hand.

"Look at that," the driver said. "These bastard Indians. This is all their doing."

"Is that for kerosene?"

"Yes, what else? They've reopened the borders, but it's going to take a while."

"Well, at least it's not as bad as it was before."

"Well, Dashain is here, and people have a lot of cooking to do. All donkeys, these politicians. This hahakar, this chaos, just because our king and the Indian prime minister couldn't stand each other's egos."

Whether there was any truth to that, Ramchandra didn't know. Rumors had it that contest of one-upmanship between King Birendra and the Indian Prime Minister Rajiv Gandhi had led India to close most of its borders to Nepal. Supposedly each felt the other hadn't shown him enough respect at political meetings. But most likely, Ramchandra thought, India was unhappy with King Birendra's purchase of military hardware from China, not to mention the way Nepal now required Indian workers to obtain permits.

"Dhotis," the three-wheeler driver cursed, spitting out his window onto the pavement. "They'll suck this country dry."

In the past few months, Ramchandra had heard similar sentiments expressed many times. Housewives lining up to buy kerosene cursed Rajiv Gandhi, and motorists fumed and blamed the Indians, "dhoti bhais," while they sat in their cars waiting to be granted the ration of a few liters of petrol. Ramchandra had nothing against the Indians who worked in Nepal—he found most of them to be pleasant and hardworking. But it was true that the Indian government liked to flex its muscles toward its neighbors.

"Can't live with them, can't live without them," Ramchandra said. Yet there was no doubt that the city was filled with growing anger. Fumes of resentment seemed to rise from the people and blend with the polluted air. As the residents of Kathmandu became more vocal in their criticism of the ruling one-party Panchayat establishment, the sense of defiance, long subdued, finally began to permeate the streets and alleys, where people openly discussed how Nepal needed radical reforms, like the ones that had brought down the Berlin Wall. The image of the lone Chinese man facing tanks in Tiananmen Square, shown on television and in newspapers, had excited people's imagination. The banned political parties, it was said, were attempting to reconcile among themselves so that they could capitalize on this growing bitterness.

Of the three houses that stood behind the Sunrise Boarding School, only one had a chicken shed next to it. A mangy dog, tied with a rope on the unkempt lawn, followed Ramchandra's steps to the door with jaundiced eyes. Chicken feathers drifted from the shed onto the veranda, and the chickens clucked in unison as he knocked on the door. A short woman with yellow eyes, not unlike the dog's, opened the door. She wore a crumpled dhoti, and there were large white blots on her neck and forehead. It occurred to him that she was an albino.

"Tell Malati that her math teacher is here to see her, all right?" Ramchandra told the maid.

Immediately, he realized his mistake. If Malati was poor, it was unlikely that her family could afford a maid. Also, the woman's authoritative stance, hand on hip, should have told him that she was not a maid. But she didn't look like Malati's mother; there was no resemblance.

"And who are you?" the woman asked.

"Ramchandra. I'm her math tutor."

"What do you need to see her for? What do you need?"

He was surprised by the roughness of her words, which, combined with her pleasant voice, had an odd effect. A baby was crying inside.

"No, no," he said. "She didn't come to the last session, so I was wondering . . ."

"Do you go to all of your students' houses when they don't come?"

He didn't respond. "All right, come inside," she said, annoyance marking her face.

She led him past a living room with a worn-out sofa, and into the kitchen, small and gloomy, with grease stains all over the walls. A yellowed poster of Goddess Laxmi, her many hands clasping her trident, conch shell, and lotus, was posted on a door in the corner. It was this door the woman opened. "Malati, someone here to see you. Says he's your teacher."

Once Ramchandra's eyes adjusted to the semidarkness, he saw Malati sitting on the floor, her hair in disarray, a baby in her lap, one of her breasts peeking out of her blouse. The baby, who couldn't have been more than a year old, was trying to find her nipple, but the wails indicated that it was having problems. Ramchandra noticed how small the room was—barely the size of a closet. Then it occurred to him that it was indeed a closet.

Malati, not looking up, continued to struggle with the baby, cooing, pushing its head gently to her breast.

"Imagine that," the woman said with a laugh. "A teacher visiting his student's home."

"How are you, Malati?" Ramchandra asked.

Malati didn't answer, but the woman did. "She is very fine, don't you see? I told her to get rid of that baby when it was still in her womb, but did she listen? And now this." She motioned toward Malati and the baby.

"Malekha Didi," Malati said to the woman, "will you please be quiet? Your voice is disturbing Rachana."

Didi. So, the woman was Malati's sister? She hadn't mentioned one, but *didi* could apply to anyone, even a stranger.

"Yes, I am the bad one now," the woman said. "I have done so much for you, and, slut that you are, you don't see what I've done."

The word *slut* stung Ramchandra. Malati finally looked up at him with a faint smile, as if to say, see what you've gotten yourself into. Then she turned again to the baby, who had calmed down and whose eyelids were becoming heavier. "I'll have to feed her Lactogen," Malati said.

"Where is Lactogen? Who's going to buy it?"

"I bought some yesterday," Malati said. "Sir, what brings you here?" Her breast was back inside her blouse, and she was rocking the baby in her lap.

Ramchandra looked at Malekha Didi, and Malati said to her, "Leave us to talk alone for a while."

Malekha Didi left, but not before warning Malati that she was to cook the morning meal after feeding the baby.

Ramchandra wanted to sit down, but the only place to sit was the cold kitchen floor, so he remained where he was and said, "I just came to see, about yesterday—"

"I'll have to make formula for the baby," she said, and got up. "Why don't we talk in the other room?"

"Is this your bedroom?"

"Yes."

"Don't bother about tea," he said. "I came by to talk."

"Let's go to the other room."

In the living room, he sat on the sofa, noticing that the carpet had large stains, and that some baby clothes were strewn about. A framed photo on a nearby table showed a younger Malati with a man about Ramchandra's age. Another photo, this one on the wall, was of the same man with the albino woman. They were standing a little apart but with an air of intimacy, which made him think they were husband and wife. There was no heater in the room, and it was cold.

Malati went into the kitchen, and when she came back, the baby was not in her arms. She held two glasses of tea, which she set on the side table before sitting beside him. To warm his hands, Ramchandra cupped a glass of tea.

"How old is your girl?" he asked.

"Eight months."

Her face, which so far he'd seen as that of a child, became transformed. He noticed lines of maturity, creases under her eyes. The room suddenly seemed different to Ramchandra, as if he wasn't sitting there, as if he was on the ceiling, looking down at the Ramchandra below. Swallowing the saliva that had filled his mouth, he asked, "Is she your sister?"

Malati smiled. "No, that's my stepmother."

"But you call her didi?"

"Yes, that seems the most appropriate."

"You'd mentioned your mother."

"My mother vanished from my life a long time ago. Malekha Didi is my mother now."

No good mother would call her daughter a slut, Ramchandra thought—that's what stepmothers are for. Of course he knew that some stepmothers treated their stepchildren with affection, but a distant memory pressed on him. A restaurant near New Road where he used to go for tea and, when he had enough money, for samosas, after finishing college and before starting a teaching job. A small boy, in a frayed shirt and loose half-pants held up by a thin rope, was constantly scolded by the woman he worked for. She criticized him for being slow, for not boiling the tea properly, for leaving the glasses dirty. The boy looked to be barely twelve, but he had an old, sad face. One day, when the woman was about to lift her hand to slap the boy, Ramchandra confronted her. She looked at him in contempt and said, "If his mother had disciplined him, I wouldn't have to do it." Later, when the woman had gone into the back room, he asked the boy why he put up with her, and the boy said he couldn't leave because this was his home; she was his stepmother.

"The tea will get cold," Malati prodded him.

He took a sip. "Do you have brothers and sisters?"

"No, just the two of us. My father passed away a few years ago."

"And the father of the child?"

"I'm not married. He doesn't live here."

Ramchandra was filled with a sweet sense of pleasure, something he'd not experienced since his late childhood. He watched this girl, her sensitive face, the sadness in her eyes, the faint lines of womanhood circling her mouth, and the voice that emerged from him came from a depth he didn't know existed. "I am so sorry about yesterday."

She must have heard the difference in his voice, for she looked at him sharply. The morning light filtered through the thin curtains, making beams of the dust in the room. Two pink clouds spread across her cheeks, perhaps signs of embarrassment at her own thoughts. She looked at him again and let a brief smile shine on her face. She prompted him toward the tea, and they both picked up their glasses.

"It was humiliating, sir," she said in a quiet voice.

"I don't know what to say. Even my wife was angry with me."

"Does your wife know you're here?"

"Yes," he lied.

"What did she say to you?"

"About my being so hard on you?"

"Yes."

"She said you were young and sensitive, and I should've been kinder."

Malati sipped her tea, pulled up her legs on the sofa, and rocked gently.

"Is your baby asleep now?"

"Yes, but I'll have to feed her soon and then help Malekha Didi."

"So you will come for your sessions again?"

She hesitated. "Do you think I'll pass the exam?"

"Of course you will."

"I feel so helpless."

"I think the problem is Ashok," he said.

"How is Ashok a problem?"

"You can't concentrate with him in the room. I'll start tutoring you alone."

She observed him calmly, again with a soft smile, and he felt uncomfortable.

"I want you to pass," he said, and before he could stop himself, he said, "And you'll come every day, not just two times a week."

"You know I don't have the money."

"I'm not asking for more money." His rational thoughts quarreled in the back of his mind. "You need to pass. I'll help you."

"Why do you have to treat me in a special way, sir?"

Her closet had reminded Ramchandra of the myriad of tiny cramped rooms, sometimes no bigger than bathrooms, where he and his mother had lived, sometimes in a relative's home, other times in a rented house in a neighborhood full of drunks and prostitutes and open drains smelling of urine and feces. In one room, the landlord had pressed himself upon his mother, and she had not screamed for the neighbors because she knew they'd think she'd invited it on herself. Ramchandra was twelve then; he'd climbed on the landlord's back, pummeling him, as tears ran down his cheeks.

"I'm not giving you any special treatment," he told Malati. "I want my students to pass. Once you become successful in a few years, you can pay me back."

She looked at him mischievously. "Will you chase after me

h the police if I don't pay you back then?" She laughed at her
joke, and crinkles formed around her eyes.

Malekha Didi appeared. "Are you going to he-he-ha-ha all
morning? Who's going to cook lunch?"

"You'd better go now, sir," Malati said.

He stood. "So, you'll come tomorrow?"

She nodded.

As he walked out of the house, Malekha Didi chuckled.

It was already nine o'clock, and his first class started at nine-
thirty, so he had no time to go home for his meal before heading to school. Ramchandra stepped into a general store near
Malati's house and called Goma on the phone at the counter.

"Where did you go? I was getting anxious."

"Have the children left for school?"

"Yes."

Ramchandra always kissed the children on their cheeks before they left for school, and now he cursed himself for not
having noted the time on the clock in Malati's house. He told
Goma he'd have to forgo lunch, that he was going straight to
school. She said she'd bring his lunch to the school around
eleven, when he had a break between classes. Despite his protests, she wouldn't budge. As he was about to hang up, she said,
"You went to see her, didn't you? That girl?"

"Yes, I was not feeling good about the whole thing."

"What did she say?"

"I apologized to her, and she says she'll come."

"You," Goma said. "Worrying about a student like that."

He wanted to tell her that Malati had a baby, that she lived in
a room that made their flat in Jaisideval seem palatial, that she
had a stepmother who didn't seem right in the head, but all he
said was goodbye, and then hung up.

The only way he could get to the school on time was by taking another three-wheeler, and he was annoyed with himself for having spent so much money that morning. This driver didn't have his meter on, which meant he was going to charge more than the usual fare for that distance. He almost shouted heated words of argument, but he made himself sit back and close his eyes. What can you expect these poor people to do? They have to eat, too, and gasoline prices kept going up. And, with Dashain around the corner, they had to worry about getting new clothes for their family and spending money on meat. In some ways, Ramchandra wished he were back in his youth with his mother, when, during Dashain, they'd go to the market and buy a kilo or two of goat meat to cook. They didn't have to worry about getting new clothes, because they had no close relatives in the city, only a few distant cousins who shunned them during festivals anyway. Now, under the watchful gaze of his in-laws, Ramchandra was constantly aware of how little he spent on his family. Last year, Mrs. Pandey, after fingering Sanu's new frock, said, "This cloth couldn't have cost more than thirty rupees, eh, Goma?" Goma had lied, said it cost about a hundred, plus thirty rupees for the stitching, and Ramchandra had seethed with anger.

The three-wheeler dropped him outside Asan, and he walked to the marketplace. At the entrance of the marketplace, the owner of a bookshop, where Ramchandra sometimes browsed for textbooks, greeted him, and Ramchandra waved back. Then he stepped into the alley where the school was, and right there, in front of the school, in the middle of the alley, was a huge mound of garbage.

On the first day he'd come to this school, the same sight had greeted him. He'd had a call from the friend of one of his college classmates. Mr. Tiwari was looking for someone to take the place of the math teacher, who had died in a bicycle accident. Ramchandra's elation at getting the phone call, which signaled that he might rise to a full-time position, was crushed when he went to the school the next day. In the narrow muddy alley where it stood, behind the Bir Hospital, piles of garbage had been dumped right in front of it. Two stray dogs, their skin covered with bruises and wounds, sniffed their way through the garbage and watched Ramchandra warily, as he stared at a faded sign on the building. It bore the school's name, in both English and Nepali, painted on the background of a lotus. The building was old and the entrance so small that even Ramchandra, who was not a tall man, had to stoop slightly to get in. After a couple of steps, he found himself in darkness and had to fumble his way through to another door. It was then that he discovered that the school was actually built around a courtyard; he heard the cacophony of voices rising from the classrooms, as children chanted their daily lessons. A boy was drinking from a tap in the middle of the courtyard; Ramchandra asked him where the office was.

Mr. Tiwari, the principal, was a genial old man with tufts of white hair growing from his nose. He wore an old suit with a bright red tie. "What to do, Ramchandra-ji? He was a very popular teacher; the students liked him. With the S.L.C. exams so near, we badly need someone."

The question on the tip of Ramchandra's tongue was, of course, about the salary, but it would have been improper to talk about money so early, and Mr. Tiwari never brought it up. He did say, "Well, if you want to do some side business, you know, you can ask some of the students with better-off parents to come to your home for tutoring." Mr. Tiwari punctuated the sentence with a wink. It was standard practice all over the country, but lately there'd been some concern, expressed in newspaper articles, that many teachers were deliberately not teaching the required material in the classroom and then telling students that if they wanted to pass the almighty S.L.C., they'd have to fork out extra cash for private tutorials. Several irate parents had even formed a group and petitioned the education minister, who had nodded in sympathy and made vague noises about "quality education for every child—in the classroom."

"I understand," Ramchandra said to Mr. Tiwari, and looked out at the courtyard, where the students had congregated after the ringing of the bell. This was not his idea of a school, one whose students wore dirty, crinkled uniforms, one that had no playground with green grass, no seesaws, no swings, no slides. Some of the younger students at the moment, in fact, were stepping into a large puddle that had formed in the center of the courtyard from last night's rain.

Now a small pack of people entered the room, and Ramchandra realized that this very room, with one desk and a few chairs, served not only as the principal's office but also as the staff room. Ramchandra craved tea. Goma always made perfect tea, with just the right amount of milk and sugar, boiled for a long time but not too long, and Ramchandra had gotten into the habit of drinking it every two hours. He'd had a cup before he left home, but now the dismal surroundings had increased his thirst.

Just then a small boy, wearing a uniform much too large for him, came in, wiping the sweat from his forehead, and asked Mr. Tiwari, "Shall I bring tea, sir?"

Mr. Tiwari looked at Ramchandra apologetically and said, "He's a poor farmer's son. Couldn't pay the fees, so we made this arrangement."

Ramchandra probably wouldn't have felt critical if Mr. Tiwari hadn't mentioned it, but now he thought, a student is the teacher's servant? The boy was smiling at him. As if sensing Ramchandra's disapproval, one of the teachers, a dark woman with a small face, said, "He's a very smart boy. He came first in fifth grade last year," and she patted the boy on the side of his head. The boy came to attention in front of Ramchandra and asked, in a well-rehearsed voice, "Shall I bring tea for our Aadarnia Sir?"

Aadarnia. Deserving Respect. Hiding his disgust, Ramchandra nodded, and the boy left, bounding out the door into the courtyard.

Mr. Tiwari introduced Ramchandra to the coterie of teachers who had crowded into the room. The small-faced woman with sharp, hawklike eyes was Bandana Miss; the tall, gangly man with the mustache was Gokul Sir; the surly man with a patch on his left eye was Khanal Sir; the man who didn't smile was Manandhar Sir; and the nice-looking woman with the bouffant hair-do was Miss Lama, originally from Darjeeling.

The boy brought in the glasses of tea, and Ramchandra, after taking a few sips, felt better. Mr. Tiwari enumerated various plans for the school, including the building of a small canteen for the students and teachers. A rich businessman was soon to make a huge donation, he said with another wink. Judging from the indifferent expressions on the other teachers' faces, Ramchandra surmised that talk of the big donation had been circulating for the past few years and would probably continue for the next few. He looked at the faces around him — the dark expressions, the taut lines, the constant shifting of eyes punctuated by vague staring into space. Yes, these people were not unlike him. They all had plans for themselves, for their small lives with their small children and their small rented flats in dark corners of the city. He felt sorry for himself, for them, for Mr. Tiwari, who was old and foolishly optimistic. And on that first day, this self-pity had, strangely, served as a salve for his disappointment at the condition of the school.

Ramchandra pinched his nose and stooped as he walked beneath the sign that read KANTIPUR SCHOOL in two languages. He went straight to the staff room to sign the attendance register, and there he found Bandana Miss, who had become the principal after Mr. Tiwari's death last year. She was in a good mood, which was unusual. "Ramchandra Sir, come, come, let's have a cup of tea," she said. She signaled that he should sit down.

"I have only a few minutes before class."

"One or two minutes late for your class. Do you think the students care?"

Bandana Miss was usually strict about her teachers' punctuality, and Ramchandra wondered what was different today. She reached beneath her desk and brought out a box. "Sweets," she said, passing the laddoos and barfis to him. "Here, take one."

"And what's the occasion?"

"My son is going to America."

A boy brought in two glasses of tea. This boy was a poor villager from the hills, who had been hired by Bandana Miss last year after she managed to coax a local Newar businessman into donating some money to the school. Bandana Miss's aggressive personality often bothered the teachers, but they had to admit that her boldness had benefited the school. Now a swing set stood in the yard, where a long queue of students formed during recess every day. Brand-new blackboards had been installed in the classrooms, and a man had been hired to fix the building's broken walls and floors.

Ramchandra sipped his tea and wondered how Bandana Miss had managed to arrange a trip to America for her son, who, he had heard, was involved in drugs. As if answering an unasked question, Bandana Miss said, "I found an American family willing to sponsor him. He's going to the district of"—she consulted a letter on her desk—"Nebraska. A very good university. One of the top schools in America." She rattled off the name of the university, but Ramchandra had never heard of it. Then again, he knew the names of only some of the famous ones, such as Harvard and MIT. As Bandana Miss outlined her plans for her son, Ramchandra's mind drifted to this morning. The dark closet with Malati and her baby, the albino stepmother. It all seemed unreal now, as he listened to Bandana Miss's talk of America and what her boy could accomplish there. "The family is going to give him a car, and soon he'll have a television set. America is a great country. Not like our Nepal. Here, you work and work, and still you have nothing to show for it. There, you work hard, and you make money, and people recognize you, and soon you become very prosperous."

Ramchandra finished his tea, congratulated Bandana Miss, and went to his class. Still thinking of Malati, he couldn't focus on his teaching. Not that his teaching needed much focus. The classes he taught were easy, and the same textbooks were used every year. In fact, the textbooks he was using had been prescribed years ago, at the time of the first education reform in the country, and they hadn't changed since then. A couple of times, especially during his first year at Kantipur School, Ramchandra had appealed to the principal. He brought in copies of new textbooks from the Tribhuvan University library, books that had innovative styles of learning. But Mr. Tiwari had smiled his genial smile and said, "Why do you want to rock the boat, Ramchandra-ji? Isn't everything working out okay? Aren't the students learning what they need to pass the S.L.C.? Besides, this is the textbook prescribed by the government, and what if students begin to fail with your textbooks?" Ramchandra hadn't argued with him, but he had talked to other teachers, and they'd also shown an apathy that, he soon discovered, seeped through the floors of the classrooms. So Ramchandra gave up trying to change the textbooks and, instead, focused on teaching his tutees well, so that his private students started to acquire high marks in the S.L.C., and his reputation as a good math tutor grew.

That evening, Ramchandra's in-laws came for a visit. Usually, they were reluctant to visit the small flat. The cramped quarters, the filthy courtyard, and the long flight of stairs up to the third floor annoyed them. They expected Ramchandra and Goma, with the children, to visit their palatial house, an expectation that irked Ramchandra, because his in-laws didn't treat their other son-in-law, Nalini's husband, Harish, the same way. Harish was a distributing agent for half a dozen big-name international companies. When it came to Nalini and Harish, Goma's parents concocted all kinds of excuses to visit them in their beautiful Chinese-brick house with the large enclosed porch near Jawalakhel. In fact, they spent so much time in Nalini's home that, during one family gathering, Harish had confided to Ramchandra that he wished they'd leave him and Nalini alone for a while. "Just because we're family doesn't mean they have to bother us every week, no, Ramchandra dai?" Ramchandra had smiled. Two sons-in-law, two opposite problems. Ramchandra would trade places with Harish any day, but of course he wouldn't say so to Harish, who was well aware of the treatment Ramchandra received from his in-laws. During gatherings when Harish was present, Goma's parents doted on him, Mrs. Pandey constantly plying him with food and drink, Mr. Pandey scolding his wife for not catering to Harish properly, while Ramchandra sat in the same room, ignored.

Harish was a tall man with pale skin and a mustache. His

business life kept him so busy that often when he appeared at a family event, he was still wearing his suit. He was in his early thirties, a few years younger than Ramchandra, and there was a boyish quality to his appearance and demeanor. He never boasted about his success in business, which was growing exponentially every year, and whenever his in-laws praised him about it, he'd quickly change the subject. Perhaps he did so, Ramchandra hoped, because he didn't like the way Goma's parents used his success as a way to criticize Ramchandra. Harish had attended well-reputed schools in Darjeeling and New Delhi, so he spoke English with ease and fluency, which delighted Mrs. Pandey, who, despite her less than adequate skills in the language, often attempted to speak it to Harish. Harish obviously felt uncomfortable doing so, because whenever she spoke to him in English, he'd respond in Nepali. That way, the whole conversation turned comical, although, of course, no one laughed. "You great son-in-law saheb," Mrs. Pandey would say. "You success business. What you think?" Harish would nod and smile, flushing slightly, and then turn to Nalini and change the subject. Or Mrs. Pandey would say, "You like dal and roti comfinaton?" And Harish would respond in Nepali that he actually preferred a combination of roti and tarkari, and didn't like the way the roti became soggy in the soupy dal. "Special," Mrs. Pandey would persist, "dal good." And she would search her mind to find the English word for mung, until finally Mr. Pandey would scold her, saying that she was harassing her jwain.

Sanu and Rakesh loved their grandparents, Rakesh more than Sanu because they doted on him more. Today it was Rakesh who alerted his parents of his grandparents' arrival. Mrs. Pandey would always announce their arrival from the courtyard, as if she were afraid she might catch someone in the act of undressing.

"Grandmother's here," Rakesh shouted and dashed down the stairs. Goma went to the window with an expectant face, and Ramchandra, as he reluctantly joined Goma, saw the tail end of a sari in the downstairs doorway. "This is a bit unusual," he muttered, and Goma's eyes pleaded with him: deal with it the best way you can. "There's nothing in the house to eat," she exclaimed, and she ran to get Sanu to fetch sweets from the neighborhood shops. Ramchandra stood at the top of the staircase, knowing he'd have to grit his teeth for the next couple of hours.

Goma's mother was a small woman with a round face, and yes, Ramchandra admitted, deceptively kind eyes. They shone in merriment when she was with her grandchildren, especially with Rakesh, about whom she often said, "My only grandson. He'll carry our family name." Her eyes also became moist at Goma's lack of comfort. "I'm too old for this," she said as she reached the top of the stairs, her husband a few steps behind, and then did a prim namaste to her son-in-law. "Son-in-law, you never come to visit us, so we thought enough was enough and decided to come here." Ramchandra laughed, and made some noises about advance warning for a proper welcome. "But how would I let you know?" Mrs. Pandey said, raising her eyebrows. "You don't have a phone." Ramchandra's application for a telephone had been languishing in the telecommunications department for four years now, and the folks there had hinted that if he were willing to be generous with about five thousand rupees, the application would be approved soon. He'd balked, swearing he'd rather do without a telephone than feed the mouths of corrupt officials, and he made arrangements with the bicycle shop, right outside the entrance of the courtyard, to receive his calls. That's where the job offer from Mr. Tiwari had come, and sometimes Ashok called there with his excuses.

Mr. Pandey, who now walked with a cane, was a thin man with a triangular face that bore a much sterner look than his wife's. His grandfather had been a close adviser to the Ranas, who, during their century-long autocratic rule, had stripped the country of its wealth. The family relationship with the Ranas had apparently imbued in Mr. Pandey a sense of entitlement, and he carried himself with his head erect, his eyes scanning for misbehavior to punish. Those eyes turned narrower and more critical whenever they fell upon Ramchandra. And today, when Mr. Pandey reached the top of the stairs, gaily aided by Rakesh, who pushed him from behind, he looked at Ramchandra with a noticeable degree of unhappiness, as if this were not a sight he deserved at the end of his journey.

The in-laws, once seated in the bedroom, again looked around, as if they were in the waiting area of a stark building where their daughter was imprisoned. "Rakesh, bring me a glass of water," Mrs. Pandey commanded, and Rakesh bounded toward the kitchen. Goma handed Sanu money to go fetch some sweets and sugar from the shops. Ramchandra eyed the money—fifty rupees.

Goma said that her parents should have let her know about their visit, but Mr. Pandey said, "You mean we have to send a messenger before we come to our daughter's house?"

"Daughter's flat," Mrs. Pandey commented. She found a packet of expensive-looking chocolate in her bag and gave it to Rakesh, who'd brought her water. "Share it with your sister."

After Goma went to the kitchen to make tea, Mr. Pandey said, "So, son-in-law, how is your school?"

"It's going well," Ramchandra replied. He was seated on the floor, as Mr. and Mrs. Pandey had taken up the bed. Rakesh was studying the chocolate wrapper.

"How many tutees do you have these days?"

"Two in the morning." He'd had an evening tutee a few weeks ago, but after a couple of sessions the student stopped coming, because Ramchandra told him that he couldn't continue unless he paid in advance.

Mrs. Pandey sighed, then looked around the bedroom and up at the ceiling, where some of the plaster was coming off.

Ramchandra avoided her eyes. "And how are you two?"

"Our lives have become very passive," Mr. Pandey said. "Nothing to do all day. We've been thinking about walking every evening, and thought we'd give it a start today by walking over here. But your mother-in-law here couldn't do it, so we came by car." The Pandeys owned a sleek red Honda.

"We should call the driver in for tea," Ramchandra said.

"Forget it," Mrs. Pandey said, and looked around the room again, as if to imply that even her driver wouldn't want to enter a dump like this.

"Did you hear of the agitation today? What do you think?" Mr. Pandey asked. The afternoon newspapers, which Ramchandra had read during tea break at school, reported that an angry mob in the city of Biratnagar had burned two buses and hurled stones at the police, who had fired tear gas, then real bullets, killing two people. One newspaper had run a scathing criticism of the government for the shootings, and talk reverberated through the city that the editor of the newspaper would be whisked away to an unknown destination. The word buzzing through the city was "khattam"—finished or stopped or gone—and after a while it acquired a special currency, rolling off citizens' tongues like a mantra. The country's situation is khattam; the prime minister, appointed by the king, is khattam; the pothole-filled, accident-prone roads are always khattam; the king, with his English education and his royal sideburns, is maha-khattam, super-gone.

"What can I say?" Ramchandra said. He didn't want to get into a political discussion with his father-in-law, who was not interested in anyone else's opinions, let alone those of his failure of a son-in-law. Clearly, he was asking only to make conversation. Even more infuriating, Mr. Pandey's allegiance was unflinching. He lambasted any inkling of rebellion and constantly praised King Mahendra, the now-deceased father not only of the current king but also of the strict one-party system. What most annoyed Ramchandra was Mr. Pandey's unwavering praise of the Ranas, tyrants who had amassed an obscene amount of wealth in their ridiculous English-style palaces while the rest of their countrymen wore tattered clothes. It was one of these Rana palaces that Mr. Pandey had inherited from his grandfather. Pandey Palace, as the family called it, the alliteration rolling off their tongues with pride, was a four-story, old, but frequently renovated structure in Bhatbhateni. Its broad balcony afforded a pleasant view of the neighborhood, and its large lawn in front was dotted with marble statues.

That the Ranas had hoarded the country's wealth while its citizens struggled to feed their families hardly entered Mr. Pandey's awareness. But it was never sufficient for Ramchandra to think that Mr. Pandey realized his complicity in enjoying the wealth his grandfather had hoarded.

"These people," Mr. Pandey said, "they don't know what they're doing."

Ramchandra remained quiet.

"They think Western-style politics have all the answers. But mark my word, son-in-law, this is the best system for Nepal."

"Maybe."

"Maybe? Maybe? That's all you can say?"

"I mean—"

"Let me tell you. I have hobnobbed with some of the most

powerful people in the country." Then he started to reel off the usual names of those he'd known during his Rana days and after, and the government bureaucrats and statesmen he could still call on whenever he needed something.

Listening to Mr. Pandey, Ramchandra couldn't help going over the reasons his in-laws considered him such a failure. He'd never made the career leap they'd expected when they joined their daughter's hand with his. After graduating, he floundered from one part-time teaching job to another, discovering competitors who were brighter than he was, or those, less bright, who had powerful uncles or cousins or in-laws to pull the strings. Time after time, Ramchandra watched helplessly as a job he thought was within reach slipped away to someone not half as qualified as he was. Occasionally, Mr. Pandey had offered to help, but Ramchandra's pride had stepped in, and he'd told his father-in-law that he'd find something through his own merit.

His relatives and friends had expected him to teach at a well-known school, perhaps St. Xavier's, which was run by white priests, or the Budhanilkantha School, nestled in the northern outskirts of the city and famous for its innovative curriculum. He'd run into teachers who taught at these English boarding schools, and they always seemed well-dressed and content. He could imagine them living in nice brick houses with television antennas on the roofs or miniature pagodas dedicated to Lord Ganesh or even Goddess Laxmi, who could, if pleased, play with the direction of the winds so that more wealth would flow into the houses. But his applications were rejected by both schools, and ultimately he'd had to accept his status as a part-timer, someone who was only temporary at the Bhanubhakta School. Sometimes he found himself repeating the word *asthai*, until the sensation of impermanence, of something fleeting and flimsy, became part of his image of himself, as if at his birth the gods had decided to stamp his forehead with a warning to those around him — TEMPORARY.

And then a few years ago, he'd found his present job, at the financially strapped Kantipur School, housed in a crumbling building in an alley where stray dogs quarreled and garbage accumulated. His monthly check of nine hundred and ninety rupees was only slightly better than what he'd made when he rushed from one school to the next, often sweating in crowded buses, across the city. But it was permanent, and now he was full time, and this realization occasionally lifted his spirits like a sharp rejuvenating breath.

He'd thought his full-time, permanent status would change his in-laws' minds, that they'd begin to see him as a full-time, permanent son-in-law. But Goma's parents had quickly shifted their focus. "You must build a house, Ramchandra babu," they said to him at family gatherings. "Without a house of one's own in this city, it doesn't matter what you do."

When Ramchandra told them it took time to build a house in Kathmandu, they shook their heads contemptuously. "Of course it takes time," Goma's father said. "But unless you start thinking about it now, how will it ever be completed? Besides, something can always be arranged to get started." Ramchandra knew what he was hinting at. The Pandeys had suggested several times that they would lend the necessary money for Ramchandra to get started on a house. They'd never approached him directly with this offer; they channeled it through Goma, who passed it on to her husband and then kept silent when Ramchandra adamantly rejected it. He would not, he said, be beholden to anyone. Especially to his in-laws, but he didn't say that to Goma. After all, who knew how long it would take him to repay the loan, and it would lie on his tired shoulders like a heavy stone for the rest of his life.

Whenever the Pandeys brought up the subject, Ramchandra turned to Goma for support, but Goma, despite her complete agreement with Ramchandra in the privacy of their bedroom, preferred not to argue with her parents. Once, when Goma was putting the newborn Sanu to bed, Ramchandra asked her, "Why didn't you say something? Perhaps if you had, they'd stop this constant criticism. We're lucky I have a full-time position now. Why don't they understand?" And Goma responded, with a guilty look, "I know, I know. Please, I'll say something the next time, I promise."

He knew she never would, so each time he'd nod with a bitter sense of understanding. He also knew that Goma's parents would never stop their criticism of him, even if he built a grand four-story house and taught at Tribhuvan University. "Are you unhappy with me?" he'd once asked Goma. "Tell me, frankly. Are you, having come from a big house and now living in this dump, are you unhappy with me?"

"Just because my parents say those things to you, don't you say them to me," she answered. "I am not that kind of a woman. Whatever you provide, I'll be happy."

And she'd meant what she'd said, because in the years that followed, she never complained about having to count paisa during festivals, about the difficulty of paying tuition for their children's school, or about wearing the same sari to several weddings because they couldn't afford a new one.

A year before he started teaching at Kantipur School, when his mother was still alive and it became obvious to Ramchandra that his in-laws' expectations of him would be a constant irritation, he'd asked his mother, with bitterness, why she thought Goma's hand had been given to him in marriage. The parents could easily have married her to someone with more money. "Maybe she was not a virgin," his mother abruptly said. "Maybe she slept around with other men, and her father was afraid no one would marry her." Ramchandra tried not to flush with embarrassment. In her old age his mother sometimes spoke her mind without regard to propriety. Ramchandra knew Goma had been a virgin the first time they made love, but he had wondered whether her parents were avoiding some sort of scandal by marrying her off to a poor student.

Ramchandra's suspicions about Goma's past surfaced again one evening during a gathering at Pandey Palace. Throughout dinner, Ramchandra had been subjected relentlessly to innuendoes by his father-in-law in the presence of all the relatives, and as the evening progressed, a dark cloud formed in Ramchandra's mind. Then, when Goma was in the kitchen, Mrs. Pandey brought out barfis. She served everyone, starting with Harish, until it was time to offer a piece to Ramchandra — and there was none left. "So foolish of me," Mrs. Pandey said. "I should have bought more." Treating the senior son-in-law like that was bad enough — Ramchandra was staring at the floor in shame — but what Mrs. Pandey said next made him feel he was burning. "But what does it matter, eh, son-in-law? This penchant for sweets is a matter of habit, after all. When one is not used to eating them, then one doesn't miss them."

As soon as Ramchandra and Goma stepped out of Pandey Palace, he blurted out to his wife what had been on his mind: that her rich parents had wedded her to him because of some past scandal, that perhaps she'd had a lover, or several lovers. Dumbfounded, Goma gasped and then started to cry, on the street, while she held little Sanu on her hip. Immediately Ramchandra regretted his accusation. She'd given no indication of a past or present lover. He'd discovered no secret notes under her clothes in the cupboard; no suspicious letters had been delivered by the postman; he'd seen no faraway look in her eyes, the kind he imagined women with lovers would have. He tried to console her, saying that he was sorry. And she replied, "I am a Hindu woman. I am not that kind."

Now, in Ramchandra's flat, Mrs. Pandey said, "Politics, politics," looking at her husband fondly as he droned on about the power-wielding people he knew. "This son-in-law knows nothing about politics," she said as if Ramchandra weren't present. "I wish Harish babu were here. He knows some politicians in the city."

Goma, who had just entered the room with a tray of tea and sweets, caught the tail end of the conversation. Ramchandra had leaned his head against the wall and almost closed his eyes. He wanted Goma to say something to her mother, but, as usual, she didn't. She merely looked at him guiltily, then set the tray on the floor. Rakesh reached for a barfi, and Goma scolded him, saying he must wait for his grandparents to start eating. Sanu peeked in through the door. "Grandmother, did you bring me the jewelry you promised?"

Mrs. Pandey had forgotten. Apparently, she had promised her granddaughter two of her very old silver necklaces, once worn by women in Rana palaces. She apologized to Sanu, who asked, "And what did you give Rakesh?" Then it was discovered that the entire bar of chocolate was sitting in Rakesh's stomach, and a ruckus ensued. Sanu accused her grandparents of playing favorites with their grandson. "I know why you like him and you hate me," Sanu said to her grandparents through her tears. "It's because he's a son, isn't it?"

Mr. Pandey, staring at Sanu, let his mouth hang open. His mind was probably stuck on some important government official in the Home Ministry. Mrs. Pandey attempted to mollify Sanu, saying of course she didn't favor one over the other, that both of them were very important to her. But when she reached to put her arm around Sanu, the girl pushed it away and said, "You think I don't know you two? You think you are such big shots, sitting in that grand house over there? And you treat Ba as if he were a dog. He's my father!"

Sanu's outburst left everyone stunned. Ramchandra had never realized that his daughter was pained by the grandparents' behavior toward him.

"Sanu! What nonsense are you uttering?" Goma exclaimed.

"And you," Sanu said to her mother. "You are frightened like a soaked cat in front of your parents." She stormed off to her room, banging the door behind her.

"What's come over her?" Ramchandra said.

"I don't know where she gets these ideas," Goma said.

Mr. and Mrs. Pandey stared at the sweets and the tea; then Mr. Pandey said, to his wife, in a loud voice, "Why didn't you bring the jewelry you promised? Why raise a young girl's expectations like that?"

"I forgot," Mrs. Pandey said. "I can't be expected to remember everything."

"Don't worry about it," Goma said. "That girl has become very bigheaded."

"Why did Didi call Ba a dog?" Rakesh asked.

"Be quiet," Goma said, ruffling her son's hair. "Why didn't you save some chocolate for your sister? Then none of this would have happened."

"Do you think our Ba is a dog, Grandma?" Rakesh asked.

Before Mrs. Pandey could answer, Goma said, "Okay, enough. Go outside and play," and she ushered Rakesh out the door.

For a while the four sipped their tea in silence. No one reached for the sweets, although Ramchandra was tempted to. He was feeling a perverse kind of glee. His daughter had told the Pandeys what they needed to hear.

"All of this will come to no good," Mr. Pandey finally said, then grabbed a piece of barfi and scrutinized it.

Everyone looked at him expectantly, for what he'd say next. "People are going to die for no reason. We need the king."

"I don't know what's happening," Goma said, apparently relieved that the conversation had shifted elsewhere. "I don't understand why people are so upset."

"People are fools," Mr. Pandey said.

"I don't think they are fools," Ramchandra said. "There's much wrong with the Panchayat system." He was pleased by his boldness.

Mr. Pandey popped the barfi into his mouth and said, "It's the best system we have."

"How can it be the best system if so many people are un-happy?"

Ramchandra thought he was going to be challenged, but he was wrong; apparently Sanu's outburst had mellowed Mr. Pandey. He chewed his barfi contentedly.

The talk gradually turned to other matters, and the closed door to the children's room was the only reminder of what had taken place. Because of the houses surrounding the courtyard, they could not see the sun go down, but they knew of its descent, behind the mountains to the west, as everything inside gradually turned gray, and a film of dust could be seen in the twilight, rising and falling, swirling in the air, fogging their view of one another, until Goma got up and turned on the light. Rakesh, his stomach filled with chocolate, had fallen asleep on the floor. The Pandeys decided it was time to leave, and Mrs. Pandey indicated she had something to say to her daughter in private. She urged the men to go downstairs. "It'll take only a minute."

Ramchandra never liked it when, at family gatherings, Mrs.

Pandey took Goma aside and whispered in her ear. When they were together like that, with the mother's mouth close to her daughter's ear, a strange expression came over Goma's face, as if she and her mother were in collusion, perhaps against him. He knew this was not true, but the way Goma looked, like a little girl sharing a secret with her childhood friend, made him feel he was an outsider. He never asked what her mother had whispered to her, but sometimes late at night, when they were alone, Goma would say, "Mother was saying . . ." and it usually turned out to be gossip about a relative or some concern of Mrs. Pandey about the health of her husband, who had bladder and stomach problems. "Does she ever say anything about me?" Ramchandra had once asked, and Goma had said, "Nothing she wouldn't tell you to your face." Somehow Ramchandra hadn't believed her, and now, as he walked down the stairs with his father-in-law, he was almost certain that Mrs. Pandey was going to say something about him to her daughter, something that had to do with buying a house, perhaps suggesting that they take a loan. He watched the back of his father-in-law's head, the wisps of hair on his scalp.

Downstairs, Mr. Pandey pulled his shawl tighter around him and said, "Son-in-law, it's time to start taking things seriously."

Across the courtyard, a silhouette appeared in one of the windows. It was Mr. Sharma, who worked in the government's insurance department. To distract his father-in-law, Ramchandra called out to his neighbor, "It's a cold evening, isn't it, Mr. Sharma?" Mr. Sharma waved back, but didn't say anything.

"Things cannot remain this way forever," Mr. Pandey said. "Look at this." He waved his hand toward the courtyard and the surrounding old houses. "Is this a decent place to live?"

Ramchandra cocked an ear toward the door for the sound of footsteps on the staircase.

Mr. Pandey sighed deeply and said, "A nice little house in Kathmandu; doesn't need to be big. Two rooms should be enough."

"In a few years," Ramchandra said.

Across the courtyard, Mr. Sharma appeared to be listening intently to their conversation.

"In a few years, in a few years. That kind of talk has been going on for too long."

"But one has to understand that mere talking about it doesn't produce a house. One needs money."

Mr. Pandey shook his head, as if money were an inconsequential factor. "One doesn't need that much. Besides, if one wants to, one can always acquire some money."

Ramchandra was thinking of what to say in reply when, at last, he heard the sounds on the staircase. Goma and her mother emerged, laughing.

Sanu didn't come out of her room for dinner, despite repeated calls, so Ramchandra went to her. She was seated on the bed, reading a book, and she didn't look up.

"Daughter, come to the kitchen. Food is getting cold."

She said she wasn't hungry.

Ramchandra went over and sat down beside her. "Are you still angry?"

Sanu shook her head.

"Then why this sullen face? Like—" he searched for a comical comparison—"a monkey who has just lost her coconut to a donkey."

Sanu didn't crack a smile.

"Come on, let's eat."

"Why doesn't Mother ever say anything?"

"They don't mean it in a bad way."

"They treat Uncle Harish differently."

"They don't mean to."

"Ba, does living in this flat make us small people?"

"I don't think so. Do you think so?"

She shook her head. "I don't think you become small or big by where you live. But I know that some of my friends at school laugh when they see my house."

"Their laughter cannot harm us."

"When do you think we'll be able to build a house of our own?"

"I don't know, Sanu." He took her hand and played with her fingers. "It might be a long time."

"How long?"

"I don't know. Maybe years."

"Will no husband want me because I live in a house like this?"

"Who told you that? Why wouldn't anyone want my pretty daughter?"

She smiled.

"Why are you worried about a husband? First, you have to study, go to a good college."

"I'm going to be a doctor."

"What kind of doctor?"

"I am going to be an animal doctor. A vete . . . a veterian." She fumbled with the word and Ramchandra laughed.

"Come, right now let's go and treat our stomachs. They're sick, and the only cure is dal-bhat." He took her hand and led her to the kitchen.

The kitchen, the smallest room in the house, had a window that overlooked the courtyard, and from it Ramchandra saw Mr. Sharma's shadow at his window.

Rakesh was already eating, and Goma served dal-bhat to Sanu and Ramchandra. The vegetable this evening was cauliflower, which they didn't have often, because it was expensive. He asked Goma why she'd bought it, and she replied that her mother had brought her two heads from the garden at Pandey Palace. The Pandeys had a gardener who took excellent care of the vegetables and the flowers. After he heard this, Ramchandra didn't ask for more cauliflower, even though it was delicious.

Seated on the wooden pirkas on the floor, the family ate quietly. Then Goma said to Sanu, "And what came over you this evening? Why did you speak to your grandparents that way?"

Sanu didn't respond, and Ramchandra signaled Goma to be quiet.

In the silence that ensued, they could hear one another chewing.

"This girl," Goma said. "She thinks she has become big."

Sanu was playing with the rice on her plate, her face dark.

"I want my children to have respect for their elders," Goma continued.

"Respect," Ramchandra said. "Maybe the elders should also learn the meaning of that word."

Rakesh, who had finished eating, was watching his parents attentively.

"And why aren't you eating?" Goma asked Sanu.

"Not hungry anymore," she mumbled.

"You can't let that go to waste. Do you know how hard your father works to feed you?"

"Okay, enough," Ramchandra said. "No more on this subject." And he coaxed Sanu to eat. She very reluctantly lifted her rice-filled fingers to her mouth.

Later, as Ramchandra and Goma were getting ready for bed, he told her, "Don't speak to her that way. She's very sensitive these days."

"I am afraid she's getting out of control," Goma said. "The

other day she argued with me about a dress that I didn't want her to wear."

"What was wrong with it?"

"It was too tight in the chest. And you know, she is getting bigger."

"She has a mind of her own."

"Too much mind of her own will make life difficult for her. She has to get married one day."

Ramchandra thought of Malati, who had brought a child into this world at such an early age, and he knew Goma was right. These days even girls from good families got themselves into trouble. "She'll be fine," he told Goma. "She is doing well at school. She likes to study. Says she wants to be a doctor."

"That's good."

He asked her what Mrs. Pandey had whispered into her ear that evening.

"Oh, nothing."

He placed his hand on her shoulder. "Am I such an outsider that you can't tell me?"

"Mother was talking about a girl from Chitwan. Her parents are very poor, and they want her to work as a servant here in the city. My sister can arrange to bring her here."

"We can't afford a servant."

"I know we can't afford one, but lately I've been very tired. All the cooking, the children . . ."

Their lack of a servant was another of the in-laws' issues. "My daughter is slaving away in your house, son-in-law," Goma's mother had remarked a few times. "How about someone just to help with the cooking and the laundry?" They'd even offered to send their own servant to help, but Ramchandra had refused. Now he wondered whether Goma had talked to her mother again about this. He studied her face. She did look tired, but, then, she usually looked this way after a visit from her parents.

"How much do they want?"

"I can negotiate for a hundred rupees a month. And she can wear Sanu's old clothes. She's only eleven years old."

"Let's think about this carefully," he said. "If we hire someone, that means even less money in savings. As it is, with Dashain this month we won't be able to set anything aside." He was about to ask why she had offered them sweets this evening, but he remembered the money he'd spent that morning, and kept quiet.

As he was about to fall asleep, he thought again of Malati, and for a brief moment, he entertained the notion of employing her as a servant. That way, she would get out of her stepmother's clutches, and he could tutor her more. But on second thought, the idea seemed ridiculous. Malati would probably balk at the idea of working as a servant in anyone's house, and, in fact, the idea made him uneasy; it was as if he were contemplating bringing home a second wife. He pushed the thought aside and concentrated on one of his beautiful vistas. This time he was on a mountain peak; the sun was rising, and snow glittered on the slopes all around. The sun cast an orange hue over everything.

3

· · · · · · ·

W HEN RAMCHANDRA WENT to the latrine in the courtyard the next morning,
with a pitcher of water and a towel, he found it occupied. Mr.
Sharma was inside, judging from the grunts and groans ema-
nating from behind the closed wooden door. He was a small
man with a goatee. His wife had died a few years earlier, and he
now spent most of his time reading religious tracts. Ramchandra glanced at his watch. He had woken up half an hour late
this morning. He usually liked to get up by six so that he could
have some time in the latrine before the other occupants of the
courtyard came down. On numerous occasions Ramchandra
had talked to the landlord about constructing bathrooms inside
the houses, but the landlord had told him the rent would then
go up by a hundred rupees. That silenced Ramchandra.

One time, when Sanu was in the latrine, some of the neighborhood boys had pried open the latch and teased her while she

tried to cover herself. She had cried the whole day, and Ramchandra had walked the streets, with a belt in hand, searching for the boys. He didn't find them, but he quarreled with the parents of one, and then went straight to the landlord, who lived two houses down the street. The landlord had dismissed his complaint, saying that the problem was with the latch, not the latrine, and he'd promised to install a sturdy latch that couldn't be opened from the outside. It had taken him a whole month to do that, and until it was installed, Ramchandra stood guard outside, with Rakesh beside him, every time Sanu needed the latrine. The structure was old and had tiny holes in the roof, so when it rained hard, water dripped on the occupant's head.

Mr. Sharma emerged after a full twenty minutes. "Oh, didn't know you were here, Ramchandra-ji. Would have come out earlier."

"That's all right," Ramchandra said and went in, with his pitcher. The stench was unbearable, and Ramchandra had to leave instantly. Resisting the urge to pinch his nose, he said, "Needs some air."

After a couple of minutes, Ramchandra entered again, and when he came out, Mr. Sharma had already started his bath at the tap. The city water flowed in abundance in this neighborhood, even though it was scarce in most parts of the city. Sometimes women from the neighborhood came to the courtyard to fill their gagros, because their own taps were dry. This had led to confrontations, the residents claiming that if the women used the tap too frequently, it would soon run dry, and the women asserting that decency demanded the insiders to grant their neighbors access to this water, which, in its ethereal form, belonged to no one. The shouts and screams and back-and-forth accusations had annoyed Ramchandra, and he finally came up with a compromise. He and his fellow residents would allow in two neighborhood families every day, and it was up to them to make the arrangements. So far, this had worked pretty well.

No one had yet come this morning, but they would soon, and Ramchandra wanted to finish bathing before the courtyard became crowded.

"That student of yours, how old is she?" Mr. Sharma said, applying soap to his armpits. "Twenty? Twenty-one? She's pretty."

Ramchandra was pouring water over his back, and it took him a moment to realize that Mr. Sharma was talking about Malati. "I don't notice such things, Sharma-ji," Ramchandra said. "Perhaps for a widower like you, they are important. For me, what's important is that I earn some income, and that the students pass the S.L.C."

Mr. Sharma laughed. "I was just making conversation, Ramchandra-ji. She is attractive. Only an observation."

Ramchandra grabbed his towel and said, "It must be hard for you, eh, Sharma-ji? All these years without your life partner." He started rubbing his back vigorously so that the heat from the friction would ward off the cold. He couldn't keep his teeth from chattering, whereas Mr. Sharma, whose head had just emerged from under the tap, seemed unaffected by the cold. Mr. Sharma said, "It's not hard at all. It's all a matter of willpower. Self-control. It's a question of bringing your mind to focus on something and exerting all your energy to bear upon it." He went on to recite some lines from the Vedas to illustrate his point, and Ramchandra's mind wandered toward Malati. He imagined her in the small chicken-feathered house in Tangal, in that cramped kitchen, frying potatoes while holding the baby in her arm, the baby's nostrils running with mucus, Malati's stepmother on the floor, sifting a pile of rice through her fingers to filter out pebbles and then tossing the pebbles behind her, to be swept up later.

With his towel, Ramchandra rubbed his belly and his crotch, and looked at Mr. Sharma, who, having realized that he'd lost his audience, was humming a song. The sacred thread he wore around his chest, a sign of his orthodox Brahminism, was shriveled, and Ramchandra couldn't help noticing, as he did every morning, the bulge in Mr. Sharma's underwear, unfazed by the cold it had just endured.

"To tell you the truth, Ramchandra-ji," Mr. Sharma said, his tone one of camaraderie and cunning, "sometimes it's hard. This life of celibacy."

Ramchandra was in no mood to hear his neighbor's confessions.

Mr. Sharma looked up at the sky. "Ever since my wife died, it's been a struggle. Sometimes I think I'll go mad. If I were in your position, with pretty young girls sitting next to me every day, I don't know what I'd do."

"Why don't you get married again?"

"That's not it," Mr. Sharma said. "I don't want a new wife. My departed wife's memory would not allow me to have someone else permanently in the house. It's just that my body sometimes . . ." And even the thought aroused him, for suddenly the bulge in his underwear stirred, and Ramchandra quickly excused himself and went upstairs.

Mr. Sharma had unsettled him, and he wondered whether it was a good idea for him to see Malati every day. But he'd already made the offer, and he'd even told Goma about it, told her that he felt sorry for the girl and had agreed to tutor her more for the same price. Goma hadn't questioned him. "Poor girl," she'd said. "You're doing the right thing."

Ramchandra combed his hair in the bedroom and went

downstairs to the bicycle shop to call Ashok and ask him to come to his session an hour later from now on.

Ashok didn't like the idea, and Ramchandra said, "I'm trying to solve a problem here, Ashok. I hope you understand."

"It's not that girl, is it, sir?" Ashok asked.

"What girl?"

"That girl you called monkey?"

"No, no."

"Strange girl. Nice-looking, though." Ashok was in one of his playful moods.

"So, is it okay?"

"Do I get a discount?"

"For what?"

"For doing you this favor?"

"No."

Ramchandra went back up to his bedroom, and he and Goma sat on the bed and drank their morning tea. Sanu and Rakesh had gone downstairs to brush their teeth and bathe.

"What are you thinking?" Goma asked. "Your mind seems far away."

Ramchandra looked at her sheepishly. "I was thinking about that girl. Looks as if she's had a hard life." He told her about the baby.

Goma shook her head. "That's not good. A young girl, having a baby without a husband. She doesn't look that kind."

"I don't think she is that kind."

"Well, don't worry about her too much. Do what you can."

Malati arrived for her tutoring session a short while after the children had left for school. She was wearing the same worn-out red kurta suruwal she'd worn the first time she came, but today she looked troubled.

"What's the matter?" Ramchandra asked as she sat down. "Is everything all right?"

She nodded and opened her textbook.

It was obvious that her mind was not on the math problems, because she chewed on her pencil and wrote slowly. When he explained the formula for compound interest, she didn't even nod with understanding; she merely kept her head lowered. After a while, Ramchandra gave her some problems to solve and left the room, saying he'd be back in a while. He went to the kitchen and drank some water. Goma had gone to the market to buy vegetables. Suddenly Ramchandra felt an urge for more tea, so he set the water to boil and looked out the window as he waited. Mr. Sharma was seated by his window, chanting, and his voice rang out clearly into the courtyard. Only after Ramchandra had poured milk and sugar into the boiling water did he realize that he should have made a glass for Malati, too. But, not wanting to wait for more water to boil, he poured himself the tea and was about to head back to the room when he saw Malati in the doorway.

"What's wrong?" he asked.

"Sir, I need to be excused today. I can't do the problems."

"Why?"

"I don't know. I can't concentrate."

"Here, I made some tea for you. Maybe this will help."

She gave him a wan smile. "I've already had my tea."

Nonetheless, he handed her the glass, which she took reluctantly. "Who's singing?"

He motioned her over to the window and pointed toward Mr. Sharma. Since the kitchen window was small, they had to stand close together to watch, and her shoulder touched his.

"What is he chanting?"

Ramchandra shrugged, his breath caught in his throat. He

saw that her eyes had a faraway look, and creases marked her forehead. He put his arm around her and drew her close. "What's bothering you?"

She stiffened, only momentarily, and placed her head on his shoulder. "Nothing is bothering me," she said in a small voice.

They stood like that for a while. He could smell the baby on her. He looked down at her face again, resting on his shoulder. The glass of tea was still in her hand, and her eyes were closed. He kissed the top of her head, then her forehead. He took the glass from her hand, placed it on the windowsill, and raised her face. Her eyes were still closed, but the creases on her forehead were gone. He kissed her lightly on the lips, and said, "Come, let's solve those problems." She shook her head and said she couldn't. "Look at me," he said. She opened her eyes. "You have to make yourself strong," he told her.

"I'm tired," she said.

"I'm tired, too. But I go on."

"You have people who love you."

"You have a daughter."

She looked toward the window again. "His voice is good," she said.

"Yes, he sings like this every morning."

"I have to go." She slipped out of his embrace and, as he followed her, walked to the bedroom. There, she picked up her books, smoothed her hair with her hand, and said, "I promise I will put my mind to it next time."

"Everything will be all right. You will pass the S.L.C."

He watched her go down the stairs and then went to the kitchen window so that he could see her leave the courtyard. Mr. Sharma briefly stopped his chanting to observe her.

Goma came home about fifteen minutes later and, noticing that Malati was gone, asked him what had happened. "She had a headache," Ramchandra said.

Goma went to the kitchen to prepare the morning meal.

Ashok arrived soon afterward and sat down with Ramchandra. "So, are you still tutoring Malati?" he asked.

"Yes."

"Has she improved any?"

"No."

"Do you think she'll pass the S.L.C.?"

"How do I know, Ashok? I don't guarantee passing or failing."

"But you have such a good reputation. It'd be a shame if she failed."

"Why don't you focus on your own exam? You think it's guaranteed that you'll pass?"

Ashok grinned. "Sir, what do you think? Don't you think I will?"

"Mere passing is not enough. You need to get good grades."

"I need to pass only because my father says so. He wants me to go to college before I take over the business."

"Not everyone has that luxury."

"Sir, why don't you start a business? I could help you. This teaching will get you nowhere. But you could be rich in a short time."

"Becoming rich is not my ambition," Ramchandra said.

After Ashok left, Goma and Ramchandra ate in the kitchen. Ramchandra could eat only half of his serving. He pushed the plate aside and said, "Save this for me. I'll have it for dinner."

"But you'll have no energy during the day."

"I just don't feel like eating." He washed his hands and mouth, got dressed, and headed for school.

He thought of Malati all day—while he taught, while he took his tea break, while he rushed a student, who'd cut his finger when playing, to Bandana Miss, while he watched her take out a first-aid kit and apply iodine and a bandage to the boy's hand. He thought of Malati as he walked home, the late afternoon traffic humming around him. He thought of her when, in Ratnapark, he saw girls her age from Padma Kanya College, wearing their saffron saris, walking along, laughter etched around their lips. He thought of her when he saw a beggar woman holding a baby in her lap, her hand stretched out for the coins people might throw in her direction.

And he thought of Goma, and the moment his mother had first shown him Goma's picture. He remembered feeling a faint tremor of excitement. She was a bit on the chubby side, but, with her large eyes, she seemed to be someone he could cuddle up to under a blanket on cold nights, someone whose belly he could caress, someone he could hold hands with and eat fritters from roadside stalls. In old age, after their children had quarreled with them and produced their own families, they'd help each other with their canes, up the stairs, on the streets. If she became ill, he'd go mad, and rush to fetch the best doctors in town. All these fantasies had converged upon him right in that instant when he saw her picture.

He'd said yes to his mother, and within a few months, he and Goma were married. The wedding was the first time Ramchandra got the sense that the Pandeys were not happy with the union. Ramchandra had expected a grand welcome at Pandey Palace when members of the wedding entourage arrived on that rainy afternoon, but the reception consisted of half-smiles, even stares. The wedding pyre was small, with only one priest, and the buffet table the guests flocked to after the ceremony had few dishes. Ramchandra did receive a large gold wedding ring from his in-laws, but when the bride's parents had to wash the feet of their son-in-law, a ritual symbolizing the godlike stature of a son-in-law, Mr. Pandey announced that it was an old ritual, one he did not want to perform. Mrs. Pandey was silent, but the distaste both of them felt for him was all over their faces. Some of Ramchandra's relatives complained, saying that not washing one's son-in-law's feet amounted to gross disrespect. A small argument broke out, and Ramchandra, worried about the way the celebration was going, raised his hand and said, "It doesn't matter. Sasura-ji is right—it is an outdated custom. Why should anyone wash my feet?"

That evening, throughout the ride in a hired taxi from Pandey Palace to his flat with his new bride, Ramchandra sat stiffly, thinking that the daughter probably shared her parents' attitude, and that he was now condemned to a lifetime of this.

After Ramchandra's mother received her new daughter-in-law, raised her bridal veil to see her face, and made the customary remarks about how beautiful she was and how she'd make a perfect daughter-in-law, Ramchandra had gone outside, saying he needed some fresh air, even though others tried to prevent him from leaving on his wedding night.

He'd walked the streets, tired from all the activity of the past few days, his mind numb with anxiety about what would happen later, once the wedding party left and he and his new wife were together, alone.

He returned to his flat about half an hour later, talked to some of his friends, and, after they left, entered the bedroom, where Goma sat on the bed, inspecting her fingers. She glanced up at him and quickly turned away. The gesture could have been charming, this quick turn of her head, which made her right earring glint under the light, but Ramchandra saw it as her rejection of him. He stood in the doorway and closed his eyes. When he opened them, he saw that she looked puzzled, as if she were saying, What's keeping you? Mustering up his courage, he took a step forward, but his eyes fell on a basket of fruit on the table. He went over to it and picked up a banana, which he brought over to her. "I don't know what time they fed you," he said, "but you must be hungry." She nodded but didn't take the banana from his hand. "Here," he said, "I'll peel it for you," and he did. "Here," and he held the naked banana close to her chin. Still, no response.

He felt awkward and sad. The daughter of rich parents, she's already unhappy with my poverty. But they'd known of his financial state and still had chosen him as her groom. He tried to find another reason. Could it be that she didn't like the way he looked? He wasn't a particularly good-looking man, but, with the broad forehead and pointed nose, his face was pleasant enough, he thought. He wondered whether she'd seen a picture of him before the marriage was arranged. He was about to put the banana on the table when he saw her shoulders heave. "What's the matter?" he asked. She covered her face with her hands, trying to suppress her laughter. "What did I say?" he said, smiling. "Why are you laughing?" And then he saw himself, holding a naked banana, on his wedding night, and trying to shove it down his wife's throat. He finally put it down and, placing his hand on her shoulder, turned her toward him and tried to pull her fingers from her face. They engaged in a little struggle. "You are a joker," she mumbled softly. Soon, he was on top of her, his chest pressing against her bosom. Laughing, he picked up the banana, pried open her fingers, and pushed it into her mouth.

4

. . . .

THE DAY AFTER he kissed Malati, Ramchandra got up before the sun rose. As he was heading out the door, Goma woke up and asked where he was going. "For a walk," he said.

"At this hour?" She glanced at the clock. "It's not even five yet."

"I'm feeling restless. I'll be back within an hour."

The only people on the streets were farmers, carrying their baskets. Groups of dogs loitered on the corners, yawning or sniffing one another. Ramchandra moved toward New Road and crossed the Tundikhel field. The grass was covered with frost, and by the time he left the field on the other side, his shoes were wet.

At the incline of Dillibazaar, a faint glow lit the eastern horizon, and some of the shopkeepers, especially those who sold tea and sweets, were opening their doors. He had an urge to walk toward Tangal, knock on Malati's door, and tell her not to come to his house anymore, that he could no longer tutor her. Or perhaps crawl into bed next to her.

By the time he reached Battisputali, his feet were humming. It was nearly six, and if he were to turn back now, it would be seven by the time he reached home, and Malati would be there. He moved toward the crossroad leading to the Pashupatinath Temple. He hadn't been to the temple for months, but his anxiety over Malati told him that this was a good time to pray to Shivaji. Men and women were walking down the slight slope toward the main gate. Some carried offerings, others were empty-handed, out for a morning walk or a chat with their friends.

Inside the temple, he stood beside the giant bull that faced the main shrine, and began to pray. He wanted to pray for something specific, but his mind went blank. So he fell back on a regular Jai Jagadish Hare, one that he heard on Radio Nepal every morning. Still, he felt that praying for a particular hope would be more powerful. Perhaps he should stand in line to get a glimpse of the four-headed Shiva. Maybe the sight of the Lord's black figure would quiet the disturbance he was feeling. He noted that the line wasn't long, as it soon would be, but he looked at his watch, became anxious, and abandoned the idea.

It was six-thirty by the time he walked out to the main road, so he hailed a three-wheeler. The driver careened through the morning traffic, and Ramchandra closed his eyes and leaned back. Only when the man asked, "Where do you want me to stop?" did Ramchandra realize he had fallen asleep. He asked the driver to stop right outside his house. He paid the fare and was about to enter the courtyard, when, on impulse, he turned around and went into the tea shop on the opposite side of the street. The shopkeeper, who knew him, was surprised. "What happened, guruji? Your wife refused to make tea for you this morning?" Ramchandra mumbled something about there not being enough milk in the house, ordered a glass of tea, and sat by the window.

At seven o'clock, Malati approached, her textbooks held against her chest. She looked frail, tired. She entered the courtyard, and Ramchandra waited, forgetting his steaming glass of tea. At seven-fifteen she came out and stood at the courtyard entrance, scanning the street. Ramchandra moved back from the window so that she wouldn't spot him. When he raised his eyes, he saw Goma seated near their bedroom window, watching Malati.

Malati waited for several minutes before walking away, with an occasional look back. Ramchandra wanted to follow her, but he knew that Goma would see him. Her eyes were following Malati until she disappeared into the crowd. Then Goma left the window. Ramchandra paid for his tea and briskly walked in the direction Malati had gone. After about one block, he spotted the red ribbon she'd tied around her hair. Now, suddenly, he didn't know what he would say to her. He could apologize for not having been there when she came, but what excuse could he give?

He followed her at a distance, keeping the red hair ribbon in sight, wishing he could see her face. He knew that she would walk all the way to Tangal, at least three kilometers, because she couldn't afford to take a three-wheeler. She moved in the direction of Indrachowk and walked into the Durbar Square area, where she stood in front of the Hanuman statue, her hands folded in prayer to the monkey god. Ramchandra slid behind a nearby temple, frightening a flock of doves, which rose into the air in a huff. As Malati walked back to the road, he followed, and the conversations of pedestrians floated around him like a song. His body became light, airy. Everything around him — the houses, the shops, the faces of people walking past — receded, and the only thing he saw clearly was the back of her head, the red ribbon in her hair.

After a while, it seemed to him that she was keeping track of him, as if she had eyes in the back of her head. So each was following the other. It was like the painting people hung above their door during Nag Panchami: two snakes about to eat each other's tails. This image gave him more energy; the sense that he too was being pursued quickened his pulse. He smiled at a couple of familiar faces, even said hello to a neighbor carrying shopping bags, but he made these gestures elsewhere, in a place different from the one he now occupied with Malati.

In the heavy crowd of shoppers in Asan, she vanished, and Ramchandra found himself squeezed between the cries of the newspaper vendors, who sang in loud voices the headlines of the day: INDIA IN COLLUSION WITH BANNED PARTIES; CLANDESTINE MEETINGS OF CPN. A cow nudged against his hip, and he gently pushed it away, only to discover that he had stepped on its droppings, which clung to his shoes.

But he had to find Malati. He tried to peer over the heads of the crowd. A flash of red, then the tilt of a shoulder. Yes, she'd already entered the street leading to Ratnapark. He ran toward her, bumping into shoppers, drawing mumbles of criticism from them. By the time he caught up to her, she was passing the co-op store of Sajha Bhandar. He stayed a few yards behind her, breathing hard, the great sense of relief making him giddy. When at last she reached the opening of Asan and its bookstores, he called out to her.

She turned around, and didn't appear surprised to see him.

"I am sorry about this morning."

"It's okay, sir. I thought you must have been occupied with something."

"I was not occupied. I don't know what happened to me."

For a moment, neither said anything more. Together they crossed the road toward Ratnapark, their shoulders touching, the cars and motorcycles weaving around them. He let his hand touch hers.

"Are you going home now?" he asked.

She nodded.

"Let's go inside the park for a while."

"Rachana is at home."

"No one to look after her?"

"Malekha Didi is taking care of her, but sometimes she gets annoyed when I'm away."

"Okay, I'll walk you home."

"It's not necessary, sir. I can go by myself."

"No, I want to." Once again, he wanted to offer some sort of apology, but he restrained himself. Suddenly, in the middle of Baghbazaar, she said, "I knew you were following me, sir."

"Then why didn't you turn around?"

She didn't respond, and they walked quietly. Finally, Ramchandra said, "I shouldn't have done what I did yesterday."

She said nothing.

As they neared Tangal, he said, "I hope you'll come tomorrow. I promise I'll be there."

"Maybe it won't work."

"No, it will work. You need to pass the S.L.C. exam. You need to get out of that house."

She eyed him carefully. "Why are you saying this? Why do I need to get out of my house?"

"Things are not right for you there."

She was about to say something, then shrugged and said only, "Sir, you needn't worry about me."

"I want things to be better for you."

"You have a family to think about."

"This doesn't take away from my family. So, you will come then?"

She nodded.

At home, Goma, seated at the window from where she'd watched Malati, was anxiously scanning the street. As soon as she spotted her husband, she left the window and went down to meet him in the courtyard.

"What happened to you?"

"Nothing happened to me. I went for a walk."

"Look at the time," she said. "That girl and Ashok have already come and gone. If you don't eat quickly and head for school, you'll miss your first class."

A wave of exhaustion washed over Ramchandra. "I lost track of time."

"What's bothering you?"

"Nothing, Goma. Let's go upstairs." He took her hand and led her up the stairs.

"You've never done anything like this before."

On the landing, he stopped and said, "Actually, I'm not feeling well. Maybe I won't go to school today."

Instinctively, her hand reached for his forehead. "It's not warm. You don't seem to have a fever. But if you weren't feeling well, why didn't you just come home? Why walk all morning?"

"No, it's not fever," he said.

He went into the bedroom and lay down, thinking Bandana Miss wouldn't be pleased if he called in sick. She didn't like last-minute phone calls about absences; they made her suspicious, she said. But what would he do if he didn't go to school? He'd go insane staying in the house, thinking.

Goma brought in a plate of his dal-bhat. "I also made some

soup," she said. "This should make you feel better. I'll go down and call Bandana Miss."

He signaled to her to stop; he'd eat first.

She watched as he ate. "Look at you. I don't know what's eating you, and why you won't tell me."

"Nothing's eating me," he said; then, smiling, "I'm eating this food." He noticed that she wasn't eating with him, so he asked her to bring her plate. She said she'd eat later.

"Maybe we should have Dr. Shrestha check you, just to make sure."

Young Dr. Shrestha, who ran a clinic in the neighborhood, had come to the house a few months earlier to tend to Rakesh and Sanu. Ramchandra reminded Goma that they hadn't paid the doctor for his last two visits. "Besides, I'm feeling better," he said. And it was true. The food had calmed him. If he rushed, he could still make it to his first class. That meant he'd have to take a three-wheeler again. It had been a bad morning.

A traffic jam near the New Road Gate delayed the three-wheeler, and Ramchandra's anxiety mounted. By the time the congestion cleared, and the three-wheeler raced in the direction of Bir Hospital, it was already past the time when his first class began.

Bandana Miss frowned as he walked in to sign the register. "You'll have to sign in late," she said.

Ramchandra pointed toward his watch. "I'm only ten minutes late."

"One minute or ten minutes. Late is late. I want everyone in this school to be punctual."

You didn't care about punctuality the other day when you were talking about your son, he wanted to say, but he simply wrote down the time of his arrival next to his signature.

"I also need to talk to you during tea break."

"About what?"

"I'll tell you then."

Ramchandra collected his book and notes and headed toward the classroom, slightly apprehensive about what Bandana Miss wanted to discuss. Malati? But that was ridiculous. She didn't have access to his thoughts.

The students were making a lot of noise, but they quieted down when he entered. He did a couple of problems on the board, but because his mind was so fuzzy, he made a few mistakes, which some of the bright students in the class didn't hesitate to point out. "Okay, okay," he said as he corrected his errors. He had to finish a particular chapter this week, but he knew he didn't have the strength to stand up during the entire class period, so he assigned the students exercises from the book and slumped in his chair. His mind went back to the morning, to Malati saying that all along she'd known he was behind her.

He woke to the angry whispers of Bandana Miss. "You don't get paid to sleep in the classroom, Ramchandra-ji."

He wiped his face. "I didn't sleep well last night."

Some students tittered at the sight of their teacher being scolded. Bandana Miss marched out of the classroom with a frown. During the next class, Ramchandra remained alert. Mr. Tiwari had never policed his teachers, which was fine at those times when it was good to let loose, to tell the students outrageous stories or allow them to work on something creative. But some teachers took advantage of Mr. Tiwari's casual attitude, and that had led to a general decline among the students' performances, clearly evident in the large number who failed the S.L.C. Ramchandra admired Bandana Miss's vigilance, but today she seemed to him too strict, and his resentment grew.

During the twenty-minute recess, he waited in the staff

room for Bandana Miss. Gokul Sir and Miss Lama were in a corner, discussing how well-to-do parents in the city were sending their children to Darjeeling and Kalimpong in India for private schooling. Gokul Sir said that it was merely a fashion, that those schools were overrated, and Miss Lama was defending her home turf, asserting that those schools had high success rates, unlike certain schools she knew where children had to slog through the city garbage before they could sit down to read. Khanal Sir was reading a book of poems by a young Nepali poet; Manandhar Sir was staring out the window at the back of the building, where some stray dogs played. The only one not here was Shailendra Sir, hired last year to teach history. He was young, about twenty-five, and was studying for his master's degree at Tribhuvan University.

When Bandana Miss finally appeared, she took Ramchandra out to the corridor.

"Is everything okay, Ramchandra-ji?" Her face was softer now. "You're the last person I'd expect to see sleeping in the classroom."

"As I said, I didn't get a good night's sleep."

"Is the family okay? Your children?"

"Everyone is fine, Bandana Miss. Only lack of sleep. Simple."

"I called you in to consult about Shailendra Sir."

Ramchandra waited.

"There are rumors in the school. He's having a relationship with a girl."

"A student?"

"Yes. Namita from tenth grade. With glasses. Always wears very nice iron-pressed uniform."

Ramchandra knew which girl she meant, and he immediately recalled seeing Shailendra with Namita a few days ago, talking and laughing outside a classroom, she leaning against the wall, his hand gesticulating near her face. At the time he'd thought nothing of it; some bonding between teachers and students was expected.

"It might just be a rumor."

"Yes, except this. I found this on the floor of the tenth-grade classroom." She handed him a paper. It was a love poem, written in flowery language, with hearts drawn all over the page. It spoke of how handsome Shailendra Sir was and how the poet was so much in love with him. It was signed by Namita.

"It's not unusual for young girls to become infatuated like this. Doesn't mean Shailendra Sir reciprocates her feelings." He handed back the note.

"She's been getting excellent grades in his class, and she's not a bright student." She took a sheaf of paper from her bag and showed him some numbers. Namita hovered in the barely passing range in most of her classes, except history, where she was at the top.

"She could be a good history student."

Bandana Miss put the papers away and said, "Just not possible. Do you know that right now, even as we speak, they are together?"

She took him by the arm, led him to one of the classrooms, and had him peek through the back door. Shailendra Sir and Namita were seated on the front bench, together, a book open on the desk before them, but they were talking.

Back at their original spot in the corridor, Ramchandra asked Bandana Miss, "And what can I do about this?"

She appeared hurt by this question. "Ramchandra-ji, I respect you a great deal. You are a good example of what a teacher should be, and that's why I was surprised when I found you dozing in the classroom. But I understand you were tired.

Now I want some advice about this situation. Namita's parents are rich, well connected. If they find out, the school's reputation will be damaged."

This school has no reputation, Ramchandra thought, but he admired Bandana Miss's attempt to uphold its dignity. "Bandana Miss, tell me. What should I do?"

"I thought perhaps you could talk to him."

"And say what?"

She was exasperated. "I shouldn't have to tell you that. Talk to him about how dangerous it is."

"What if he denies everything and gets angry?"

"If you tell him, he won't get angry. I could tell him, but he always sulks when he's with me."

"All right, I'll talk to him," Ramchandra said. "But the rest is up to him. If he gets angry, I won't say anything further."

The end-of-recess bell rang, and they saw Shailendra Sir and Namita leave the classroom. Shailendra Sir noticed them, moved away from Namita, and walked toward the staff room, greeting them as he passed.

All day Ramchandra looked for an opportunity to talk to Shailendra. His initial dread vanished when he realized that it was distracting him from concentrating on Malati. As he wrote a problem on the board, or had a student recite a multiplication table, Ramchandra rehearsed what he would say. He tried various openings. Some were soft: "Shailendra babu, as an older person, I reserve the right to say certain things to you for your own benefit." Others were more blunt: "Shailendra, her parents will take you to court and hang you." The range of openings became a game for Ramchandra, and often he lost track of which trigonometry problem he was trying to teach his ninth-grade class. He kept glancing toward the corridor for a glimpse of Shailendra, or of Shailendra and Namita together, giggling and whispering, until finally Aloo, named so because of his potato-like head, commented, "Sir, are you expecting someone? The headmiss, perhaps?"

Ramchandra knew he'd find Shailendra in the staff room after classes were over, but he didn't want to pull him aside there, because that would arouse suspicion in the other teachers. When, finally, he saw Shailendra walking by the classroom, in a hurry, possibly toward the bathroom. Ramchandra gave his students a problem to solve from the textbook and hurried out to the corridor. Shailendra was already inside the bathroom, so Ramchandra headed in, too.

He stood before the urinal next to Shailendra, said something about how he couldn't wait for the day to be over. Shailendra agreed, though he had to attend a couple of night classes. The bathroom, with three urinals and two in-ground toilets, had been recently renovated, thanks to Bandana Miss's efforts, and was cleaned regularly, so it was much more bearable than it had been during Mr. Tiwari's tenure, when urine and feces floated on the floor.

Once they were done and were walking out, Ramchandra asked Shailendra, "So, any plans for your wedding?"

Shailendra, surprised, said, "No. Not until I finish my master's degree."

Ramchandra paused for a moment and went on. "There are some rumors in the school, Shailendra-ji."

"About my marriage?"

In a nearby classroom, fourth-graders were chanting the names of the country's fourteen states.

"No. About Namita."

Shailendra frowned. "What? What about her?"

"I know they're not true," Ramchandra said. "But you ought to be careful."

"What are people saying? I've done nothing." He started fiddling with his ear.

"Whatever it is," Ramchandra said, "it's best that you not associate with her outside the classroom."

Shailendra started to explain, but Ramchandra put his hand up. "Shailendra-ji, whatever it is, I am only doing this for your sake. It is not good when people talk about you. It is not good for a teacher to have any kind of extracurricular relationship with a student."

"But I'm helping her with her history."

"And I am merely advising you. The rest is up to you." Ramchandra touched his arm. "You are young; you have a full life ahead of you. Don't do anything foolish." And he left Shailendra rubbing his ear, staring at him.

For the rest of the school day, Ramchandra's head rang with fragments of his own voice, and those of Bandana Miss, about a teacher-student relationship, so by the time he left the school, his temples were throbbing with pain.

He went home, gulped two tablets of Citamol, and lay down on the bed. Sanu and Rakesh came into the room.

"Where were you all morning?" Sanu asked.

He made up an excuse.

"Malati and Ashok came. I think Malati was disappointed."

"And Ashok was not?"

"Ashok was smiling," Rakesh said.

Rakesh brought over some drawings he'd done at school, and for a while the three huddled together, commenting on the pictures, suggesting how Rakesh could make them better. Goma brought him tea. "Are you not feeling well again?"

"No, just a headache today," Ramchandra said. "Why don't we go to the cinema this evening?"

Sanu and Rakesh began shouting in excitement. They'd been

pestering their parents for days, and Goma had put her foot down each time, saying that the cinemas they showed these days were not appropriate for children.

"What about your headache?"

"It's already gone," Ramchandra lied.

"And where's the money going to come from?" Goma said, with a frown.

Ramchandra waved his hand in the air. "Money comes, money goes. One needs to enjoy life once in a while." *If only I really believed that*, he thought ruefully. But he did need a diversion, something to get him out of the confines of this house and his thoughts.

"That's a strong philosophy," Goma said. "That'll really get us far, with rent to pay and tuition and books for the children. Someone will also give us a house with utmost respect."

Sanu looked at Goma pleadingly. "Mother, we never do anything fun. We haven't even gone to the Ramailo Mela this year, as you promised."

"So, why don't we go to Ramailo Mela instead?" Ramchandra suggested.

Sanu and Rakesh became even more excited. Goma was conducting an internal battle, he could tell. She enjoyed watching the people, all dressed up, walking around, buying ice cream or riding the Ferris wheel. But she was also thinking of the cost, how much it would chip away at their savings.

Ramchandra did some quick calculations. Seven rupees for two adults at the fair, and three-fifty each for the children, which made a total of twenty-one rupees. And some for the rides, so they'd probably spend thirty to thirty-five rupees. At the cinema, they might have to purchase tickets on the black market, and that would cost nearly fifty, maybe more. Either way, they'd be able to put aside very little this month. "Maybe we shouldn't go. Maybe we should stay home and play carom instead. Or cards. That'll also be fun, won't it?"

The children's faces dropped. Sanu said nothing, and Rakesh looked as if he were about to cry. The parents exchanged glances. "Okay, we can go to Ramailo Mela," Ramchandra finally said. "But only one ride."

"Ice cream?" Rakesh asked.

"In this weather?" Goma said. "You'll catch a cold."

"If you insist, Mr. Rakesh Icecreamwallah," Ramchandra said, "but only the cheap kind."

There was a long line outside Bhrikuti Mandap, and Ramchandra was annoyed to find that the prices had been raised since last year. Now the total came to thirty rupees. But once they were inside, and the children's faces were shining with joy, Ramchandra couldn't regret the outing.

Throngs of people walked around under the bright lights from the stalls. In the middle of the grounds, on a large patch of grass, stood a giant wheel that penetrated the sky, and the whistle of the children's train came around a corner. People from the stalls shouted in loud voices, advertising their wares. Some even stepped out and acted like clowns to solicit customers. One sold unidentifiable dark objects in serious-looking jars — medicine, Ramchandra was told. But most of the stalls had games, which usually involved throwing a hoop, a ball, or some other object onto something else — an action that involved a degree of precision. Few people won anything, Ramchandra noticed, and when they did, it was usually something small and disappointing.

Sanu and Rakesh got on the Ferris wheel, and Ramchandra and Goma watched them disappear up in the sky and come down again, up and down, their faces flushed. They ate gol-gappas served by a man from a cart; judging by the vendor's dark skin and his accent, Ramchandra figured he was from India. They watched, fascinated, as he broke open the top of each paper-thin wafer with the tip of his thumb, filled it with mashed vegetables, and dipped it into the bowl of spiced water, from which it emerged ready for the plate. The wafers disintegrated on their tongues, delicious, as the spicy water tickled the roofs of their mouths.

Ramchandra recalled his conversation with the three-wheeler driver the other day, and he asked the gol-gappa man, "Where in India are you from?"

"I am not an Indian, hajoor," the man said with a smile. "I am Nepali, from Rautahat."

Ramchandra was embarrassed.

"But you're not the first one. Many people call me Indian. Some even treat me badly. Once a bunch of teenagers toppled my cart."

"People don't know the truth," Goma said.

"Delicious," Ramchandra said to the man as he paid. "Go to the police if someone harasses you. Don't sit quiet."

"The police are no better," the man said. And he gave an extra gol-gappa to Rakesh. "I have a son back in the village your age," he said.

Rakesh took the gol-gappa with glee and asked the man his son's name. When the vendor said, "Rakesh," everyone burst out laughing, and Rakesh blushed. Ramchandra explained the coincidence to the bewildered vendor, who, smiling, gave Rakesh one more gol-gappa. "Then you are my son."

Rakesh wanted to try his hand at a children's shooting range, and Ramchandra carefully counted out the ten rupees demanded by the man behind the stall. Ramchandra had to help his son steady the toy gun and aim it at the stuffed deer and owls and bears in the foliage a few feet away. Rakesh missed all his marks, and complained that he would have fared better without his father's help. Sanu became entranced by a pink doll with large blue eyes on display at a store. "Made in Japan," the storekeeper said. She looked pleadingly at Ramchandra, who walked away when he discovered that the doll cost twenty-five rupees. Sanu was so disappointed that Ramchandra silently queried Goma, who signaled no. Ramchandra took Goma aside and said, "Her birthday is coming soon. Why don't we buy it and save it for her birthday?"

"You do what you want to do," she said. "But don't keep pestering me about your living in a hellhole."

Ramchandra returned to the store and purchased the doll. "This is not for right now," he told Sanu. "This is for someone special's special birthday." Sanu asked if she could hold the doll for a little while, and Ramchandra handed it to her and said, "Aren't you too old to be playing with this?"

"But she's so pretty. I'll give it to my daughter and tell her she got it from her grandfather."

He realized then that he hadn't been thinking about Malati for a while, and this awareness led him to think about her, which made him despondent. Now, in this festive atmosphere, he couldn't help wondering what it would be like to come here with Malati, to hold her hand while they visited the stalls. He imagined them disappearing behind a stall and sitting on the grass to talk, his head in her lap, observing the people enjoying the activities while they remained unseen. He had a very clear picture of what she would wear: something he'd bought for her. A bright red kurta suruwal, with small mirrored sequins in which he could see parts of his face; a pearl necklace that he would buy her at a jewelry stall; and a pair of kohlapuri sandals like those he'd just noticed in a shoe shop. She would look radiant, and as he walked beside her, he would squeeze her hand, rubbing his thumb across her palm.

This juvenile fantasy saddened him, and Goma, noting the change in his face, asked whether his headache had come back.

"Perhaps those gol-gappas didn't sit well with me," he said.

"We aren't going to leave now, are we?" Sanu said. "We haven't been to the bingo hall yet." In Sanu's school they often played bingo, and she loved the game.

"Okay, we'll go play bingo, then head home." Ramchandra quit trying to add up the cost; this was an expensive evening, and that was that.

Inside the hall, Sanu purchased the bingo tickets and sat down with Goma and Rakesh to play; Ramchandra stood to the side, leaning against the wall, listening to the rhythmic intonation of the man who announced the numbers. Outside, the day had given way to the gray haziness of dusk. He closed his eyes, and instantly conjured up an image of Malati, this time wearing a bright red sari, like a bride. She was smiling at him. Ramchandra jerked his eyes open. Goma was calling him from her seat a few yards away. She pointed to the front, and said, "Isn't that one of your teachers?" He looked in that direction, and saw Shailendra and, with him, Namita. They sat close to each other, their shoulders rubbing. Shailendra whispered something in Namita's ear, and she let out a laugh.

Before they headed home, Rakesh reminded his parents about the ice cream, so, with a sigh of resignation, Ramchandra bought two pistachio ice cream cones. As they exited Bhrikuti Mandap and walked toward Shahid Gate, Goma asked whether the woman with Shailendra was his wife. Goma had met Shailendra last year at the annual school picnic, and had commented on what a polite young man he was. "She looked awfully young," she said.

Ramchandra told her about Bandana Miss's conversation with him that morning, and his subsequent talk with Shailendra. "It's not right, what he's doing," he said. "The girl is too young, and she's a student. She's probably in awe of him. He's taking advantage of her."

"Perhaps he's helpless."

Her statement surprised him. "Helpless? About what? He's a teacher. He should know better."

"People have their own reasoning."

Rakesh and Sanu were walking in front of them, arms around each other, lost in their ice cream.

After a while Ramchandra said, "I'm surprised that you're supporting him."

"I didn't say I'm supporting him. I just said we can't judge people without knowing what's ailing them."

It occurred to him that she might be thinking of his judgment of her parents, and this annoyed him. But he didn't want to argue with her on this fine evening, when the children were happy and the air was nippy and refreshing, so he said, "That can't be love. If he loves her, he should ask for her hand in marriage."

"Maybe he will. Maybe he's waiting for the right moment."

"How would you feel if one of Sanu's teachers did something like that?"

"Sanu is too young." Then she added, "Well, not all that young. She's already started."

It took a moment for Ramchandra to understand. "Already?"

"Yes, last week. She was complaining of pain, and there was blood."

Ramchandra looked at his daughter, who was now singing in her brother's ear.

They started to discuss again the idea of hiring that servant girl from Chitwan, but Ramchandra, still going over the conversation about Shailendra, still counting up the expenses of the evening, said, "We'd have to feed her, buy her clothes."

"If she works for us, though, I'll have time to sew. Garment businesses are really picking up in the city; this is a good time to start." Goma had long harbored the wish to start a sewing business at home to augment their income. She had the Singer machine she'd brought with her when they got married, and she was good at sewing. She could start by making petticoats and blouses, altering clothes for women in the neighborhood, and then branch out into making clothes for garment shops on a contractual basis. Ramchandra had initially opposed the idea, thinking that it was somehow beneath a teacher's wife to work as a common tailor. But Goma had raised the issue many times, and he himself had seen that the culture of the city was changing. Even Brahmins were opening shops these days; some were even selling alcohol. What would be the harm, if sewing made her happy and, more important, added to the family income?

"Okay, let's arrange to have her come," he said.

That evening, the children, happy after the excursion to the fair, asked Ramchandra to continue the story he'd started the other day. He pleaded a headache, but Rakesh said that without the story he wouldn't be able to sleep. And since Rakesh often turned his threats into reality, Ramchandra gave in. He had to recall what he'd told them: poor girl living with her mother; father left years ago to work in the city; now rich village merchant wants to marry her.

"So, this girl, Mandakini, didn't like the merchant. But—"

"That's not her name," Rakesh said. "She had a different name last time. What was it?"

"Malati," Sanu said. "Ba's student's name."

"Well, it's different now, okay?"

"But how can her name change?" Sanu protested. "It was Malati before, so it has to be Malati now."

Goma, who had just finished washing the dishes, peeked in. "What are you saying about that girl?"

Sanu explained to her mother, and Goma looked at Ramchandra with annoyance. "Couldn't you find any other name to use?"

"That's why I wanted to change it now."

"Don't use her name," Goma said sharply, and moved away, pulling the children's door nearly shut.

"See? Now you made your mother angry at me," Ramchandra whispered jokingly to the children, who giggled. But he could tell that Goma had sensed something; it was on her face. He shifted back to the story.

"As the day of the wedding approached, the girl, Mandakini, became sadder and sadder. She went to the local temple and prayed to Lord Shiva to save her from marrying a man her father's age. She visited the local palm reader, and he traced the lines on her hand and told her that she would be very rich but very unhappy. She climbed a mountain and, from the top, looked down on the thin, milky white river that ran between two steep gorges, and she closed her eyes and asked the deity who resided there to make something happen so that she wouldn't have to marry that old merchant with the glinting eyes.

"But nothing happened until the evening of the wedding, when the old merchant came riding on his elephant and the ceremonies began. Then, right in the middle of the priest's chanting, an unbelievable thing happened, something that made everyone's jaw fall open.

"And that's it for today," Ramchandra said, not knowing where to go next. "To be continued." The children protested, but not too much, perhaps thinking the story might go on too long.

Back in his room, Ramchandra saw that Goma was already asleep, or was pretending to be. When he got into bed, he caressed her back and waited. Finally she turned to him.

"Are you angry with me?" he whispered.

"There's too much of that girl in this house," she said.

"I was merely fishing for a name."

"What's on your mind?" Goma asked.

"Nothing's on my mind. Why?"

"You've been very distracted these days. I keep feeling you're not telling me something."

"There's nothing," he said. "I'm tired." He rolled over the other way and closed his eyes.

"Shall I give you a massage?" she asked softly, and, just to keep her from questioning him, he nodded.

She started on his lower back. Her hands were warm; they felt surprisingly good. He imagined them to be Malati's hands, and his pleasure intensified. He turned over again, and, his eyes still closed, reached for her breasts. Goma laughed softly. "What are you doing? I thought you were tired."

He lifted her gown and pulled down her underwear. It had been quite some time since they had allowed themselves this.

His penis was hard, and as he entered her, he shut his eyes. Malati floated enticingly into his mind, but he pushed her away and focused on one of his fantasy scenes: a park, with radiant flowers, daisies and hibiscus and camellias and rhododendrons, frogs croaking, a colorful parrot perched on a branch, the sky blue, like a crystal lake. As his mind became brighter, he opened his eyes and looked at Goma, who was now moaning.

5

· · · · · · · ·

From where they stood, on an elevation on the opposite side of the river, they could clearly see the stone steps that led up from the ghat to the Pashupatinath Temple. Devotees moved up and down the stairs, some descending to the bank to dip their bodies in the holy Bagmati River; others climbing to enter the temple, and perhaps the main shrine, of which only the upper tier and the shining gold pagoda were visible to Ramchandra and Malati. The gazebo inside the temple complex that overlooked the river, usually crowded with chanting devotees and a harmonium player, was deserted today, except for a man, perhaps a laborer, taking a nap. Occasionally one of numerous bells around the temple sounded—a devotee waking a god for a blessing.

On the bank of the river below them, a woman was washing clothes, the soapsuds drifting south, past the bridge. The river was filthy, its color resembling sewage water; the deep black must contain some desperate sin, Ramchandra was sure, even though the river was revered as the sustainer of life. Still, a naked boy of about twelve was taking a bath, pinching his nose and immersing himself in the muck, then coming out with a whoop. Against the wall of the ghat sat a sadhu, on this cold day dressed in only a loincloth. His body was smeared with ash—all signs of the ascetic life he'd devoted to Lord Shiva. He held a small chillum in his hands, and occasionally inhaled from it, blowing the hashish smoke into the morning air, his eyes on the boy.

"It must be difficult to abandon everything in order to live as an ascetic," Malati said. Today she wore a blue sari; it made her look serene, pure. "No family, no home," she said. "Don't know where you're going to be next month."

"There's a certain charm to it, don't you think? Imagine the freedom you'd have."

They were standing, their bodies touching, and now she moved back and sat down on a stone platform. He joined her and took her hand. "How's Rachana?"

"She's with Malekha Didi."

"She's such a lovely baby," he said, although he'd caught only a glimpse of Malati's daughter, that day when he first went to her house.

"All babies are lovely," she said distractedly, then looked at him and said, sharply, "I don't know what I'm doing here with you."

Earlier that morning, when they'd finished the tutoring session, she had readily agreed to meet him at the temple. After she'd left, he'd gone downstairs to the shop and called the school, telling Bandana Miss that he didn't feel well and wouldn't be able to come. "A little sickness should not prevent you from teaching," she'd said. "How am I going to find a substitute on such short notice?" Ramchandra had coughed viciously, said he was burning with fever, and hung up. Then, after his morning meal, he'd left the house as if he were going to the school. He didn't know what Malati would tell her stepmother, whether she had to lie to her at all, what her stepmother would think of her meeting her tutor like this. But she'd been happy to be with him and had talked to him gaily, until now, when her mood shifted. A tension line on her forehead was clearly visible. Perhaps she was a moody girl, he thought, like the monsoon sky, clear one moment and the next filled with dark clouds.

He had no answer for her, so he reached out and touched her face.

She drew away. "Someone will see, sir."

"Let them see," he said, trying to sound nonchalant. "What difference does it make?"

"It makes all the difference," she said. "Goma bhauju will learn about this. Everything will fall apart."

He was annoyed. "Then why did you agree to meet me?"

"I wanted to see you." She inspected her fingernails.

"You'd have seen me tomorrow morning, during the session."

"What about you? Why did you ask me to meet you here?" she asked in a challenging tone.

"I wanted to see you in the open air, in the sunlight."

"Why?"

"So that I could get a different perspective, see your face clearly."

Her challenge dissolved, and she probed his face with her large eyes. "Do you like what you see?"

He touched her lips.

"Sir." This time she didn't turn away.

He kissed her, grinding his lips into hers, hard, and she said, "Let's go someplace else. Everyone will see us here."

They wandered through the woods behind them and finally found shelter in a ruined, abandoned temple. Inside, it was nearly dark; a stone statue of Lord Ganesh lay in the corner, the lower half of its elephant trunk broken. Someone had painted a red mustache above the statue's upper lip so that it looked like a warrior with a broken nose. Cobwebs hung from the corners, and the floor was dusty. Ramchandra wrapped his hand around Malati's waist and pulled her toward him. This time she responded. She ground her groin against him, and he felt himself rise. They explored each other's mouths, and he squeezed her breasts. She began to moan. He lowered her to the floor — and at once, both of them sneezed from the dust. They laughed. His lips against hers, he fumbled with the buttons of her blouse. She stroked the back of his head.

He felt a tug at his trousers and thought it was her hand, but then he turned and saw a large monkey. It was an arm's length away, watching them. Ramchandra waved a hand to shoo away the monkey, but it blinked once and kept gazing, its eyes watery, as if the creature were saddened by the sight of the two. Malati let out a cry. Ramchandra heaved himself up from the floor and was looking for something to throw at the monkey when two more monkeys entered the temple. All three sat on their haunches and observed Ramchandra and Malati. "Do something," Malati cried, and Ramchandra, scanning the floor, saw the broken elephant trunk lying beside the statue. He picked it up and hurled it at the animals, who merely ducked their heads. A few more monkeys now stood at the entrance of the temple.

"Hurry!" Ramchandra told Malati. "Let's go." But Malati was frozen on the floor. One of the monkeys approached her and, grabbing the end of her sari, tugged at it, and it began to unwind. Another monkey joined the effort, and soon there was a tug of war between the monkeys and Malati. Malati was screaming, pulling the edges of her sari, while the monkeys, chattering, tugged with great vigor. Ramchandra threatened and shouted, but the monkeys at the entrance had sidled toward him, some of them baring their teeth. Then, incredibly, in one swift motion Malati's sari was in a large monkey's hand, part of it covering its body so that it looked as if it was the one wearing the blue sari. It ran out the entrance, the sari trailing behind. Malati, in her petticoat and her blouse, feebly tried to cover her chest with her hands, while she whimpered and the tears streamed down her face. And then, as if it had all been a big show, the monkeys left the temple, one by one.

Ramchandra went to Malati and put his hand on her shoulder. She jerked it away, and buried her face in her knees. Scratch marks covered her legs, and her hair was disheveled. Ramchandra stood there, helpless, afraid to touch her again. But he had an idea. "Stay right here," he said. "I'll be back soon."

"I don't want to be here alone," she said in a muffled voice.

"I'll only be a few minutes."

He walked out and headed toward the main Temple of Pashupatinath, wondering whether the gods had sent the monkeys as punishment for what he was doing. After he crossed the small bridge, he found a shop that displayed saris and, cursing himself over and over, bought a cotton dhoti for seventy rupees. It was a cheap-looking bright red dhoti, the kind village women wore when they came to the city to sing and dance and fast for the festival of Teej.

When he returned, Malati was in the same position. She took the sari silently, and as she put it on, he turned away. They walked out of the temple, down the steps toward Guheswori, and when she told him she wanted to walk home alone, he didn't object.

★

It was only eleven o'clock, and Ramchandra wondered whether he should go to the school to teach some classes. Bandana Miss might be partly appeased. If he hurried, he could get there during the lunch break and teach his three remaining classes. But the prospect of standing in front of the classroom and solving mathematical problems on the board depressed him. His mind whirled with images of Malati, crouching on the floor in her petticoat and bra, monkey scratches on her thighs, and her face contorted in terror as the monkeys unrobed her.

Ramchandra headed toward the city. If he went home, Goma would ask why he'd left school early. He walked past Jai Nepal, where a movie with Amitabh Bachchan was playing. The façade of the building was adorned with a giant poster of the current feature, showing the actor with a red bandana around his head. He looked angry, with glaring eyes and a defiant stance. In the background was the figure of a dancing woman, the heroine, lifting her buxom chest in the air. Ramchandra had seen one of Amitabh Bachchan's films, one in which he played a mild-mannered friend to another film star who was very popular at that time. But now the same actor had become famous as "an angry young man," and youngsters in Kathmandu tied red bandanas around their heads and scowled at one another in the street.

Ramchandra hadn't been to a movie theater for several years. Before the children were born, he and Goma used to go every six months or so, even though they'd had to count their rupees carefully. Goma would dress in her best sari, and Ramchandra would wear his daura suruwal and would oil and comb his hair. Before they entered the dim auditorium, Ramchandra would offer to buy some fritters, but Goma always refused, saying, "Why eat this trash when I can cook better food for you at home?" Ramchandra didn't remember the movies as much as he remembered their shoulders touching in the dark. A couple of times Ramchandra had put his hand on Goma's thigh, tickled by the thought the others around him couldn't see what he was doing, and she, embarrassed, had immediately pushed his hand away. But he had been persistent, and eventually she didn't object. He even suspected that she was smiling at his touch. He could barely concentrate on the screen, and by the time the movie finished, he would have an erection. Once they reached home, she'd head to the kitchen to make tea, but he'd hold her and guide her toward the bedroom.

For a moment Ramchandra was engrossed in these memories, until he realized he had an idiotic grin on his face. He immediately straightened himself up.

Outside the gate of the Royal Palace, he stopped to observe the guard, who stood perfectly still with a rifle on his shoulder. Ramchandra couldn't imagine standing like that for hours—it must take endless stamina. What did the man think about as he stood there? His face was expressionless; his eyes stared blankly at the street in front of him. Did he think of his wife in the village? Was he even married? Did he have a girl somewhere he was hoping to marry, or would he allow his parents to negotiate his marriage for him, as Ramchandra had done? Or was he fearful that, with all the political demonstrations going on, an agitated crowd might knock him down and storm the palace? As if the soldier could read Ramchandra's thoughts, he said, sharply, "What are you staring at? Move on!" Ramchandra wanted to say, "Brother, is this job hard?" The man was once again looking forward, but out of the corner of his mouth he muttered, "Move on, I said." Someone shouted from inside the small guardhouse by the gate, "Eh, who is it? Who are you talking to?"

Ramchandra walked away and crossed the street toward Durbar Marg, with its rows of hotels and fancy restaurants.

He stopped outside the bakery of the Annapurna Hotel, and looked at the cakes and pastries on display. He'd always wondered how much these cakes cost. Sometimes he'd had the urge to walk in and buy something for Sanu and Rakesh, especially Rakesh, who had a sweet tooth, but he knew the price of one of those cakes would probably buy him a two-week supply of rice. Adjoining the bakery was one of the hotel's restaurants, with clear glass windows that allowed the pedestrians to see who was eating what inside. He noticed some Indian families at the tables, and a few white foreigners, one of whom smiled at him and waved. Ramchandra, feeling self-conscious, walked on.

Just as he reached the Ghantaghar clock tower, it began to ring. It was noon, and he had at least another two hours before he could go home without arousing Goma's curiosity. Opposite the tower was Tri Chandra College, and, on impulse, Ramchandra walked through the gate. Students sat on the lawn in small clusters, enjoying the late autumn sun. Their voices were loud, boisterous, and Ramchandra remembered his own college days: the gaiety, the sound of his friends' laughter, the mental clarity he had when he woke in the morning, the way the afternoon expanded before him, the deep, smiling world of sleep that he fell into at night. And now? What was happening to him now? He tried to see himself through the eyes of his in-laws, and what he saw was a small man among rich, powerful men, a man who was worthless unless he continually moved toward better jobs and bigger houses.

Ramchandra entered a building and walked aimlessly through the corridors, occasionally peeking into classrooms, where teachers were lecturing and students were listening, with bored expressions. He should have been in one of these classrooms, teaching college students, and once again this thought pulled him toward that dark pit where he frequently fell these days. But now he stopped in the corridor and recalled Malati—not the battered and bruised Malati of this morning but the one who'd come to his door asking for help, the one who'd told him that she'd heard he was a good teacher. On the second floor of the building, Ramchandra saw three girls in a corner, giggling. If Malati passed the S.L.C. exam, she would become one of these girls.

A noise startled him, and he saw one student chasing another. The chaser, passing close to Ramchandra, held a knife. Suddenly, three students appeared quickly and tackled the man. They threw him to the ground so violently that his head struck the floor with a smack. They kicked him, and one of them wrenched away the knife and held it close to the face of the man on the ground. "Motherfucker," he said, and slashed the man's right cheek. Blood poured from the gash and covered the man's face.

Ramchandra ran down the stairs. Others ran past him up the stairs, shouting, "Where are those panchays?" He quickly walked down the corridor toward the main entrance, as streams of students, all talking at once, left the classrooms. On the lawn, more students were craning their necks, trying to see what was happening on the second floor. "Who was that student with the knife?" Ramchandra asked one of the students.

"How would I know?" the student said. "I can't tell the difference between a panchay and a communist and a Congressi. They all look alike to me. I came to the city to get a degree, but the village was better."

Ramchandra left the campus just as a police van drew up and some helmeted men ran into Tri Chandra. He went to the park and sat on the platform of one of the stone umbrellas that were scattered in the park. A few people were reclining on the grass, dozing or reading a newspaper. Two homeless boys, with jute sacks on their backs, were fishing for empty cans and bottles. They jostled each other, then one smacked the other on the head and fled, and the chase began. Ramchandra, watching the two bedraggled and toughened boys, thought that they were much like his own children, who fought and kidded with each other in similar ways. Impulsively, Ramchandra called out to them, and when one of the boys came over, he dug into his pocket and took out two rupees. "Go eat some ice cream," he said in a stern voice, as if he were scolding. The boy looked at the money in his hand and said, "With two rupees? We couldn't even get peanuts with this." Ramchandra gave him another rupee and said, "Go. I don't have any more." The kid shook his head and showed the money to his companion. "He said it's for ice cream." And they both chanted, "Ice cream man," and ran away. "Donkeys," Ramchandra muttered to himself, but he felt good, having given them even that small amount of money. The two boys had run out of the park and were crossing the street toward some fritter stalls. The sun's warmth was at its peak for the day, and Ramchandra felt its heat on his shoulders. He reclined on the platform. The sun hovered in the sky like a soft simmering yolk, and soon he felt drowsy.

He woke to the sound of his name and was startled to see Goma standing in front of him. "What are you doing here?" For a moment he thought he was dreaming, but there she was, holding a plastic bag, wearing that familiar dark-green sari she wore when she ran errands.

"Why are you sleeping here? What happened to school?"

"I don't know what happened," he said, his tongue thick with grogginess.

"You haven't been drinking?" It was more a statement than a

question. In their thirteen years of marriage, he'd rarely had a drink.

"No, no," he said, wiping his face with his hand and hopping off the platform. "There was an accident at school, so the classes were canceled." He was in the process of concocting an elaborate story about the accident when she asked him why he didn't simply go home. He hadn't been feeling well, he said, and wanted to catch his breath but had ended up dozing. He asked what had brought her to the park, and she said that she'd spotted his daura suruwal from the pharmacy near Bir Hospital, where she'd gone to get cough medicine for Rakesh. He'd been sent home early from school because he was coughing. Ramchandra recalled his own fake cough this morning when he'd lied to Bandana Miss, and wondered whether his lying had made his son ill. He dismissed the superstitious thought.

"How much did it cost?" he asked Goma. "For the cough syrup?"

"Don't ask," Goma said. "The children's health is important."

And so they walked home together, and as the sun's warmth waned, a cool wind blew across the city, and women tightened their shawls, and men put on the coats they'd taken off. Light fell on Ramchandra and Goma at an angle when they entered the courtyard; as she preceded him up the stairs, Ramchandra watched his wife's behind, shifting with each step, and he assured himself that she had no suspicions or doubts about him. Instead of feeling guilty, he was pleased and proud, not because he was getting away with something, but because Goma accepted him as a complete man, someone who needed no tinkering to be perfect. And he knew, even as Malati brought him so much pleasure, that she would never see him the way Goma did, that even if Malati began to love him, there'd be gaps and holes in her perception of him that her love, no matter how genuine, could never fill.

To his surprise, Malati did come. She had red blotches on her face, and a scratch that ran all the way from her left eye down to her chin. When Goma asked her what had happened, Malati said that Rachana had done it in a fit of rage. "Quite a feisty girl," Goma commented. "She'll be a handful when she grows up." During the lesson, when Ramchandra asked Malati how she was feeling, she laughed softly. "Wasn't that incredible?" she asked. "I'd never imagined something like that happening to me. Bad luck seems to have a particular liking for me." And she laughed again. Ramchandra was relieved by her ability to bounce back. "I thought you wouldn't come," he whispered to her, running his finger up her arm. Her eyes followed his finger, a faint smile curving her lips, and when his finger reached her chin, she locked her eyes into his. "I am determined to pass the S.L.C.," she said. "If anyone can make me pass, it's you."

Half an hour later, after the children were dressed and sent to school, Rakesh's cough a bit better, Goma left for the market to get kerosene, saying that she'd probably have to stand in line and wouldn't be back for a long time. A few minutes after her departure, there was a crash on the street below. Startled, they both rose from the floor and rushed to the window, where they stood shoulder to shoulder. A crowd had gathered around a three-wheeler, the side of which had been smashed by a car now off to the side, its left bumper dented. People shouted and gave instructions, and soon a bloody body was lifted out of the three-wheeler. The injured man was groaning. The people holding him set him down on the street, and someone called for water, which the tea shopkeeper brought over in a jar. The driver of the car, a man in a business suit, was being held by three young men, who were also jabbing him with their fists.

"Just because you're wearing a suit and tie and driving a car doesn't mean you can destroy poor folks," one of the men said. The driver, while battling the fists, attempted to offer an explanation.

"That could have been me," Ramchandra said. "These days I seem to be taking three-wheelers all the time."

"You shouldn't say such things."

He saw that she had on a large chandan tika. Had she gone to the Pashupatinath Temple this morning?

The commotion below lessened after the young men made the driver take the injured man to the hospital. Some people still milled around, going over the details of the accident. The shopkeeper looked up and said to Ramchandra at the window, "This is more interesting than tutoring, isn't it, Ramchandra-ji?"

Ramchandra and Malati sat down on the floor again, but they'd lost interest in tackling the math.

"Do you want to study?" he asked.

"What do you want to do?" She was smiling.

He slid closer to her and took her hand. She'd chewed her fingernails, which looked frayed.

"That's a bad habit," he said.

"I do it when I worry."

"What are you worried about now?"

"So many things," she said. "But I don't want to bother you with them."

"Tell me one thing you worry about."

"About passing the S.L.C. But here I am, not studying."

"I'll make sure you pass."

"But how? You're holding my hand right now."

He let go and said, "Okay, let's do another couple of problems."

"I'm in no mood."

"See? How can it work this way?"

They fell silent for a while. He found it hard to believe that the thin body beside him had harbored and finally pushed out a living, breathing baby. He eyed her belly, and, pretending to pick lint from her kurta suruwal, ran his hand across her stomach and noted that it was flat. After Goma had given birth to Sanu, she'd put on about twenty kilos, and had had to hold his arm while climbing the stairs. Her cheeks had become puffy, and her fingers had swollen. He'd paid no attention to her weight gain, although he missed sleeping with her; tradition demanded that mother and baby sleep together.

"Why don't you tell me about Rachana's father?" he asked.

"There's nothing to tell. He's not in our lives anymore."

"What happened?"

She seemed reluctant, but he waited patiently. Her eyes measured him, checking to see whether he would judge her.

At first she spoke with some difficulty. Gradually, she relaxed and spoke with ease. Ramchandra listened intently, watching her face: how her nose twitched when she conjured up an image, how she lowered her eyes when a thought saddened her.

Rachana's father was a taxi driver who had followed Malati from a bus stop near her house to school. He was very handsome, with curly hair and a mustache that ran down to his chin. He wore rings on all his fingers, and he sang Hindi songs through the window of the taxi: *mere sapano ki rani kab ayegi tu*—oh, the queen of my dreams, when will you come to me? He whispered that she looked very pretty in her uniform—the red frock and white blouse—and offered to give her a ride to school. He'd feel like a king, he said, if she'd allow him to chauffeur her to school. Since the school was only a few neighborhoods away, she merely smiled and walked on. One day he didn't appear, and she kept turning back to see if he'd come. The next day she waited at the bus stop until she saw the taxi.

"Did you miss me?" he asked, his elbow on the window. The cigarette on his lips moved up and down as he spoke.

This time she got in. As they reached the school, he asked whether she really wanted to go to her classes that day. She saw her friends by the gate, waiting for her, because they had a habit of walking in together. "If I don't, where will we go?" she asked. He smiled and pressed the accelerator. They drove to Balaju, sat near the water spouts, and he told her of his dying mother and his tyrant brother, and she told him that she was fatherless, that she had a stepmother who sometimes treated her as stepdaughters were often treated. From his back pocket, he produced a gift: a small mirror. She would be able to see herself throughout the day to remind her how beautiful she was.

Every day he gave her a ride, and eventually she stopped going to school. They roamed the city all day in his taxi. He took her sightseeing in the valley: the top of the Swayambhunath Temple, the woods of Gokarna, even all the way to the Dakshinkali Temple, where they stood in front of the goddess and proclaimed their love for each other. Then they started making love in the jungles of Balaju, a few hundred yards up from the very place where they'd come the first time she'd gotten into the taxi with him.

When she discovered she was pregnant, she considered an abortion, but she didn't have the heart for it. She told him she was pregnant, and at first he said that he'd marry her, that he'd come and see her stepmother soon. But he didn't come at all for a few days. She waited for him near the bus stop, her hands in front of her belly as if to hide her shame, even though it was too early for her to show. His absence forced her to attend school again, and she managed to take her final exams, and pass, just before her belly started to bulge. One afternoon she went searching for his house near the banks of the Bagmati River in Thapathali. After two hours of knocking on different doors, she found it. A woman opened the door, and when Malati told her whom she was looking for, the woman said, "My husband has gone to Birgunj for a few days. Who are you?"

Malati made some excuse and walked away.

"That's it," Malati said to Ramchandra. "And I haven't heard from him since."

She rose from her cross-legged position, and started looking at the pictures on the wall. She eyed them closely, spending time in front of each. She didn't ask him any questions about the people in them, but her absorption prompted Ramchandra to go into the other room to get the photo albums Goma had kept over the years.

"This will be our math for today," he said, and they sat down once again. She flipped the pages, lingering on the photographs of Sanu and Rakesh when they were younger. She spent time with the photos as if she were looking at pictures of her own family. She asked a few questions about when and where the pictures were taken, and he'd answer and sit back to watch her face. When she became aware of his gaze, she asked solemnly, "Why are you looking at me like that?" He was about to touch her face, to trace her lips with his finger, when he heard footsteps on the stairs. He started to collect the albums, and Goma appeared at the door, holding a plastic container of kerosene. Outside, a truck honked its horn.

"Back already?" Ramchandra asked. His face grew hot.

"The situation must be getting better. The line wasn't as long today."

Ramchandra glanced at Malati, whose face betrayed nothing.

"No studying today?" Goma asked. Her face, too, revealed no emotion.

"Sir was just showing me pictures of Sanu and Rakesh," Malati said.

Goma set down the container by the doorstep and entered. "Which pictures?" and she sat beside Malati. She didn't look at Ramchandra, but, together with Malati, she went through the albums. She talked about the circumstances behind some of the pictures, ones Ramchandra didn't know or had forgotten. Goma rarely forgot anything, and Ramchandra, too, found himself drawn into the particulars she mentioned. It surprised him, for instance, that one photograph of him with Goma, standing under the Ghantaghar clock tower, was taken by a colleague from one of the schools where he'd previously taught. "Why were we together that day?" he asked Goma, and she said they were about to board a bus in Ratnapark for a picnic arranged by some friends. Ramchandra tried to recall that picnic, but he had absolutely no memory of it. When they reached the pages of marriage photos, Malati said to Goma, "You look lovely, bhauju."

"Yes, I was young," Goma said, looking at Ramchandra. "Now, this body has become old and tired."

"You're not that old," Malati said, putting a hand on Goma's arm.

"Well, I'm certainly not as young as you are."

"I don't feel young."

Goma took Malati's hand and said, "You have much to look forward to in life."

They could be sisters, Ramchandra thought, and their intimacy made him uneasy. "Nearly time for Ashok," he said.

Goma said to Malati, "Let's go to the other room and finish looking."

Malati glanced at him as they left, as if to say, "You were nervous for no reason."

Ashok arrived. Ramchandra demonstrated certain calculus shortcuts to him, but remained alert to the faint murmuring behind the wall separating the two rooms. He started making

mistakes. Ashok gleefully pointed them out, and even commented, with a sly smile, "Sir, if you took the S.L.C. now, I
don't know whether you'd pass." Ramchandra was taken aback
by the student's brazenness and thought of scolding him, but all
he said was "Don't joke with me." He gave Ashok a problem to
solve and left the room. Standing near the children's room, he
heard laughter — Malati's. Then she said something he couldn't
decipher that was followed by Goma's laughter. Ramchandra
leaned closer and put his ear against the small crack in the door.
He caught words like "foolish" and "embarrassed" and became
convinced that they were talking about him. Ashok appeared
beside him. "I thought you were going to the bathroom," he
whispered, and Ramchandra was about to usher him back to
their room when the door opened and Malati came out, still
smiling. "I'll see you tomorrow, sir," she told Ramchandra, and
bounded down the stairs, clutching something in her hand.

"Is the tutoring over?" Goma called from inside.

Ramchandra told Ashok to go back and finish his problem,
and said to Goma, "What was all that noise about?"

"That girl," Goma said, shaking her head. She was putting
the albums in a cupboard.

"What happened?"

"Nothing," she said. "We were talking."

"About what?"

"Why all these questions?" she asked. "I didn't ask this many
questions when I found you giving her lessons on our photographs."

"What do you mean?"

"I mean nothing."

"Then why are you so prickly?"

Goma closed the cupboard, put away the key, and said, "I
gave her an extra copy of our wedding photo."

"Why?" Ramchandra asked. "You barely know her."

"She said I looked beautiful, and I couldn't resist." She began arranging the children's bed, tightening the sheets, smoothing the pillows. "Besides, you know her quite well by now, don't you?"

Ramchandra didn't know what to say.

Later, when Goma served him dal-bhat, she was quiet, and because her earlier question remained with him, he also said nothing. At one point he asked her to eat, too, and she silently served herself. They could hear each other chew. Goma made soft, slurping sounds with her mouth fully closed, and Ramchandra stuffed large morsels into his mouth with his fingers and chewed with large movements. When he heard Goma make a sound like a hiccup, he looked over and saw that she was trying to suppress laughter. "What?" he asked. She turned serious again, but a short while later made the same sound.

"What's the matter with you? One moment sulking, the next moment giggling."

"You sound like a slow train when you eat," she said. "Approaching the station, wheezing and snorting."

"At least a train is a sign of progress. You, you sound like an old woman with no teeth. Only flabby gums going *chap, chap.*"

She covered her mouth, laughed, then remembered something and became solemn.

"I don't know what you're thinking," Ramchandra said. "Whatever it is, you're wrong."

"It's just that I've never seen you show so much interest in a student before," Goma said.

"I feel sorry for her. She has problems. She doesn't have anyone in her life."

"Sometimes, these days, you seem to think about her more than about us, about Sanu and Rakesh."

He reached out and touched her arm. "What nonsense. You

are my family. I just feel some compassion for that girl and want to help her." He added, "Want her to feel that she too has someone she can rely on."

Goma considered this. "She's a sweet girl," she finally said. "Old for her age."

"She's had a rough life. It's hard to lose your mother, then lose your father. Imagine how alone you'd feel."

"I hope that if something happens to one of us, the other will take care of Sanu and Rakesh."

"Don't utter such nonsense. We're both in good health. We'll both be here to see our children become married, settled, and give us grandchildren."

Just as they finished eating, Goma said, "I'll invite Malati for lunch this Saturday. Poor girl; I feel bad for her. So young and already with a child."

Friday evening, the day of Ghatasthapana, the start of the Dashain festival, they went to Harish and Nalini's house in Jawalakhel for dinner. The bus was overflowing, so they had to stand and hold the bar that ran across the ceiling. The bus reeked of sweat, and someone must have taken off his shoes, because a strong whiff of old socks assaulted them. Sanu was squeezed between two men, and in Thapathali, Ramchandra noticed that one of them had his crotch pressed against her body. The man, who was bald, was looking at her in a way that made Ramchandra angry. "Why are you crowding her?" Ramchandra asked him in a belligerent voice, and the man responded calmly that the bus was crowded, that Ramchandra should take a taxi if he didn't like the crowd. "What an idiot," Ramchandra said loudly.

"What did you say?" the man shouted across the heads.

"Let it go," Goma told Ramchandra and reached out to pull Sanu closer to her.

"What are you doing?" asked the other man pressed against Sanu. "There's no space."

Goma managed to bring Sanu near her, and the rest of the bus ride was uneventful, although when the bald man went to get off at Kupondole and had to pass Ramchandra, he said, "I let you go only because you're here with your family."

Ramchandra thought it best not to respond, but the incident left a sour taste in his mouth. If they hadn't had to worry about money, they could have traveled in a three-wheeler. He studied his daughter, who was looking out the window. He noticed the small protrusions of her breasts, the long earrings she wore. She looked pretty.

They got off at Jawalakhel, and as they walked toward Nalini's house, Ramchandra pointed out St. Xavier's School to Rakesh. "That's where I want you to study in a couple of years." The fee was not too high, even though the school was considered one of the best in the country. Whenever Ramchandra came across the Xavier schoolboys, in their smart white pants and blue shirts with ties, he heard them rattling away in English, as if they'd been born with that tongue. In citywide debate competitions in English, the Xavier boys always won first prize. They often acted condescendingly toward students at schools like Kantipur, and Ramchandra didn't care for their arrogance. But there was something attractive about their sense of confidence, and he wanted Rakesh to gain that self-assurance.

Rakesh examined the huge yellow building, a Rana palace converted into a school by the Jesuits. Some students, wearing their uniforms, loitered outside the gate to the oval driveway. One of them jostled another and said, "Give me some money, yaare." Rakesh heard this and started chanting "yaare."

"Can we look inside?" Sanu asked.

Goma was afraid they'd be late, but Ramchandra said it would take only a few minutes. They passed the gate and were heading down the driveway when a guard, appearing out of no-where, told them they couldn't go inside without permission. Ramchandra explained that his son was going to attend the school soon, but the guard was adamant. "No visitors allowed without permission."

"But I have permission," Ramchandra lied. "One of the teachers invited me. I am also a teacher at Kantipur School."

The guard wasn't impressed, and asked the name of the teacher. When Ramchandra fumbled, the guard shooed them away.

"I told you we shouldn't have gone," Goma said.

Ramchandra cursed the guard, then the school, then the for-eign priests, and said, "Just wait until my son gets in. I'll come here every day, and this very guard will salute me."

Sanu and Goma exchanged smiles. Sanu took her father's hand, and said, "What about me, Ba? Will I have to attend St. Mary's?" St. Mary's, a sister school run by nuns, was next to St. Xavier's.

"Do you want to?" Ramchandra asked.

"Not really. I'm happy where I am. I have friends there."

They ate dinner in the enclosed glass porch next to the dining room. Two heaters hummed on the porch, so they didn't feel at all cold, despite the weather outside. An old man, who'd previously worked for the Pandeys, served the food on elegant china: chicken chili, egg curry, roasted lamb, raita, samosas, to-mato soup. Over the years Nalini had acquired a reputation as an excellent cook, and sometimes the food she served was like that one might find in the restaurant of a five-star hotel—so delicious its taste, so immaculate its presentation. Both chil-dren looked uncomfortable, faced with the cutlery—the soup spoon, the two forks. They sat, their hands folded, and waited for the adults to begin. They were not as enthusiastic about visiting their aunt and uncle as they were about going to Pandey Palace. Harish was aloof; he barely acknowledged their presence. Every time they saw him, Sanu complained, it was like meeting a stranger. Nalini, on the other hand, talked to the children as if they were adults and barely showed any affection. Five years younger than Goma, Nalini was thin, with eyes that seemed to be pleading for rescue. She always wore expensive jewelry and a bright kurta suruwal, even when she worked about the house. She moved slowly, as if she were assessing the utility of every movement she made. Ramchandra found her difficult to talk to. Only Goma was completely at ease with Nalini. Goma chattered away while her sister, with those imploring eyes, listened to every word. With Harish, Goma was respectful, and when Sanu complained, later, about how distant Harish was, Goma said that he was a nice man, just not very sociable.

"You could easily work as a chief cook," Goma said now as she tasted a piece of chicken, "in any high-class restaurant in this town."

Ramchandra nodded and made some appreciative noises. He actually preferred Goma's cooking, which was more down-to-earth and homey. But Nalini had spent a lot of time preparing this meal. With so much food, he wondered why Nalini hadn't invited her parents.

"How is your exercise class?" Goma asked. "What do you call them? Arabiks?"

"Aerobics," Sanu corrected her.

Nalini gave Sanu a wan smile and said, "I dropped it."

"Why?"

"It took too much effort."

"Don't you get bored, sitting at home all day?" Goma asked.

Despite five years of marriage, Harish and Nalini had no children, which was a source of great disappointment to Mr. and Mrs. Pandey, although they never directly commented on it. "They're waiting for the right time," Mrs. Pandey would say to Goma. Her mother's face, however, betrayed her worry. Goma had prodded Nalini a few times, but Nalini had been tight-lipped. The lack of children had given rise to speculation among the extended family. Some said that Harish was impotent; others were sure that Nalini couldn't bear children. Mr. and Mrs. Pandey vigorously defended their younger daughter and son-in-law, often chastising those relatives for gossiping.

Watching Nalini and Harish together, Ramchandra had often wondered what kind of marriage they had. They acted more like office colleagues than husband and wife. Each was formal with the other, never raising a voice or stating a complaint. Not once had Ramchandra seen Nalini touch her husband. They didn't exchange glances as married couples often did in company. No signals. There was a curious distance between them, so that even when they sat next to each other on the sofa, they appeared far apart. Ramchandra had voiced this observation to Goma one night, and she reprimanded him. "Not everyone relates to each other in the same way. How do you know what they do when no one else is around? They love each other. I know that for a fact."

"See, that's what I mean," Ramchandra had said. "Have you ever heard one of them scold the other as you just scolded me?"

"If there's nothing to scold about, then why scold? Perhaps they don't like to wash their dirty linen in public."

Ramchandra had let it go. But now, as he watched Nalini walk to the kitchen to get more tomato soup, which Rakesh was devouring like a wolf, it occurred to him that Harish and

Nalini most likely weren't intimate in bed. That's why they didn't have a child. He dismissed this theory instantly; he was assuming too much. Goma was right. Of course they behaved differently when they were alone. To distract himself from speculating more about their sexual life, Ramchandra started asking Harish about his business.

In the middle of dinner, there was a knock on the door. "Did you invite anyone else?" Harish asked Nalini, who shook her head. The old servant went to open the door, and as soon as he heard the voices of the visitors, Ramchandra groaned silently.

"Who's here?" Mr. Pandey said, walking in. Rakesh jumped up from his chair and went to his grandfather, expecting a gift.

"Had I known you were here, I'd have definitely brought something," Mr. Pandey said, patting the boy on the head. "But who invited us?"

Mrs. Pandey followed her husband, appraised the food on the table, and said to Goma and Ramchandra, in a peevish voice, "Oh, I think we came at the wrong time."

The servant brought two chairs from the kitchen.

"But we're not invited," Mrs. Pandey said. "Otherwise we'd have received a phone call. Even during Dashain, no one thinks about us anymore."

Flustered, Nalini said, "It was a last-minute arrangement."

"So, we've become strangers now?" Mrs. Pandey said. "Or have we become a burden?"

"Shut up," Mr. Pandey told his wife, waving his cane at her, "and sit down."

The servant brought more food to the table, and once Mrs. Pandey tasted some of her daughter's cooking, her mood improved. She reached into her bag and took out two silver earrings, which she dangled across the table at Sanu. "Look what

I've been carrying in my bag day in and day out, just for my dear granddaughter." Sanu looked at the earrings and pursed her lips. Goma said, "Go ahead, Sanu, don't be angry anymore."

"I don't want them," Sanu said.

Goma rebuked her. "Don't be foolish."

Sanu folded her arms across her chest and repeated, "I said I don't want them. Didn't you hear?"

Mrs. Pandey kept swinging the earrings in front of Sanu.

"Sanu, take the earrings," Goma said. "Don't act like that."

"I'll take them only if Hajurba and Hajurma stop saying those things to my father."

"What things?" Mr. Pandey asked. He drank some water. "Who's been teaching her such nonsense?"

"No one," Ramchandra said. "My daughter has a mind of her own." He didn't know where his boldness came from, but something had loosened inside his chest.

"Be quiet," Goma said to Ramchandra. "Is that a thing to say?"

"What did I say? I only said she speaks what's on her mind."

Mrs. Pandey glared at Ramchandra, put the earrings back into her purse, and said, "I'll find someone else to give them to."

Sanu got up. "Go, go! Who needs your earrings? I spit upon your earrings."

"Sanu, don't talk that way," Ramchandra cautioned.

"Great," Mr. Pandey said to Ramchandra. "First you teach her to talk that way, and then you pretend you're innocent." He was clearly angry at Ramchandra, but was controlling himself.

"Please, let us eat our food in peace," Harish said.

"There's no peace in this family," Mrs. Pandey said. "Otherwise, why would we hear such things from our granddaughter?"

There was a brief silence. Everyone stared at the food.

"Come, let's eat," Goma said. "This is over now."

"I'm not eating," Sanu said, and went inside the house.

"You shouldn't encourage her," Goma said to Ramchandra.

He felt a sting of anger. "How did I encourage her? You think she doesn't hear things that other people constantly say about me?"

Now Mrs. Pandey got up. "If by other people you mean us, fine; then we've become other people. But all we want is that our daughter live a comfortable life. That's all we've asked."

"Why are you arguing?" Rakesh said in a small voice.

"Always criticizing, always complaining," Ramchandra said to Mrs. Pandey. Again he felt a rush of heat, and he knew he was about to cause more trouble for himself, but he couldn't stop. "You treat me as if I were a street vendor," he said. "If you wanted a rich son-in-law, you should have married your daughter to someone else."

Goma, who had been holding her head in her hands, said, "I can't listen to this," and left the porch, opened the main door, and went outside.

The servant nervously started piling more food on everyone's plate. Harish, who so far had been playing with his rice, said, "Is this necessary?"

"Yes, this is necessary," Ramchandra said. "This has gone too far." His hands were trembling, so he hid them under the table. "There's clearly a distinction between how you are treated and how we are treated."

"Son-in-law, we have never thought badly of you," Mr. Pandey said. "We're only trying to help."

"And a great help you are," Ramchandra said. "You make me feel this small every time you talk to me." He indicated about an inch between his thumb and forefinger.

Mrs. Pandey appealed to the ceiling. "Hare Bhagwan, why

are we subjected to this? We've never made any distinction between the two of you."

"Let it go," Nalini said. She looked as if she was about
to cry.

Ramchandra picked up a spoon and started tapping the
table. He was breathing hard and sweating inside his vest. He
wished Goma would come back, just so that she could see that
he hadn't backed down, that he wasn't going to take it any longer. No one spoke. Ramchandra wanted to leave, but he was
determined not to make the first move; he sat there, tapping
the table lightly with the spoon, until Rakesh reached over
and snatched it away. "Is this a fight?" Rakesh said. No one responded.

"The food will get cold," Nalini said.

"The hell with the food," Mrs. Pandey said, getting up from
her chair, her face flushed. "Now I know the truth. Now I know
what you really think of us. I will not stay in this room any longer." She slapped her husband's back. "Get up. What are you
doing, sitting there like an idiot? We're not wanted here."

"Mother," Nalini implored. But Mr. Pandey obeyed his wife
meekly. They walked out the main door, and, a few moments
later, Goma entered, her face solemn. "You've done a great job
today," she said to Ramchandra. Nalini went over, wrapped
her arm around her sister, and led her to the bedroom. Harish got up and mumbled something about having to use the
bathroom. Ramchandra and Rakesh stared at each other; then
Rakesh started to cry, and it took some time for Ramchandra to
soothe him. "Go get your mother and sister," he said. "We have
to leave."

"But I haven't finished eating yet."

"We'll eat at home."

"But the food at home isn't this good."

"Son, please do as I say."

Rakesh left, and Ramchandra sat there, the servant standing behind him. In the silence, Ramchandra could hear the man breathe, could feel the man's eyes burrowing into his back. He turned around and asked, "Will you get me some water?" The servant pointed to the glass of water in front of Ramchandra. He drank it, listening to his own gurgles. Soon he heard the muted voices of Nalini and Goma coming from the bedroom. Where was Sanu? Where did Harish disappear to? Doubts about himself began to nip at him, but he angrily brushed them aside. The Pandeys needed to hear what he'd said, and he hoped they'd start treating him better. But part of him knew that this would not happen.

He closed his eyes and conjured up the image of Malati in a bright red kurta suruwal, her face clean and eager, and slowly the warmth of pleasure entered him. The harsh words, the strained faces of his in-laws, dissolved, and he was left with a sweet sensation in his throat, his chest.

He felt a hand on his shoulder. Sanu said, "Ba, are you crying?"

He took her hand and said, "No."

"Should I not have said those things?"

Of course you should have, he thought, but he said, "Perhaps this was not the right time. Your mother is upset."

Her face was gloomy. She sat down next to him. "What's going to happen?"

"I don't know. I think we should leave."

Goma, her eyes puffy, came out of the bedroom with Nalini and Rakesh. Nalini was caressing her back. After a moment, Nalini went to look for Harish so that he could drive them back to Jaisideval. Goma stood by the door, saying nothing. Rakesh examined the family pictures on the wall.

"This food is only half eaten, gone to waste," the servant said.

In the car, Ramchandra sat in the front with Rakesh on his lap, and Goma, Sanu, and Nalini sat in the back. No one spoke for a long time, until Harish cleared his throat and said something about how the weather was supposed to warm up considerably in the days to come. Ramchandra added that warm weather, without any rain, would probably lead to more dust in the city, which was already filthy.

At Jaisideval, the four of them trudged up the stairs, and Goma went straight to bed. Rakesh complained that he was hungry, so Ramchandra rummaged around in the kitchen and discovered some leftover cauliflower and rice. Sanu stood by the door, her face glum. When Ramchandra asked whether she wanted to eat, too, she shook her head. He tucked the children into their bed, noting that Sanu, with her growing body, would soon have to sleep apart from her brother. He turned off the light and went to his room.

In bed, he lay staring at the ceiling. He could hear Goma's soft breathing. Her back was turned to him, but he knew she was awake. A while later he said, "It had become too much, Goma. Don't you understand?"

Slowly, she turned toward him. "They are my parents. Don't you understand? Was all of that necessary?"

"It was bound to happen. You know how your parents always treat me."

"They don't think badly of you. They just want a better life for both of us."

That sounded exactly like the Pandeys, but he didn't want to argue with Goma this late. "We can't take back what's happened," he finally said.

"I'm worried about Sanu. That attitude toward her elders, especially her grandparents, who love her so much; that doesn't bode well."

"She's a sensitive girl, that's all."

"And you encourage her."

"I have never encouraged her," he said sharply. "If you want to keep blaming me, maybe we shouldn't talk right now." He turned away and closed his eyes. He could hear her breathing hard. Then, gradually, her breath became softer.

Soon, he felt her hand on his shoulder. "How is she? Sanu? What is she saying?"

"I think you'd better talk to her. She's miserable."

"I'll make up to her tomorrow."

Turning around to face her, he asked, "Do you still want Malati to come for lunch tomorrow?"

"Oh, I nearly forgot that," Goma said. "Yes, I've already asked her, and she seemed eager to come. I told her to bring her daughter, too."

"We should think of something we can play together so that Sanu and Rakesh will also enjoy themselves."

"Why don't we play carom?"

Ramchandra wondered whether he and Malati could be partners, and then realized what a ridiculous thought that was. He clasped Goma in his arms. "Let's forget about what happened today and get a good night's sleep. What are you cooking tomorrow?"

"I'll go to the market early and buy some squash and goat meat."

"Goat meat is expensive these days. What? Forty rupees a kilo?"

"What's the point of inviting someone if we don't feed them properly? I'm tired of counting each paisa."

"Okay, okay," he said. "I'm just suggesting that we watch our money." He nuzzled Goma's breasts.

The tension was dissipating, but he knew that there was

much more to come, that the next time he saw his in-laws, the strain from this argument would hover in the air, creating even more distance between them. Mrs. Pandey was not the forgiving kind. She would be resentful, and Goma would reflect her mother's attitude. But he didn't want to think that far ahead, so he pressed his face deeper into his wife's bosom.

As if she were materializing from Ramchandra's daydreams, Malati appeared at their door in a bright red kurta suruwal, with Rachana straddling her hip. Two silver earrings dangled from her ears, and around her wrists were bangles that tinkled as she talked and moved her hands. "We hadn't set a time, but I thought ten o'clock might be when you eat."

"Yes, yes," Goma said. "You came at the right time." She smiled at the baby. "Looks just like you," she said. "Same nose, same eyes."

Ramchandra looked at Rachana from where he sat on the bed. Yes, indeed, Malati's daughter looked like her, something he hadn't noticed before. He wondered whether Rachana also showed any likeness to her father.

"Sit, sit," Goma said, and when Malati attempted to sit on the floor, Goma caught her arm and said, "Not today. Today you're not a student. So, on the bed," and she asked Ramchandra to move so that Malati could sit comfortably. He stood up, his arms dangling awkwardly by his side. Rakesh came running in, acted shy around Malati, and then started making faces at Rachana, who began to cry. Ramchandra scolded Rakesh and shooed him out of the room. When Sanu entered, she sat beside Malati and asked if she could hold the baby. "You might drop her," Goma said. Sanu said she was a grown-up now. Malati carefully passed the baby to her, and Sanu held the little one in the crook of her arm. She cooed softly at Rachana, and everyone watched and smiled. "She'll make a good mother," Malati said.

They drank tea and made small talk. Malati expressed her anxiety about the exams. Ramchandra assured her that she'd do fine. Goma told Ramchandra that he should tutor her more, that perhaps he could tutor her even during the festival, except, perhaps, on the day of the Tika, when they'd be visiting relatives. "No, no," Malati said, "I obviously can't impose that on you. You must celebrate the festival, too. Besides, I can't pay any more than what I already pay." Goma said that it was no imposition, that Ramchandra would gladly do it. And who said anything about more payment? Goma looked at Ramchandra, who said, "Of course, you should come during the festival, except on the day of the Tika, and don't talk about more payment."

The baby was passed around, and when she came to Ramchandra, he held her awkwardly. Rachana smiled at him and said something that sounded like "ba, ba." Everyone laughed, including Malati. Goma joked, "Maybe she thinks you're her father," and Ramchandra felt embarrassed. He kissed the baby and, out of the corner of his eye, looked at Malati, who, once again, had that soft smile on her lips. Goma went to the kitchen to check on the food, and Sanu followed her. For a while Ramchandra and Malati were alone, except for the baby and Rakesh, who was engrossed in his toy army truck.

"I am glad you're here," Ramchandra said. "I thought you might not come."

"Why wouldn't I come?" Malati said, looking at the baby, now in her lap. "Goma bhauju invited me with such an open heart."

"She likes you."

"I like her too. She's so gentle."

Ramchandra pointed toward Rachana. "Is she hungry?"

"She ate before she came, but you never know."

"You can feed her now," he said.

"Not in front of you!" she said.

Rakesh looked up from his toy. "Is the baby hungry?"

"Maybe," Malati said.

"Can I watch her eat?"

"She doesn't eat dal-bhat like us," Ramchandra said. "She drinks her mother's milk."

"I want to watch her eat," Rakesh said.

As if prompted by Rakesh, the baby started clawing at Malati's breast.

"Looks as though she's hungry," Ramchandra said. "Why don't you go to the next room and feed her?"

He escorted Malati to the children's room, and just as he was shutting the door, Rakesh slipped inside.

In the kitchen, Goma was stirring the goat meat, and Sanu was shelling green peas. "It smells great in here," he said.

Goma didn't respond. From the back she looked tense, so he asked, "What's the matter?"

"Nothing," she said.

He looked at Sanu, and saw that she once again had a sullen face. "What happened?"

"I can't deal with your daughter anymore."

"What happened?"

"She refuses to apologize to her grandparents."

"And why did you have to bring it up now? They're not here, are they?"

Goma put the ladle into the stew and faced him. "I was just talking to her, trying to make things right. She cannot keep treating her grandparents this way."

"You told me you'd make up with her, and the first chance you get, you argue again."

Their voices had grown louder. It's a replay of last night, Ramchandra thought. Sanu had stopped shelling the peas and was staring at the floor.

"You seem not to realize what your daughter has become."

"My daughter is fine," Ramchandra said. "Perhaps you should realize what you've become." He couldn't remember the last time they'd argued like this.

"What have I become? All I want is my children to respect their elders. Is that too much to ask?"

"The elders who want respect should respect others."

"They haven't been disrespectful of anyone."

"How can you say that? How can you stand there in front of your daughter and pretend that nothing's wrong with the way your parents behave?"

Goma's face suddenly became transformed, and she started to cry. Sanu leaped from the floor and went to her mother. Goma pulled her hand away and turned her back to them. Father and daughter exchanged glances, and Ramchandra motioned to Sanu to go to her mother again. Sanu stood near her and said, "If it's that important to you, Mother, I'll apologize."

Goma didn't respond. Ramchandra placed his hand on her shoulder. "Okay, enough. We have a guest in the house. What will she think?"

"This whole thing gives me a headache," Goma said.

"All right. Sanu will apologize, so please stop worrying."

It took a few minutes for Goma to regain her composure. Then she embraced Sanu.

They heard the children's room door open, and Malati and Rakesh appeared in the kitchen doorway. Malati obviously sensed that something untoward had happened; she looked uncomfortable. Goma smiled and said, "The food should be ready in a few minutes. Is your daughter sleeping?"

Malati nodded. She was standing close to Ramchandra, and

as Sanu left the room, Malati had to shift closer. Now their shoulders touched. Briefly, Goma turned back to her masu, stirring the meat, scooping up gravy to smell it, and Ramchandra let his small finger caress Malati's wrist. She blushed.

"Taste it and tell me how it is," Goma said. She put a piece of meat and some gravy in a bowl and gave it to Ramchandra. He tasted it and made appreciative noises. "Delicious," he said, and as Goma turned toward her cooking again, he looked at Malati directly and said, "Delicious." Only then did he notice that Rakesh, who had been fiddling with the religious calendar hanging on the wall by the entrance, was watching him.

They ate in the kitchen while the baby slept in the children's room. Malati had a funny way of eating. She'd scoop up the rice with her fingers, lower her head, and thrust the food into her mouth, keeping her head lowered while she chewed, as if she were embarrassed to have anyone watch her eat. "How is it?" Goma asked, and they waited while Malati finished swallowing. "It's delicious." Ramchandra became mesmerized by the movement of her slender fingers cradling the food and then putting it into her mouth. Her bangles tinkled. Goma asked him whether the meat had enough salt, and he nodded, unable to talk. "Tell me if it's not good," Goma said, laughing. "I can take it." She explained to Malati that Ramchandra never criticized her cooking, which was good, but she didn't know whether he was being completely honest.

Mr. Sharma across the courtyard began to chant his religious hymns at his window, and abruptly Malati looked up.

Ramchandra said, "Seems that our neighbor is late today."

"On Saturdays he wakes up late," Goma said.

"Mr. Sharma is funny," Sanu said.

"Why?"

"He stares at me."

"He doesn't stare at me," Rakesh said.

"When did he stare at you?" Ramchandra asked Sanu.

"Every time I'm in the courtyard, he looks at me, as if I've done something wrong."

Ramchandra recalled Mr. Sharma's comment about Malati. He stopped chewing, drank some water, and said to his daughter, "The next time he does it, ask him why he's staring."

"There you go again," Goma said, "teaching her to mouth back to adults."

"But why does he look at her like that? What's his motive?"

"He's just a strange man," Goma said. She'd finished eating and was extracting threads of goat meat from between her teeth, her palm covering her mouth. "He means no harm."

"How do you know that? He's lived alone too long."

"Calm down," Goma said. "Why are you so hot? Is the food heating up your brain?"

After they were finished, they washed their hands and mouths at the sink. Ramchandra looked out the window toward Mr. Sharma, who was rocking as he chanted. He looked up and waved at Ramchandra, who didn't wave back.

They all sat in the bedroom and settled into a game of carom. The board had been a gift from the Pandeys to Sanu when she turned six, and over the years the paint had peeled off, so some spots were rough. Often one of the small counters would zoom across the board and get stuck right before it hit the mark, so Goma brought some powder and sprinkled it on the board's surface. Ramchandra asked, "Okay, who is whose partner?" Both Sanu and Rakesh wanted to partner with Malati, and there was a brief argument before Sanu gave in to her brother. "I'll watch," Goma said, because only four could play.

The counters were arranged and the game began. Malati turned out to be an expert player. She'd align the master counter with great care, hit the designated piece, and it would deftly plop into the corner hole. Rakesh was delighted with his partner's virtuosity, and they won every game.

"Where did you learn to play like that?" Ramchandra asked.

She said her father was a big fan, and they'd had a large board at home when she was a child. "I might be a math monkey, sir," she said with a smile, "but I'm certainly not a carom monkey."

Liking the sound of those words, Rakesh turned to Ramchandra and started chanting that it was his father who was the carom monkey. It was true; Ramchandra was clumsy at the game.

The baby started crying, so Malati hurried to the children's room. Goma said she was feeling sleepy, and, with a yawn, lay down on the bed. Sanu and Rakesh went down to the courtyard to skip rope. Ramchandra sat on the floor near the bed, one hand massaging Goma's foot. "The meat feels heavy in my stomach," Goma said drowsily. Soon, she was snoring, the faint rasping breath that had lulled Ramchandra to sleep so many times. He kept rubbing her foot, aware that he and Malati were the only ones awake. From the next room came the soft gurgling sounds of the baby. Ramchandra let go of Goma's foot and stood up. A truck whizzed by outside, making such a ruckus that Goma's eyes fluttered. She shifted and went back to sleep. In the courtyard, Sanu and Rakesh were counting as they skipped rope.

Ramchandra stood near the door of the children's room, which was slightly ajar. Malati was softly singing a lullaby. As he pushed the door open, she looked up from the floor, where she sat nursing the baby. For a brief moment, she attempted to cover her breast, but then her face relaxed, and she smiled. Ramchandra put an index finger to his lips, shut the door behind him, and sat beside her. Leaning his head against her shoulder, he closed his eyes and soon felt her palm on his chin. She caressed him. The baby was sucking hard on her nipple. "Where is everyone?" she whispered. He whispered that Goma was asleep. He opened his eyes and watched her breast, then reached out to stroke it. He could feel himself getting hard. The baby stopped sucking and fell asleep. Ramchandra bent down and took Malati's nipple in his mouth. His head was so close to the baby's that he could feel the up and down of her tiny chest. He sucked briefly, then sat up. The room seemed to be moving. He put his hand on Malati's chin. "What's happening?" he said. Her eyes became moist. "Sir, sir," she said, "what are you doing?" He leaned over and kissed her fully on the lips. Goma might wake at any minute next door, yet here he was, smelling Malati, sucking her body.

Around four, after they had tea and pakodas, Malati left, and Ramchandra's mind became numb. The others kept talking about her, saying what a sweet girl she was. Goma said that she'd like to invite her again—she was so popular with the children. Sanu said Malati had invited her to her house to learn how to sew, and that she couldn't wait to go. She asked Ramchandra to take her to Malati's house one day soon.

Sanu and Rakesh sat down to do their homework, and Goma began to prepare the evening meal. Ramchandra told her that he needed some fresh air; he put on a sweater and left the house.

The evening was chilly. He walked around aimlessly. The dusky sky was filled with kites. As he traversed New Road, with its brightly lit shops, its shoppers carrying bags and looking happy and tired in anticipation of the festival, he knew he'd taken another step toward Malati. The significance of what lay ahead seemed immense. He stood beneath the large peepul tree, its long branches covering the sky, and looked around. Under streetlamps and shadows, newspaper vendors and shoe-shine boys advertised their wares. Small groups of men milled about, discussing the rumbling of the nation. Ramchandra stood and listened. Last night, painted slogans decrying the Panchayat rule had appeared on the walls of alleys and houses in Patan, and bands of policemen had begun patrolling the streets to catch the culprits. Newspapers reported the mysterious disappearance of some political activists.

Before he was married, Ramchandra used to come here in the evening to smoke and discuss the politics of the day with friends and strangers. They would buy the local newspapers and argue vehemently about whether a certain politician was corrupt, whether India would barge into Nepal and declare it a part of its own territory, as it had done to Sikkim, and, in whispers, whether eventually the monarchy would be ousted from Nepal and replaced by the kind of democracy found in Western countries. Of course, at that time such vocal protests against the government and the king were unthinkable, so the evening arguments were conducted with secrecy. Ramchandra and his friends downed glasses of tea over the course of the evening, smoked one Gainda cigarette after another, and found great satisfaction in their own words, which blended with the smoke and circled up to the sky.

Even though Ramchandra and his mother lived in dingy apartments, life was uncomplicated for him then, as he struggled each evening to pay his share of the cigarettes and tea.

Now, his temples started to throb, so he walked into a small restaurant and bar in Indrachowk and asked for a glass of the local rum. It burned his throat as it went down. He drank another and laughed to himself as he doled out the money. My house is sinking into my stomach, he thought, and it'll stay there and eat my innards.

Gradually the voices in his mind became muted, and he walked home, on unsteady feet, as he hummed a tune from his younger days, a popular folk song: *rato bhaley kwaink kwaink*— about a red rooster and how the singer, while feeding it to a pregnant woman, gobbled down the head. The buoyancy of the song made him smile, but when he entered his courtyard, he thought of what had happened inside his apartment today, and the song took on a menacing tone.

Goma smelled the alcohol on his breath and was surprised. He told her he'd run into one of his old friends, who'd coaxed him into having a drink. She accepted the explanation with a degree of suspicion, and said nothing about the expense.

He woke around two, his heart beating wildly, his throat parched. He reached for the jug of water Goma usually placed beside the bed, but he couldn't find it. In the darkness, he got up, made his way to the kitchen, and, standing by the window, drank a glass of water. Mr. Sharma's light was on, and Ramchandra could see him move back and forth. The man seemed to be talking to himself, every now and then he lifted his hand toward the ceiling and said something. Ramchandra recalled Sanu's comments about him, and his disgust seemed to move physically inside him; nauseated, he stood by the sink and retched. In that moment, breathing hard, his eyes blurry, his hands clutching the side of the sink, Ramchandra knew he had to do something.

He went to his room and sat on the bed. Goma's mouth was slightly ajar, her eyes partly open. This was how she slept, and during the first months of their marriage, he'd been amused by those eyes that never fully closed. He'd teased her, saying she wanted to keep an eye on him all the time, even in the darkness of the night, so that he wouldn't escape. In frivolous moments, when she was asleep, he'd taken some sugar and sprinkled it into her open mouth. She'd wake up, her tongue tasting the sweetness, and scold him, and he'd laugh.

Now, he placed his hand on her hip and jiggled it. She woke up instantly, saying, "What? What?"

"I have to tell you something."

"What time is it?" She sat up and turned on the bedside lamp. "Why are you up?"

"It's about Malati and me."

She stared at him. "What about you two?"

"There's something going on."

Her face became very still.

"I've kissed her."

"Are you still drunk?" she said softly.

He shook his head. A strange sound floated up from the courtyard, like the howling of a distant dog. Then it became more clear; Mr. Sharma was chanting. Goma lay down.

"Goma."

"Why did you do it?"

"I don't know." He picked a piece of lint from the bed. "I don't know what's come over me. I don't know why—"

"I think I understand." Her face was slightly turned away. "You don't want me anymore."

"That's not true."

"Please leave the room."

"Goma." He placed a hand on her arm.

She moved away. "Please."

He wanted to tell her more, tell her that he could not control himself, that perhaps if she helped him, he could. But with no response from her, he left the room and went to the kitchen, where he sat on the cold floor.

He had no idea how long he sat there, and whether he'd dozed off. But a gray light appeared in the window, and Mr.

Sharma's chanting had stopped. Silence surrounded Ramchandra.

Goma stood in the doorway. "I will leave for Pandey Palace with the children," she said.

"With the day of Tika so near? Maybe you can go after that," he offered.

"It doesn't make any difference," she said. And she was right. After a moment, she said, "I don't know what I'll tell the children."

He had nothing to say.

"Perhaps we should get a servant, to feed you and wash the dishes and your clothes."

"How long will you be gone?"

She didn't answer his question. "I'll send my parents' servant for a few days, until we find someone permanent. It's good that your school is closed for these few weeks of the festival. You'll have some time to cook for yourself."

"What about that girl from Chitwan?"

"She'll be too hard for you to train. I'll keep her with me, there. Her father is supposed to bring her to the city in a couple of days."

"Sanu will be unhappy in Pandey Palace."

"I'll start to pack now."

She lingered as if she were waiting for his permission. Then she entered the kitchen, set some water to boil for tea, and stood by the window. He watched her. She made the tea and set it before him. "Aren't you going to have some?" he asked.

"I don't feel like it right now." She hesitated, as if she expected him to say something. But a lump had formed in his throat; he couldn't talk. He sipped the tea. It tasted bitter—she'd forgotten the sugar.

"I'll start packing now," she repeated, and left.

Later, he heard her wake the children. Rakesh sounded excited about going to his grandparents so early in the morning, probably pleased that he'd spend the next few days of the festival at Pandey Palace, where he'd be given money and gifts. Sanu sounded querulous. Ramchandra heard her ask Goma whether her father was coming, too. When Goma didn't respond, Sanu asked again, and Goma scolded her. No one came to the kitchen, and soon footsteps descended the stairs.

6
. . . .

FOR A LONG TIME Ramchandra sat in the kitchen, listening to the birds chirping in the guava tree in the courtyard. The gray light had given way to a golden hue that painted the courtyard, and people were waking in the surrounding houses. Someone coughed, then gargled by a window. The old lady living in the apartment above Mr. Sharma tuned her sitar.

Ramchandra put his head between his knees, and tried to make sense of what had happened, but the lack of sleep confounded him; he couldn't think. He went to the bedroom to see what Goma had packed. All her clothes from the closet were gone. In the children's bedroom, one of Rakesh's shoes had been left behind. Ramchandra picked it up and thought it might serve as an excuse for him to go to Pandey Palace and urge Goma to come home. He'd plead with her; he'd tell her it was all a mistake, that he'd slipped in a moment of confusion.

But he wasn't sure that it wouldn't happen again. Even now, as he rehearsed what he'd say to Goma, his thoughts linked themselves into a chain that led him to Malati. She would arrive soon for her session; this thought entered his mind like a breeze. He began to imagine what they would do together. Perhaps he'd cook lunch for her. Or she would cook for him. Then he became ashamed. Goma and his children had left, and here he was, thinking about someone he'd known for only a few months.

It occurred to him that he and Malati may have had some connection in a past life. Usually he scoffed at belief in reincarnation, but right now he couldn't think of any other explanation. How else could he account for his surge of anticipation at Malati's arrival, in this pathetic apartment, the morning his family had left him? Even this hellhole didn't seem bad now. He looked around the bedroom. The sparse furnishings: a bed and a small bedside table with a lamp, some photographs on the wall, a religious calendar of Goddess Kali with her fangs showing and decapitated heads at her feet. That was it. And yes, the traffic noise. As he imagined spending the afternoon in bed with Malati, his body trembled, and he quickly walked back to the kitchen.

He set some rice to boil, and found some green onions and potatoes in the cupboard. But there was no meat in the refrigerator; he'd have to buy some. Quickly he put on his clothes and went downstairs. There was a meat shop only a few yards away. He usually avoided the place because it was expensive, and the shopkeeper sold terrible meat, with bones that appeared only after he got the package home. But Malati would be here any minute, and he didn't have time to go to the shop down the block.

Back in the apartment after buying the chicken, Ramchandra chopped onions and cut the meat into small pieces. As he was about to turn on the kerosene stove, he heard footsteps on the staircase and went out to the landing. Malati was wearing the same old kurta suruwal she'd worn the first time she'd come to him. She smiled up at him. The long scratch on her left cheek made her even more beautiful, he thought. He held out his hand. She didn't offer hers, but motioned with her head to find out whether Goma was inside.

"They all went to her parents' house."

"So early? Something happened?"

"No, just a visit," he said. "How are you feeling?"

"Fine," she said shyly.

"No tutoring today," he said. "We're going to cook."

"No tutoring?"

"I bought some chicken for you." She looked disappointed, so he asked, "What? You don't want to cook?"

"Sir, the S.L.C. exams are nearly here. At this rate, I won't pass."

"I'll make sure you pass."

She crossed her arms and said, "Sir, give me your honest opinion. Where do you think I stand?"

"You've made some significant progress," he said, matching her serious tone. "My honest evaluation: you will pass."

"You aren't lying to me?"

"Why would I lie to you?" She still needed a few more days of intense studying, but right now he was ready to say anything to reassure her.

His confidence seemed to buoy her up, for she said, "Okay, we can cook and eat, and then we can study."

Her proximity made him catch his breath. "What about Rachana?"

"Malekha Didi is in a good mood today. She got a big order

of chicken for a Dashain party, so she won't mind if I'm late. What shall we cook?"

She turned out to be a very efficient cook. There was a quickness to her movements that was a pleasure to watch. She seemed to know instinctively where things were, so even before he could tell her where to find the coriander, she was sprinkling it on the potatoes. In contrast, Goma's movements in the kitchen were slow, even though her meals were delicious. Goma would worry about how much salt to add to the food, or what amount of oil was best. Malati appeared to cook without thinking. Her hands flew in all directions.

Their bodies inevitably touched, and he smelled the fragrance of jasmine in her hair. At one point, when she was stirring the chicken, he put his arms around her from behind. She leaned her head back against his shoulder and said, "Sir, why are you doing this to me?"

"I'm not doing anything to you," he whispered. He was getting an erection, and she felt it, because she pushed him away and said, "You are shameless."

They sat to eat, and when he offered her some food from his hand, she opened her mouth wide. Then she did the same to him. They fed each other, and any thought of Goma and the children in the house began to fade like a memory. Outside in the courtyard, Mr. Sharma was singing a hymn as he took his bath.

After they'd finished eating, Ramchandra led her to the bedroom. He lay down and pulled her on top of him. He kissed her and stroked her breasts, which began to rise under his touch. He put his lips to her breasts over her dress and licked them. "Sir, sir," she said. She had closed her eyes and was beginning to moan. He felt under her kurta and unraveled the string that tied her trousers. He helped her out of her suruwal, her panties, her kurta, and her bra. She straddled him, completely nude, her arms covering her breasts in shyness. Her face was flushed crimson, as if she were his bashful bride. The monkey scratches ran down her right forearm, and on her leg he saw small boils. He thrust his pelvis under her, and gradually she responded to his movement. Her hands moved away from her breasts, exposing her nipples, and she fumbled with the string on his suruwal. Soon, he too was naked.

A shout was heard on the street, and for a moment both lay still. But the call was for someone else. The *rat-rat-rat* of a motorcycle rose from the street into the room, but the sound no longer bothered Ramchandra. A great serenity came over him. There was more light in the room now—the sun had moved higher—and all the objects were brighter. He smiled at Malati, who seemed to be waiting for a signal. Her face was serious. He felt like laughing at his chain of thoughts. Of course, it was serious business. He was about to make love to his student right in his bedroom, on the very bed where he had slept with his wife a few hours ago, the very bed where his children had played with each other. His wife and children were gone, and this was serious business. A burst of melancholy and amazing joy erupted inside Ramchandra, and he quickly entered Malati, who started rocking on top of him. Her earlier bashfulness vanished, and now she moved with the same quickness she'd displayed in the kitchen. She bent over and took his head in her hands and kissed him on the mouth. "Sir, sir," she said.

"Goma," he cried as he ejaculated, but the first syllable got stuck in this throat and it came out as "O ma," repeatedly, as if he were calling his mother in distress.

They must have fallen asleep, for both were startled by the sound of footsteps on the stairs. Malati hurriedly began to put on her clothes, and Ramchandra rushed to close the door. He latched it from the inside and leaned against it, holding his breath. At first, he thought that Goma had come back to get something. But the footsteps were heavy, and something clicked inside Ramchandra's head at the sound of a rap on the door. Ashok, he mouthed to Malati, who was struggling to tie her suruwal. "Sir? Anyone in there?"

"One minute," Ramchandra shouted. He picked up his clothes and put them on.

"Should I hide?" Malati whispered.

"There's no place to hide," he whispered back. "Just pretend nothing is wrong." He said loudly to Ashok, "Why are you here? There's no tutoring today."

"I know, sir. I came for something else."

When Ramchandra opened the door, Ashok was grinning. "I was wondering if I'd entered the wrong house." His eyes fell upon Malati, and the smile on his face became bigger. "Namaste, Malati," he said.

Malati mumbled something and sat on the bed.

Ramchandra didn't invite Ashok in. "Everything all right, Ashok?"

"Of course, sir. Why wouldn't everything be all right?" He stretched his neck to look past Ramchandra toward Malati. "How's the tutoring going?"

"Fine."

"You think you'll pass?"

"Of course she'll pass," Ramchandra said testily. "What about you, though? You think that smile is going to impress the S.L.C. examiners?"

"Better to smile than to cry," Ashok said. "But I didn't come here to disturb anyone, sir. I came to give you this. It's from my father." He handed an envelope to Ramchandra, who opened it and saw a hundred-rupee bill. "Dashain bonus. He wants you to make sure that I pass."

"No teacher can give that kind of guarantee. You know that."

"I know, sir. I just wish I were given some special attention, too." Again he smiled at Malati, who got up, mumbled that she was late for something, and left. Soon, Ashok also left.

Ramchandra went to the kitchen and washed his face with water from a jug. Then he headed outside, but he got no farther than the New Road Gate when a wave of nausea swept over him. He sat down on the street, right near a newspaper vendor who had spread out his wares in front of a shop. The vendor rushed to him, lifted him up by the arm, and asked what had happened. "I'm fine," Ramchandra said. He brushed off the dust from his pants and walked toward Bhatbhateni.

Every few hundred yards, he found himself out of breath, disoriented, and had to find a place to sit. By the time he reached Pandey Palace, beads of perspiration were running down his neck, even though the air was cold. For a moment he stood outside the gate, catching his breath, wondering what to say. The Pandeys' large Alsatian dog came bounding toward the gate, barking. It recognized Ramchandra and wagged its tail. He opened the gate and walked in, the dog dancing around him.

Mr. Pandey was on the porch, smoking his hookah, and when Ramchandra did his namaste, Mr. Pandey motioned to him to sit beside him.

"What happened at home?" Mr. Pandey asked.

"Just a minor disagreement," Ramchandra said.

"Goma has never done such a thing."

"Sometimes with a family there are arguments. It's not a big deal." He glanced inside. "Is she in there?"

"I think she's sleeping. The children have gone to the market with their grandmother."

A servant brought Ramchandra a glass of tea, which he gladly accepted. There was hardly any conversation between the two men. Mr. Pandey seemed to be lost in his own world.

Ramchandra set his glass on the floor and said, "I'll go talk to her." Mr. Pandey didn't look at him. He walked up the stairs and knocked on the door of one of the bedrooms, and Goma answered that she didn't want anything to eat.

"It's me," he said.

She didn't come to the door despite his repeated pleas. After a while he went down to the porch, and Mr. Pandey asked, "So, it's serious, eh? You must have done something really bad, son-in-law. I don't like to meddle in other people's business, but whatever it is, you'd better fix it now." Before Ramchandra could answer, Mr. Pandey pointed to the rose garden and said, "That bastard gardener is not doing his job. Look how those roses are turning out." He tried to engage Ramchandra in a discussion about the pamphlets people were reading, filled with articles mocking the royal family, calling them names. "Spewing venom against royalty," Mr. Pandey said. "What has this godforsaken country come to?"

Ramchandra abruptly cut him off. "I'll come back later," he said and headed toward the gate. The Pandeys' Honda passed him a few hundred yards down the road, and he caught a glimpse of Sanu and Rakesh in the back seat, talking to their grandmother. He waved. They didn't see him, but for a brief moment Ramchandra thought they were pretending not to see him, as if they were already looking at him through their mother's eyes.

Ramchandra wandered around the streets for a while, and, as the emptiness inside him grew, set off toward Tangal.

Malati's stepmother opened the door. "Oh, the professor," she said, tightening her lips. She invited him in and called Malati, who came to the living room holding Rachana.

"So, how is my daughter doing with her studying for the S.L.C.?" Malekha Didi asked.

"I think she'll pass."

"You only think? Or will she actually pass?"

"She'll pass."

Malati asked Ramchandra to sit down, and, handing Rachana to Malekha Didi, went to the kitchen to make tea. Malekha Didi kissed the baby, who was straining her neck to look at Ramchandra. He snapped his fingers at the baby and said to Malekha Didi, "She looks just like her mother."

"Maybe she looks like her father, too. We don't know." Abruptly she added, "What's happening between you and Malati?"

"What do you mean?"

"You two . . . are you?" Her face twisted into an obscene smile.

"There's nothing."

Malati returned and asked what they were talking about, and Malekha Didi said she'd been inquiring about the two of them. "You," Malati said to her stepmother, slapping her on the shoulder. "There's nothing. You are so nosy."

The conversation was too casual; it made Ramchandra uneasy. After Malati brought in the tea, Malekha Didi talked about her recent coup, the large order of chicken for a wedding party. Ramchandra listened, but her words flew past him; his mind was on Goma and the children. A short while later, Malekha Didi handed Rachana to Malati and went outside.

"You don't look well," Malati said.

"Goma has left with the children."

"I know—" Then what he'd said seemed to dawn on her. "You mean . . . she knows?"

"I told her."

She stared at him.

"I couldn't not tell her. It was eating me."

She set Rachana on the floor and covered her eyes with her hands. "What will she think of me?"

"It's not your problem. It's mine."

For a long time, Malati kept her hands over her eyes. When she revealed her face again, he saw that she looked startled. She glanced at the door, as if expecting Goma to appear. "What are we going to do?"

"I don't know. I went to her parents' house, but she wouldn't open the door."

"The children . . . ?"

"They think they're with their grandparents just for a while."

Malati rested her chin in her hand and said, "I am not right in the head."

"What are you saying?"

"I'm strange; I don't know what I'm doing. Everyone is better off without me." She began to cry. "Bhauju treated me like a sister, and I betrayed her trust."

Ramchandra shook his head. This was not what he'd come here for. He hated this kind of self-pity, so he said, "That's going to do no good, Malati. This isn't your fault."

"Why is my life like this?"

"Stop it," he said, a bit louder.

She stopped, walked over to him, and took his hand. "I am so sorry this happened," she whispered.

He ran his index finger across her chin, wiping away the tears. "I don't know what's happened."

She stroked his hair, and soon they were kissing. "I am so

sorry," she repeated again and again. She grew passionate as she uttered those words, and it was he who gently pushed her away, saying, "Your stepmother will come," even though he found comfort in her kisses. Rachana had stood up and, holding the sofa arm, began wailing.

"What are we going to do?" Malati said. "Bhauju must hate me."

"She never hates people."

"What will you do this afternoon?"

"I don't know. I'll go home and try to sleep. This evening I'll try to talk to her again."

"Why don't you stay with me?" she said. "Here?"

"What about Malekha Didi?"

"She's going to leave in about an hour. She's spending the day with her elderly mother in Bhaktapur."

"Then I'll come back after an hour," he said.

As he passed Malekha Didi, near the chicken shed, she called out, "Oh, professor-ji, what makes you leave so early? You had enough time with our Malati?"

Ramchandra looked around to see whether the neighbors had heard her. "I have some work to do."

"Don't leave her alone. She needs you." She laughed. Vulgarly, thought Ramchandra.

The sun had taken some of the chill from the morning air. What would he do for an hour? He walked toward Bhatbhateni again. Much of his disorientation had vanished, and he walked quickly. Two blocks from Pandey Palace he ran into an old friend, a teacher from his days of working as a part-timer. They chatted for a while. The friend asked about his family, and Ramchandra said everything was fine.

He walked past the Pandey Palace gate, then turned around. Goma was sitting by herself on the porch, looking toward the garden. He couldn't make out her facial expression, but he heard Rakesh shout something from inside the house. When Goma turned her head to respond, Ramchandra quickly moved to the side so that she wouldn't see him. He leaned against the wall, his eyes closed. Slowly, he moved toward the gate and peeked in. She had gone inside.

He circled the block a few times and then went to Malati.

The city was alive with the energy of the festival. A parade walked the street of Ranipokhari on the day of Fulpati. The next day, goats, sheep, and buffalo were slaughtered at the numerous Devi Temples throughout the city. People consumed meat as a divine blessing from the goddess. They fried goat blood and ate it with relish. They boiled goats' testicles, dipped them in salt and chili powder. Goat ears were barbecued on gas stoves and passed around to the children. People ate until their stomachs were bloated, until they became sick and had to be rushed to the hospital. Other people ate until, heavy with food, they fell asleep, dreaming of riches raining on them directly from the open mouths of the ferocious Durga.

For a brief while, people forgot the city's tensions, ignored the newspapers that spoke of a revolution brewing in dark corners of its streets. Occasionally rumors rippled through the city: the king is contemplating martial law; the communists are plotting to massacre the royal family; the Indians are working with the panchays to crush any rebellion. Such talk appeared and disappeared, and the spirit of the festival made the city's streets cheerful.

On the night before Tika, Ramchandra lay in bed in Malati's closet-sized room, Malati beside him and Rachana sleeping against the wall. The bed was so small that Ramchandra's left arm dangled over the side. Under the blanket, both he and Malati were naked, shivering slightly because it was cold.

They'd done their lovemaking carefully, because of the lack of space and their fear of squashing Rachana. They'd moved slowly, their hips grinding against each other. Even at the height of excitement, Ramchandra couldn't thrust his hips at her, for fear of shaking Rachana, but he found that this control made the experience even more pleasurable.

After they were done and she'd closed her eyes for a few minutes, she said, as if the idea had come to her in a dream, "Bhauju must hate me." For a long time, he tried to console her, but she had cried out, "I am wrecking a family. I should stop studying with you."

In annoyance, he'd retorted, "Then why don't you? What's stopping you?"

"I don't know," she said. She shivered. "I don't know why I feel this way about you."

"What do you feel about me?" he asked softly.

She took his hand in hers. "When I'm with you, I feel that I am really someone."

"But you are really someone, even without me."

She shook her head. "Look at my life. What do I have? This"—she gestured around the room. "That little girl who doesn't have a father? And Malekha Didi. She could kick me out of this house any moment, and then where would I go?"

"What kind of a woman is she? She seems . . ." He wanted to say *vulgar*, but that would sound too harsh. "She's like a different kind of person."

"She's unpredictable. One day full moon, the other day no moon."

He reached over her and stroked Rachana's head. "Does she care about you? And Rachana?"

"I know she loves Rachana, but sometimes she doesn't want to see her face."

"And you? Does she love you?"

Malati lifted her arms and stretched. "Sometimes she does. Other times she treats me the way any stepmother would."

"You don't have to live with her, you know."

"But where would I go? How would I take care of Rachana? That's why I want to pass the S.L.C., so that I can go to college, get a good job, move to a place of my own."

She paused, as if she were envisioning the possibilities. Then she said, "Now the exams are only a few weeks away, and I'm afraid I won't pass."

"You will," he assured her. "If you focus on getting out from the clutches of that woman, you will."

"Malekha Didi isn't so bad," Malati said, although she didn't sound convinced of her own words. "She could have thrown me out of the house, but she didn't."

"She seems strange."

"I think it's because of her dubi," Malati said, referring to Malekha Didi's albino skin. "She must have suffered all her life. You know how people in our society act toward anyone of that color."

"How did she end up marrying your father?"

Malati said that after her mother ran off to India with a truck driver, taking all the money and jewelry in the house, she and her father had come to Kathmandu. Malekha Didi had helped her father get a job in a government office in Singha Durbar. Malati didn't remember when her father and Malekha Didi became lovers, but she knew that her father began spending more and more time at Malekha Didi's house. Soon, they moved in with her, and the two adults slept together in the same bedroom. When Malati was sixteen, they got married in a small temple ceremony, and about three months after that, her father was hit by a motorcycle outside Singha Durbar and died in the hospital of a brain hemorrhage.

"Whatever Malekha Didi's faults, she really loved my father."

Ramchandra played with her navel, and they fell asleep again. They woke near dawn to the crying of Rachana, who was hungry. Ramchandra's watch read six o'clock. Across the city, people were preparing for Tika, getting their jamara ready, cooking food for the people who'd flock to their houses throughout the day to receive tika, planning when and how they'd go to their elders to receive tika. And here he was, in this cramped room with Malati. He should go somewhere, do something, but what? Malekha Didi had asked that he stay today and put tika on Malati and Rachana, and he'd said yes, he'd like to. But right now, he grieved at the thought of being away from his children, from Goma, on this important day.

He watched Malati try to feed her daughter, who was shying away from her mother's breast.

"I have to make some formula for her," Malati said. "Can you watch her for a second?"

Ramchandra picked up the crying baby, and Malati went to the kitchen. Rachana didn't stop crying, so he sang to her, a song he used to sing to Sanu when she was a baby cradled in his arms. Sanu would gradually stop crying and look intensely at his face, as if she were savoring each sound. But the song didn't work for Rachana, who began to wail even louder.

When Malati came back with the bottle, Ramchandra said, "I think I'd better leave now."

"Where will you go?"

He shrugged. "I'll probably go to Pandey Palace to see if I'll be allowed to put tika on the children."

"Will you come back here for tika?"

"I'll try. Let's see how it goes at Pandey Palace."

★

In Naxal, a swing had been set up on a small field between a school and a row of houses. Children in brand-new clothes were swinging high on the babiyo rope that dangled from tall bamboo sticks. Some children already had the bright red tika on their foreheads, with the yellow jamara tucked behind their ears. The lullaby he'd sung to Rachana echoed in Ramchandra's mind. Looking warm but happy, families walked the streets, dressed in their freshly tailored clothes, going to their relatives to get and to give tika. It was the day of victory over evil, when Lord Rama slew the monster Ravana, when Lord Durga triumphed over Mahisasur, the terrible demon that, in the guise of a buffalo, had wreaked havoc, piercing the air with its razor-sharp horns.

Laughter, shouting—all the joy of festivity—rang through the air under the clear blue sky. When Ramchandra passed some people he knew, they looked curiously at him in his crumpled clothes.

In the cluster of shops in Bhatbhateni, he found a telephone and called Pandey Palace. Mrs. Pandey answered, but when Ramchandra asked for Goma, she muttered, "Too many phone calls in this house," banged the receiver down on something, and went to fetch Goma.

Ramchandra waited a long time for Goma to come to the phone. She didn't say anything, but her breathing told him she was there.

"Goma, today is Tika. Please come home."

After more silence, she said, "There's nothing to come home to."

"I miss the children."

She said nothing.

"At least let me come over and put tika on the children. Otherwise . . ." His voice caught in his throat, and he coughed.

Two other voices, a man's and a woman's, echoed within the wires like distant bells in a cross-connection. Ramchandra heard terms of endearment and then the woman's voice saying that she'd written a poem for the man. "Okay, you can come and visit them," Goma said. "But only for tika. They won't leave with you."

Is it a love poem? the man asked, and Goma hung up.

Ramchandra checked his wallet; he wanted to give something to the children. He had about two hundred rupees and would give each of them fifty. He'd never before given them such a large sum — usually he gave them no more than twenty rupees — but money was the least of his concerns right now.

To his consternation, it was Nalini who opened the door at Pandey Palace. As soon as she saw Ramchandra, she pursed her lips and said, "The children will be with you shortly. You can sit in the living room."

Her coldness stung Ramchandra. Had Goma told her what had happened? He waited a long time, wondering where everyone was, why no one offered him a cup of tea. Then Sanu and Rakesh came in, wearing their new clothes, and already with their tika and jamara. Ramchandra immediately noticed Sanu's somber face. Rakesh jumped into his lap. "Ba, look how much Grandfather gave me," and opened his fist to reveal a hundred-rupee bill. Even on his most generous day, Ramchandra couldn't keep up with his in-laws. But he acted pleased, hugged his son, and kissed him on the cheek. Sanu remained at a distance until he called her to him. He patted her arm and asked, "And how much did you get?"

"Why are we here, Ba? I don't want to be here."

"It's only for a short time."

"Did you and Mother have a fight?"

"Is that what she told you?"

"She hasn't told us anything. She stays in bed most of the time. Even today she hasn't done anything. She hasn't put tika on us. Only Hajurba and Hajurma have."

"Now that I'm here, your mother will come down." He asked Rakesh to get his mother. While he was gone, Sanu sat quietly on the edge of the sofa, her hands folded in her lap.

Rakesh returned to say that Goma wasn't feeling well. Then Nalini appeared with a tray of tika and jamara and said, "Here it is. Just leave it here when you're done, brother-in-law."

"I haven't even greeted your parents." He didn't want to, but he thought he had to say something. "And this is such an auspicious day."

She kept her head averted and walked away.

The children sat down in front of him, and, reciting the prayer Om Jayanti Mangalakali Bhadrakali Kapalini, which he always had some difficulty remembering, Ramchandra dipped his fingertips into the rice-yogurt mixture, colored bright red, and dabbed it on Sanu's forehead. Then he placed a few strands of jamara on her hair. He leaned over to touch her feet with his forehead. That usually made Sanu titter, but today she maintained her serious look. Ramchandra gave her the fifty-rupee bill and recited the blessing of happiness and prosperity. When it was Rakesh's turn, the performance was repeated, except that the son was to touch the father's feet. At that point, Rakesh rebelled, saying it wasn't fair that his sister didn't have to do this. He thrust his feet at his father, and Ramchandra, overcome by love for his son, and giving in to the sorrow that was spreading its wings inside his body, leaned over and put his forehead on his son's feet.

7

· · · · · · ·

THE DAYS CREPT ON, and Goma and the children didn't come home. He felt their absence in his bones, his chest, the membranes of his throat so that at times it was difficult for him to speak.

Initially, he went to Pandey Palace almost every day, first calling the house to say he'd be coming, and then spending some time with the children in the living room. He was offered none of the hospitality that was usually accorded to a son-in-law, not even tea. The Pandeys were obviously avoiding him as much as they could. Perhaps they saw this as an opportunity to wrest their daughter away from a son-in-law who was nothing but a failure. When he did encounter Mr. Pandey, the old man was more interested in talking about politics than about Ramchandra's rift with Goma. And Mrs. Pandey hardly showed her face. Their opinion of him was so low, Ramchandra thought with much bitterness, that they didn't even care about society's criticism of women who lived separated from their husbands. Good riddance, he could hear them saying silently.

One day, to a servant who had come down with the children, he insisted that he talk to Goma, and she appeared. He sent the children away and talked to her. She listened but said she couldn't come back to the house right now. She seemed lethargic, as if the whole matter had tired her. Darkness circled her eyes, like Nalini's. "I'm not tutoring her anymore," Ramchandra lied, but the information had no effect on Goma. "Not right now," she said. When he reached out to hug her, she slipped away from him and left the room.

After that, he no longer asked to see her and she no longer came down. What hurt him even more was that, with each visit, he could tell that Sanu had grown to enjoy living at Pandey Palace. She showed him a frock her grandmother had bought for her, talked about the gardener, with whom she'd developed a friendship. And there was the girl from Chitwan, Hasina, a few years younger than Sanu, a scrawny child with a sassy mouth. Sanu adored her. Every time Ramchandra went to Pandey Palace, he found the two together. When he asked Sanu whether she missed home, she became serious and said, "Of course I do. I want to go home." But he knew she thought that's what he wanted to hear. Rakesh was his usual jovial self. He'd ask about some of his friends from the surrounding houses in the courtyard, but then lose interest and go running upstairs.

Amidst everything was Malati. She no longer talked of Goma, and when Ramchandra brought up her absence, Malati said, "I'll never be able to show my face to her again." He watched her carefully, trying to judge what she was really thinking. He didn't doubt her sincerity, but often he sensed that part of her—something that defined her, made her a person—remained elusive. He found himself trying to figure out what she was thinking. Sometimes, when she stood looking out the living room window, the expression on her face confounded him. It was sadness, yes, but it was also longing, a craving for something he could not comprehend. And this expression, accentuated by the afternoon rays streaming through the window curtains, made him feel that even as she was in the room with him physically, she was somewhere else emotionally, laughing with someone else, whispering an urgent detail into someone else's ear, someone with whom she was truly Malati, Malati who knew how to enjoy life, Malati who got what she wanted. He saw her in this alternate life so vividly that the Malati in front of him became a mere shadow, a poor cousin. His own words made him shake his head. Poor cousin? Of course she was poor, and so was he. And as if hearing his thoughts, she'd look at him and smile.

The city had brightened in anticipation of Tihar. Around the outer walls of their houses many inhabitants had already wrapped strings of lights that blinked and winked all evening long. Those people who were rich left them on all night, and the faint glow illuminated the street, sometimes revealing a roaming band of dogs. In Ranipokhari, the entire periphery of the pond was illuminated, and so was the bridge that led to the Shiva shrine in the center. The lights, reflected in the water, seemed to be swaying when a breeze ruffled the surface. A couple of times in the evening Ramchandra stood by the black railings that surrounded the pond and watched. He thought of the children, how excited they'd become during Tihar, when they could play with firecrackers and join a straggly band of neighborhood children to go to each house in the area and play deusi. When Sanu and Rakesh came to their own house with their friends, Ramchandra would make sure that he extracted enough entertainment out of them before he gave them any money. Often, in the courtyard, he'd ask Rakesh to sing a popular tune and Sanu to dance. Goma would come down to watch her children, and she and Ramchandra would exchange looks of pride as Sanu and Rakesh and their friends shook their hips and flailed their arms.

All across the city people congregated in living rooms to play cards—flush, paplu, twenty-nine, marriage. They'd sit in a circle on the floor and hurl money at the center. They'd drink, argue, and maybe leave the room in a huff. The women of the house would bring endless cups of tea and spicy minced meat, or hover behind their husbands and uncles to watch what was at stake. Children eyed the money hungrily, crying "bakshish" whenever someone made a large haul. Some went bankrupt in minutes; others stuffed their pockets with cash and strutted down the streets. Ramchandra had been invited by a few people to join them in playing tas, but he declined. He'd never liked gambling, mostly because he was always poor. He'd never understood how people could risk their money so thoughtlessly.

Malati had begun to improve in her math. She had mastered compound interest and mensuration, and Ramchandra was becoming convinced that, with more intensive sessions, she would definitely pass the S.L.C. She started to come earlier to the house, so Ramchandra had to get up before sunrise to take his bath and make himself a cup of tea. Now he tutored her for nearly two hours. But once she'd left, the morning stretched before him like a long yawn.

The school was closed for the festival, so he had the days to himself, and after Malati left, his mind immediately went to Goma and the children. A servant boy from Pandey Palace came every morning to cook for Ramchandra so that he wouldn't have to worry about his meals. The boy, a chubby young man with a thin mustache, cooked well and left enough for dinner, but that portion often went to waste, because Ramchandra would end up eating at Malati's house. A couple of times Ramchandra tried to pry from the boy some information about Goma—what she did all day, whether she mentioned his name—but the boy didn't know enough or, if he did, was under instructions not to tell Ramchandra.

Ramchandra spent the afternoons in Malati's house, where they made love in her room, sometimes even with Malekha Didi puttering around in the kitchen. She apparently had become used to Ramchandra's presence, for she often brought him tea and biscuits without Malati's prompting. One day, while Malati was washing Rachana's clothes in the bathroom, Malekha Didi told Ramchandra that her skin disfigurement had subjected her to ridicule and contempt when she was a child in a village outside Kathmandu. She spoke to Ramchandra as if he were her older brother, as if he would understand precisely what she had suffered, and he wanted to live up to that role, so he shook his head and said, "Tsk, tsk," as she described her suffering. Once, she reached out and touched him as she talked, and, strangely, he felt moved.

On the morning of Laxmi Puja, when all the people in the city were praying to the goddess to make them wealthy, Ramchandra prayed to the small picture of Laxmi in his kitchen and lit a few sticks of incense. Every year he had prayed to Laxmi, asking her to do something about his financial situation. As he stood, his palms joined in front of her, he would picture a house, just a small house, with enough room for his small family. This year, a house no longer seemed important. He asked that his wife and children come back to him. At dusk he called Pandey Palace to see whether he'd be invited there, but no one picked up the phone. Probably they were outside, enjoying the lights or playing with the firecrackers. He didn't go to Malati's house that day; he stayed by the window in Jaisideval, looking at the street. Groups of boys and girls came by, dancing, beating the madal. Some entered the courtyard and began their chant, asking for money or anything the household could provide. Ramchandra turned off the light in the flat and watched them from the window.

Even on the day of Bhai Tika, two days later, when Sanu would perform puja on Rakesh, tightening the bond between a sister and a brother, Ramchandra got no call from Pandey Palace. On that evening, he did go to Malati's house, and Malekha Didi insisted that she put tika on him, make him her brother. Ramchandra didn't like the idea, but how could he say no? So he let her, and then, reluctantly, gave her a twenty-rupee note as dakshina.

Around nine o'clock, after they'd eaten dinner, they heard thunder, and soon rain was clattering on the roof. Chickens in the nearby shack began to scream. Chewing the betel nut Malekha Didi had passed around, Ramchandra waited for the rain to subside. But it came down even harder, and the ceaseless noise of the torrent made him drowsy. The next thing he knew, he was being led to Malati's room by Malekha Didi. He kept saying that he had to go home, but he couldn't keep his eyes open.

He woke to a silence that told him the rain had died down. Malati was sleeping beside him, Rachana squeezed in the corner. He put his hand on Malati's hip, hoping his touch would wake her. But she was in deep sleep, and his thoughts kept getting louder—accusing, cajoling, condemning—until he forced himself to sit up and shake his head and groan out loud. Even that didn't wake Malati, although the baby did cry and thrash around in her sleep.

Softly, Ramchandra got out of bed, and, finding his way in the darkness (and this tormented him even more: how familiar he had become with the interior of this house), he moved to the main door and left.

The streets were shiny from the rain, and he had no idea what time it was. Hardly anyone was out. Occasionally a car hurtled past, and from one car a drunk shouted something incomprehensible, though to Ramchandra it sounded like an admonition, a warning. With frightened steps, he walked in the direction of Pandey Palace. The rain returned, a drizzle that soaked him by the time he reached the house and stood in front of the gate. The roof was bright with colorful electric lights. All the rooms were dark, except for one window on the second floor. That was Goma's bedroom before she married. Could she be there, awake? Where were the children sleeping? He grabbed the iron bars, leaned his forehead against them, and closed his eyes.

The sound of screeching tires startled him; it was a police van. A uniformed policeman got out and asked what he was doing at the gate of this house.

"I'm just taking a rest."

The policeman came closer. "Are you trying to sneak in, huh? That's what it looks like." With his right hand, he waved a baton in the air. "Are you trying to bomb this house? Are you a communist? Which party do you belong to?"

"No party." Ramchandra's eyes started to water. "I'm resting."

"Drunk? Are you a drunk? I'll take you to jail."

Another cop shouted from inside the van, "What's going on?"

"I think he was trying to go inside to steal."

"This is my sasurali," Ramchandra said.

"Yes, of course." The policeman laughed. "If you don't move on, I'll take you to your real in-laws' house. Down at the station." He struck Ramchandra hard on the shoulder. "Move on."

Ramchandra clasped his right shoulder with his left hand and bent over. "Vamoosh," the policeman said before getting back in the van. Ramchandra, his shoulder flaming, stumbled away. He imagined coming to Pandey Palace in the light of the morning and telling Goma what had happened. He pictured her rubbing some tiger balm on the spot, the heat of the ointment and her soothing fingers making his pain evaporate.

He couldn't remember how he managed to get home; his mind was a blur. But he staggered up the stairs and flopped down on the bed. The pain in his shoulder kept him from lying on his right side. Through the window, he saw the full moon, the same moon that appeared outside Goma's window, the same moon that shone above Malati's house, except that she wouldn't be able to see it from her windowless room. Throughout the night he imagined noises in his apartment, footsteps creaking up the stairs, the clank of dishes in the kitchen.

After the police incident, Ramchandra was reluctant to visit Pandey Palace. He thought of his children constantly, but the realization that Goma had given up on him, that she had severed their relationship, made him numb. As Tihar drew to an end, instead of visiting Sanu and Rakesh he only talked to them on the phone. He had found a phone for public use in a shop in Malati's neighborhood. For privacy he could take the phone inside a small room, the cord winding over rice sacks and kerosene containers, and he called the children every evening. But these conversations had begun to acquire a lethargic tone. Sanu and Rakesh had nothing to report to their father, and he had nothing to say that interested them. Rakesh once reminded Ramchandra that the story he had started, about the poor girl, had never been completed. Ramchandra assured him that the final installment would be delivered as soon as they came home.

One day the inevitable happened. Malati came in the evening for an extra session, and she ended up staying the night.

After the session, he had encouraged her to eat dinner with him, and they ate the meal that the boy had cooked for Ramchandra that morning. They made love, then fell asleep. He woke a few hours later and watched her. Her lips twitched as she slept, and occasionally her eyebrows fluttered. A couple of times she whimpered, troubled by something in her dreams. Ramchandra felt a deep affection for her, not unlike what he felt for his children when he watched them sleep. Well, Malati was a child, he thought. He reached over and kissed her, and she opened her eyes. "Ama, what time is it?" she cried. And when she saw that it was already eleven, she panicked. "Malekha Didi will kill me," she said and hurriedly put on her clothes.

"You're not going home at this time of the night."

"But I have to."

Ramchandra thought about walking home with her, but at this time of night many drunks were staggering in the streets, and there was no telling what they'd do when they saw a young woman. So he suggested they call Malekha Didi and tell her Malati would be home early the next morning.

"But where can I call from?"

The shop that had the phone would be closed by now, but Ramchandra knew the shopkeeper slept inside because he was afraid of thieves. Ramchandra would have to wake him; there was no other way.

They trudged downstairs, and Ramchandra rapped on the shop's door. The shopkeeper's sleepy voice asked who it was, and when Ramchandra identified himself, the shopkeeper didn't believe him. "I'll call the police," he threatened. Only after a long moment did he open the door, and then he scolded Ramchandra for waking him. When the man saw Malati, he became even more irate. "This doesn't look good," he told Ramchandra. Everyone in the neighborhood by now had heard that Goma and the children had left. Ramchandra calmed him down, saying that he misunderstood the situation, and signaled Malati toward the phone.

Her conversation with Malekha Didi didn't go well. Malati sounded defensive and apologetic, repeating, "What to do? I fell asleep. I'm sorry." Malekha Didi's rough voice crackled over the phone, and Ramchandra flinched with embarrassment as he heard the words "slut" and "harlot." The shopkeeper pretended he wasn't listening, but his forehead tightened. Ramchandra snatched the phone from Malati and said to Malekha Didi, "This is Ramchandra here. It was a mistake. She'll be there to-morrow morning. Please calm down."

His voice apparently triggered something in the woman, for she started cursing him in terms he'd never heard before. "Motherfucker. Pig's ass." Ramchandra handed the phone back to Malati and looked apologetically at the shopkeeper, who stood at the counter, ready to snatch the phone away. Malati was saying, "Please don't say such things, Malekha Didi. Please." And then she hung up, because Malekha Didi had slammed down the phone.

Ramchandra gave the shopkeeper an extra five rupees, which he took with a grunt.

Back upstairs, Malati sat on the bed, unable to sleep. "She hasn't been this angry in a long time."

"But I don't understand," Ramchandra said. "She didn't mind me sleeping at her house. Why is she so particular about this?"

"She's always been unpredictable," Malati said. "Now, I'm not sure she'll welcome you to the house anymore."

Neither of them slept well the rest of that night, and around four o'clock, Ramchandra got up to make tea.

"I'll make it," Malati said.

While she was boiling the water, he put his arms around her. "I don't know whether I'll be able to see you for a while."

She poured some milk into the boiling tea.

"Did you hear what I said?"

She mumbled something he couldn't decipher.

"I'm going to Pandey Palace today and ask Goma to come back," he said.

She stirred the tea.

"Even if she doesn't come back immediately, it's best if you and I don't see each other."

"If that's what you think is right."

"But it means that I may not be able to tutor you anymore."

Her face was sad as she poured the tea. The light in Mr. Sharma's window had come on, and he was peering in their direction, so they moved to the bedroom. Ramchandra held Malati's hand and said, "Everything will be all right in your life." He told her that she should concentrate on the chapters on quadratic equations and probability, since those were her weak areas. He stroked her face.

"I have brought nothing but trouble for you," she said.

"It's my fate. I have to deal with this."

At five o'clock, even before light began spreading across the Kathmandu sky, Malati headed toward home and Rachana.

Ramchandra stood in front of the Ganesh statue in the kitchen and prayed, asking the elephant god to make his day successful. The prayer gave him a boost of confidence.

The shopkeeper with the phone sniggered at him as he walked by. "When is Goma bhauju coming back home, Ramchandra-ji?" he asked.

"Today," Ramchandra said.

The air was colder than it had been the past few weeks, and Ramchandra tightened the muffler around his neck. He walked briskly, pretending he felt more confident, hoping that this affectation would spread into his surroundings and impress Goma so that she would return with the children.

By hook or by crook, he repeated to himself, I am going to get them back today.

When he entered the gate of Pandey Palace, he saw Mr. and Mrs. Pandey sitting on the porch. He greeted them with a smile, and asked after their well-being. Their cool reception didn't deflect him. He said, "I have come to take Goma and the children home."

"That will depend on her," Mrs. Pandey said.

Mr. Pandey, staring into the distance, acted as if Ramchandra weren't there.

Ramchandra leaned against the porch banister. "You could try to persuade her."

"Why should we try to persuade her, son-in-law?" Mrs. Pandey said. "What have you given to our daughter other than unhappiness? And now you've done something that has shown your true nature."

"What did she tell you?"

"She hasn't told us anything, but that's because our daughter is a sweet girl and won't speak badly of you. Whatever you did, it must be pretty bad. Otherwise, why would she have left you?"

"That's right," Mr. Pandey said, although he didn't look at either of them.

Ramchandra was furious. "You've found a good excuse, haven't you? This was all you needed, a move from Goma. And now you'll do anything to separate us. I couldn't even spend Dashain and Tihar with my family."

"What are we doing?" Mrs. Pandey said. Her face was turning red. "We're doing nothing. Whatever is happening is between Goma and you; it has nothing to do with us."

"You've never held me in any regard." He wanted to hurt them. "You don't want to see us together; that's what the problem is."

"Yes, that's what it is," Mr. Pandey said, rising to his feet and looking at Ramchandra threateningly. "What are you going to do? What have you done to our daughter?"

Ramchandra also stood, in case Mr. Pandey lunged at him. "You are miserable people," he said. "You are status-hungry, money-conscious, miserable people." He didn't know where his courage was coming from. This was hardly a good start to getting back his wife and children, but he couldn't stop his tongue. "You will burn in hell for your treatment of me."

Mr. Pandey sat down, obviously debating whether he should physically tackle his son-in-law.

"Hell?" Mrs. Pandey said. "It's you who has put us through hell all these years. With your dingy apartment, with your miserable job."

The screen door creaked and out stepped Goma.

"You are going home with me today," Ramchandra said.

"See what your husband is doing?" Mrs. Pandey said. "Like a lowly cobbler, he's come to argue with us."

"What happened?" Goma asked Ramchandra.

"Nothing happened," he said. "Get the children ready so that we can go home."

"She's not going anywhere with you," Mrs. Pandey said.

Ramchandra took a step toward his mother-in-law. "And why not? And who are you to say that?"

Mrs. Pandey called to her servants (and she kept many of them), presumably to have them throw out Ramchandra.

"Why don't you go inside, Mother, so that we can talk?" Goma said.

"I don't want him here."

"He's my husband," Goma said. "He has a right to come here."

Three servants had appeared, but Goma asked them to go inside. Mr. and Mrs. Pandey also left, reluctantly.

"And why are you acting like a hoodlum?" Goma asked.

"Let's go home, Goma. This is too much. I can't take it anymore."

"So, it's all about you, then? What about me?"

He took her hand. "Please. Let's go home and talk about this."

"There's nothing to talk about, is there? You've already made your decision."

"It's not like that."

"What is it like, then?"

Ramchandra said, in a tearful voice, "I need help. I can't live without you and the children. What happened was because something's not right with me, and only you can help me. No one else."

"Oh, so you hurt me, and now you want me to cure you? I am not a magician."

"Goma, please."

"I told Sanu yesterday what happened."

Ramchandra stared at her in disbelief. "Why did you do such a thing?"

"Why shouldn't I? She's been asking me what happened. She's been depressed."

"And your telling her made her happy?" He didn't want to argue with Goma, but he was sickened by the thought of Sanu looking at him with scorn.

"She's old enough to deal with the truth."

He was silent, then said, "I thought she was happy here."

"She's a sensitive girl. She was pretending, so that I wouldn't worry about her."

Ramchandra sat down in the chair vacated by his father-in-law. "Goma, let's go home."

She turned toward the gate. "What will I do there?"

"It's your home. It belongs to you."

The door burst open, and Sanu and Rakesh came out. Rakesh immediately complained to his father about his not having visited in a long time. Sanu remained at a distance, avoiding his eyes.

"Go pack your belongings. We're going back to Jaisideval."

Rakesh looked at his mother. "So soon? You didn't tell us about this."

Goma patted him on the head.

"What about school, then?" Rakesh asked, a trace of hope on his face.

"We'll worry about that once we get home," Ramchandra said.

Sanu went inside.

Ramchandra waited breathlessly for Goma's response.

"All right," she told Rakesh. "It's time for us to go home."

The taxi ride to Jaisideval was filled with silence. Even Rakesh stopped his usual chattering and pressed his nose against the window to blow vapor on the glass. Sanu sat with hands in her lap, her eyes on the crowded streets. Earlier, after she had vanished into the house, they had had to search for her. She was found in the back garden, lying on the grass and staring at the sky. Ramchandra wanted to apologize to her, but he let Goma approach their daughter and ask that she get ready. For a long moment Sanu didn't move; then, muttering under her breath, she went in to pack her things.

The taxi driver was singing an old Nepali song, one that proclaimed heartbreak despite the protagonist's chasing a damsel named Sani up and down the slopes and crossing the river of Bijapur: *Ukali orali chadhera, Bijapur khola tarera, Sanilai bolaunda boldina, parnu pir paryo.* Just to break the tension, Ramchandra first hummed along with the driver. And replacing "Sani" with "Sanu," he started singing. Rakesh began to belt out the song too, poking Sanu at each mention of her name. Ramchandra, who was sitting beside the driver, turned around and said to his daughter, "So, Sanu, who is chasing you, eh?" Sanu didn't smile, and Goma said to Ramchandra, coldly, "You don't need to teach my children about chasing and grabbing."

Ramchandra stopped, and Rakesh went back to pressing his nose against the window. Only the taxi driver continued humming.

As they got out of the taxi, the neighbors watched. The tea shopkeeper stared at them while he was giving change to a customer. A coin slipped through his fingers and clanked its way down the street. A neighbor smiled and nodded. Inside the courtyard, Mr. Sharma leaned on his windowsill, unsmiling, and Ramchandra observed him carefully to see how he looked at Sanu, but Mr. Sharma was watching Goma.

They trudged up the stairs, and for a brief moment Goma stood on the landing, as if she felt traces of Malati's presence. "I'm going to sleep in the children's room," she told Ramchandra. Sanu headed toward her room, and Rakesh went to a neighbor's window and shouted to his courtyard friends. Ramchandra had to remind him that they'd all gone to school. It was already nine o'clock, and his school reopened today, too. He'd leave it to Goma to decide whether the children should go.

As if reading his thoughts, Goma said, "Okay, get dressed for school."

Rakesh pouted with disappointment. "But we haven't had anything to eat. And school's already started."

"I'll give you money for snacks. Come on."

She went to the children's room with the bags and helped them get ready.

Sanu, passing Ramchandra on her way down the stairs, didn't meet his eyes.

After the children had left, the apartment was silent. Goma stayed in the kitchen. Ramchandra sniffed the bedroom for the scent of Malati in the air. He peeked inside the kitchen: Goma was sitting on a pirka in a corner, her knees pulled up, her fingers doodling figures on the floor.

"What shall we eat this morning?" he asked.

"I don't need to eat. I'll cook something for you."

"There's nothing to cook."

"I'll go to the market."

"No need to cook only for me," he said. Two thousand explanations, apologies, excuses floated through his mind, but all he could do, too, was doodle on the floor.

A loud rap sounded on the door downstairs. "Who could it be?" Ramchandra said. For a moment he didn't move, thinking that this moment with Goma was too important to break. But the rapping continued, followed by footsteps on the stairs. He went to the landing and saw Malati coming up, holding Rachana on her hip. Sucking in his breath, he bounded down the stairs, and nudged her to go back down. She started to speak, and he shook his head vigorously. In the courtyard, he whispered, "Goma is back."

"I am so sorry, sir," she said. "Malekha Didi kicked me out of the house."

"Why?"

"She said she's angry about everything."

"But you haven't done anything."

"I pleaded with her. It was of no use."

"Where are your things?"

"She threw everything out on the front porch. Says if I don't pick it all up by this evening, she'll throw it into the street."

Mr. Sharma had come back to his window and was watching. Ramchandra glared at him, then he thought hard and said to Malati, "Okay, right now I'm talking to Goma. Why don't you come to the school at around eleven, and we'll find a solution." He asked whether she'd had anything to eat, and she shook her head, so he fished in his pockets and found a twenty-rupee note for her. He told her the directions to get to his school. "If I'm teaching, just wait outside the door. I'll find you."

"How is bhauju?" she whispered.

"She'll be fine."

"I am so sorry about this, sir," she said, her eyes welling up. "But I didn't know where else to go."

"Don't be sorry. Okay, go now."

He went upstairs. Goma was in the kitchen, sitting in the same position. It was nearly time for him to get to school. He hadn't planned on going there today, because he hoped to spend time with Goma and find ways to reconcile, but he couldn't leave Malati in the lurch. "I'd better get dressed," he said to Goma, who didn't look up.

As he went to the bedroom, he heard her say, in a low voice, "It was Malati, wasn't it?" He said nothing, just stood in the doorway, his back to her.

"What does she want?"

"Nothing. She wanted nothing. It's over between us."

"She's in trouble, isn't she?"

"Yes, but it's not a big deal."

She said nothing more, so he got dressed. His stomach was rumbling. Maybe he could eat a samosa during the break.

He went back to the kitchen. Goma was now standing by the window, looking out.

"I am leaving," he said.

She turned. Her face had a strange expression, a combination of pain and resolve, and he was slightly afraid of what thoughts were running through her mind. "What are you going to do about her?" she asked.

"It's over, Goma. Trust me. Please. I have learned my lesson."

"Are you going to leave her, just like that?"

"It was a momentary thing, a lapse. It'll happen no more."

"A fine man you are," she said. "Where is she going to go?"

"What do you mean?"

"Didn't she tell you her stepmother kicked her out of the house?"

How had she heard that? Had she come down the stairs to listen to them?

"Yes, but that's her problem, not ours."

Goma gave a short, bitter laugh. "A fine, noble man you are."

"I've asked her to come to the school," he admitted. "I'll give her some money."

"You'll give her money? Is she a prostitute?"

"What do you want me to do, Goma? I don't know what to do."

They were silent. Then Goma said, "Ask her to come here."

"Come here?"

"Yes, here, to this miserable apartment."

Ramchandra laughed.

"Yes, you two can sleep in the bedroom. I'll sleep with the children."

Ramchandra leaned against the doorway. Goma was dead

serious. "Is this your way of punishing me? Saying such things?"

"I am not punishing you. You asked me to help you."

"How will this help me?"

"Don't you see?" she said, shaking her head, as if he were a child who couldn't see the obvious. "You've found something in her you haven't found in me. You have to decide for yourself exactly what that is. And the only way to do so is by being honest, by living with her, as if you were husband and wife."

"What nonsense, Goma. This is not a Hindi film."

"She needs help right now, doesn't she? She can't walk the streets with that child on her hip. The city will swallow her up. She'll become a prostitute."

Ramchandra groaned.

"And you need help of another kind. You need to find out what it is you crave. So this is the only way."

"Impossible," he said. "Goma, you've lost your senses."

"Yes, indeed," she said. "I'm the one who's lost my senses."

"What will the children think?" he finally said. He thought of his daughter, and a moan escaped his mouth. "I can't do it. What will Sanu think?"

"I'll explain things to her."

"She's only thirteen years old. How do you expect her to understand?"

"You don't know your daughter."

"She'll hate me for the rest of her life. Goma, this is absurd."

"What you did with her, without my knowledge, is more absurd than this."

"No, no."

"So what will you tell her today at school?"

"I don't know."

She came closer to him. "Listen to me." Her voice was firm. "What you've done is irreparable. If you two want to be together, I'm not going to stand in your way."

He leaned against her shoulder and cried. "What kind of a woman are you? You're asking me to bring someone home, as if she were my second wife. That's unnatural. It's wrong."

"Says who?"

"Society won't accept it."

"Why are you concerned about society now?"

"People will condemn us. They'll laugh at you."

"I don't care who laughs at me."

"What about your parents?"

"This is not their problem, therefore not theirs to solve."

The room spun, and Ramchandra sat down on the floor. "This is wrong, this is wrong."

"It's the only way. The only way we can reach the truth. The only way I'll be satisfied living with you from now on. Otherwise, our relationship will always be cold, as it has been these past weeks."

"Please don't do this to me, Goma."

"I'm doing nothing to you. I'm offering a solution to a problem that you caused. I'm offering a roof to a girl who has been left homeless. If you have a better solution, let me hear it."

Ramchandra closed his eyes. "I need a glass of water."

She brought him one, and he gulped it down. She brought him another one, and he drank it, too.

"Go and bring her home. I'll get the rooms ready," Goma said, and went into the children's room.

Ramchandra stood up and ran down the stairs.

At school, he dreaded Malati's arrival. The students could tell he was distracted and became restive. Some even talked to each other while he outlined a math problem on the board. In his second period, when he was teaching the tenth grade and was writing on the board, something hit him hard on the back. He turned around, and on the floor was a dead rat. The students usually didn't play pranks on him as they did to the other teachers, and he'd always assumed, with a degree of smugness, that they respected him. Now he glared at the snickering students, and his eyes fell on one, in the middle of the classroom, a tall, lanky boy with long hair and a red bandana tied around his head. The school rules explicitly forbade extraneous clothing, such as a bandana or a hat, but some of the senior students ignored the rule. Bandana Miss also disliked long hair, and she'd had arguments with this particular student.

"Okay, who did this?" Ramchandra said loudly. "Mukesh, get up."

Mukesh lazily got to his feet. "You need something, sir?"

"Come with me to Bandana Miss's office."

"For what, sir?"

The rest of the students were laughing. "Yes, he did it, sir. He's a naughty, naughty boy," someone called out.

Mukesh looked around the classroom with a smile. "Evidence, my dear comrades. Where is the evidence?"

"Okay, that's it. Don't blame me if you fail your S.L.C. You, come with me." He pointed to Mukesh, picked up the dead rat by its tail, which brought howls of laughter from his students, and left the classroom. Mukesh followed, his hands in his pockets. Ramchandra noticed a string tied around the rat's limp neck, holding a small note. It read: "The future of Panchayat."

Ramchandra wanted to laugh at the practical joke, but this was a rat, and it had been thrown at him, a teacher. "You want to be expelled? Is that why you do these things?" Ramchandra said.

Bandana Miss was on the phone, but once she saw the rat dangling from Ramchandra's hand, she ended her conversation.

Ramchandra told her what had happened.

"I didn't do it," Mukesh said. His eyes dared Ramchandra.

"He threw it at me while I was writing on the board."

"Did you see him throw it?" Bandana Miss asked. She didn't even glance at the note around the rat's neck.

"I didn't, but I know he's the one."

"Prove it," Mukesh said.

Ramchandra, suddenly remembering that he was holding the rat, dropped it on the floor.

"Ramchandra-ji," Bandana Miss said, "pick that up immediately, and both of you, leave my room. It's the first day of school. I have much work to finish."

"Bandana Miss—"

Bandana Miss smacked her forehead with her palm. "Ramchandra-ji, you didn't see him throw it, so there's nothing I can do. Now please leave. I have to prepare for a school board meeting."

In the hallway, Mukesh said, "Sir, you targeted me for no reason. What's your problem? Are you a panchay, a Panchayat lover?"

Ramchandra contemptuously waved him away and walked down the hall, the rat dangling from his hand, much to the amusement of students passing by.

"Is that your new love, sir?" someone said loudly.

Ramchandra took the rat to the office boy, who was basking in the sun in the courtyard. "This is your problem now," he said.

The rest of the period was relatively quiet, and Ramchandra once again thought of what he should tell Malati when she arrived. Occasionally he lifted his hand to his nose to see whether the rat smell still lingered.

Malati was waiting in the staff room, her eyes puffy. Rachana was fidgeting in her lap. Two teachers, both women, were sitting in a corner, looking in their direction and whispering.

He had about twenty minutes before the next class, so he signaled Malati to follow him to the small tea shop in the alley outside the school. He rarely went there, because the shop buzzed with flies, but it was the only place he could talk to her in private.

Two students were drinking tea inside the shop, and to his dismay Ramchandra saw that one was Mukesh, who snickered at him as he sat down on a bench with Malati.

"You look tired," he told her.

Rachana smiled up at him.

"Any luck finding a place?"

"I don't know anywhere to go," Malati said. She didn't touch the tea in front of her.

Ramchandra ordered samosas for both of them. "You must be hungry."

"I'm not hungry," she said in a small voice.

Mukesh and his friend were listening intently.

"Goma wants me to bring you home."

Malati looked at him with disbelief. "What are you saying?"

"She wants to offer you shelter; that's what I am saying."

"After knowing all about—"

"Yes, yes, you don't have to say it." He glanced at the students.

"But how can I even show my face to her? This is absurd. Isn't she angry with me?"

Ramchandra shook his head. The samosas arrived, and Ramchandra asked her to eat, but she didn't. "She's not angry with me?"

Ramchandra took a bite. The samosa was old, and dripping with oil. He set it back on the plate. "I don't know what she's feeling. She thinks it's the best solution."

"The best solution," Malati muttered. The shock was visible on her face. After a moment, she said, "I can't do that. How can I do that?"

"What choice do you have?"

She leaned her head against the wall and closed her eyes. He placed his hand on her forearm. "It's better than begging on the streets."

"But after what I've done to bhauju."

The school bell rang, and the two boys made their way past Ramchandra's table. "Having fun, sir?" Mukesh said as he walked by. Ramchandra had to get back for the next period, but this needed to be resolved.

"The decision is yours. How much money do you have?"

"I have only two hundred rupees."

"That's not enough to rent even a room."

"What am I going to do? What will happen to her?" She stroked Rachana's head.

"So, we have no choice, then."

She closed her eyes again.

"Why don't you go to Jaisideval now? Goma will be there."

"What will I say to her?"

"You don't need to say anything to her. This was her idea."

"I'll wait for you. I can't face bhauju by myself."

"But I won't be done until four o'clock."

"That's fine. I'll wait here."

Ramchandra talked to the shopkeeper and gave him some money so that Malati could stay until he'd finished his classes. He kissed her on the forehead before he left the shop. He was already fifteen minutes late.

Bandana Miss accosted him in the hallway. "This is not good, Ramchandra Sir. Sleeping in class, and now late for class."

"I had urgent business to attend to."

"Everything is urgent, isn't it? Who was that girl?"

"An acquaintance."

"Ramchandra Sir, I've been hearing some things. Of all people, I would expect you—"

"I am already late for my class. Why are you delaying me?"

"What is your relationship with her?"

"She's a friend's daughter."

"Let's hope that's true. You are a teacher. I asked you to talk to Shailendra because I thought you were a good man."

"Bandana Miss. Please. Keep your lecturing to yourself." He brushed past her and walked to his classroom.

By four o'clock it was raining. Holding a newspaper above his head, Ramchandra ran to the tea shop, where he found Malati crouched in a corner, her eyes closed and Rachana in her lap, playing with her necklace. He woke her, and she scrambled to her feet, startled. He calmed her down, led her outside. The rain was coming down harder, and they stood in the doorway. "This isn't going to subside for a while," the shopkeeper said. "May as well have a cup of tea." They drank more tea and listened to the rain. Rachana started bawling, and Malati went to a corner and breast-fed her.

The rain eventually turned into a drizzle, and they decided to move on. Ramchandra held the newspaper above Malati's head as they walked through the puddles in the alleys toward Bir Hospital, where he thought they'd find a three-wheeler —although part of him hoped they wouldn't, so that he wouldn't have to spend more money. As was always the case in bad weather, all the taxis were taken. People scurried about, either finding shelter or braving the rain to finish their errands. "Should we wait and take a bus?" Ramchandra asked her, and she shrugged. "No, this isn't too bad. Let's walk."

By the time they reached New Road, they were completely soaked. He looked at her. She was beautiful, with the rain glistening on her face. And she was young; he had to remind himself that she was indeed young, only twenty-one. She clasped his hand and asked, "Do you love me?" For a moment he thought she was crazy to ask that question at this moment, but she was watching him, waiting for an answer, and when he said, "Yes," her eyes filled with a look that told him she knew exactly what she was doing.

In Jaisideval, as they climbed the stairs, Malati slowed down. "Come on," he urged her. They could hear the children's voices as they reached the landing.

Goma appeared at the door, the children behind her. "You could have taken a taxi," Goma said to Ramchandra. "That baby will catch a cold." She went into the children's room and came back with a towel, which she wrapped around the baby, whom she lifted from Malati's arms. "You could have simply waited for the rain to die down," she told Ramchandra.

He had nothing to say. This was a crazy dream from which he'd wake up at any moment.

Malati kept looking at the floor. No one seemed to know what was to happen next. Then Goma took the baby, who had fallen asleep, into the children's room. When she came out, she said, "Why don't you two go inside the bedroom, and I'll bring you some food."

Suddenly, Malati knelt at Goma's feet. "Bhauju, please forgive me."

Goma bent down and lifted her up. "What's the matter with you? There's no time for this nonsense. You have to put on some dry clothes." She asked Ramchandra where Malati's belongings were.

He shrugged.

"They're still on the porch at the house," Malati said.

"I'll have my parents' servant bring them here after you two have eaten."

There was energy in her voice, as if the sight of Malati had transformed her. There was a new personality on her face, and Ramchandra could hardly believe that this was the wife he'd lived with all these years.

"Will you forgive me, bhauju?" Malati asked.

"I don't have that power. You'll have to forgive yourself."

Rakesh, who had been listening intently, asked, "Forgive for what? What mischief did she do?"

"That's none of your concern, wise boy," Goma said.

Sanu said nothing, and Goma asked both of the children to go into the room and look after the baby; they were to call her when Rachana woke up. Then she brought a dhoti to Malati. "You can wear this until your clothes arrive this evening. Come, don't stand there in those wet clothes, both of you." And she shooed them into the bedroom and went to the kitchen.

"What's happening, sir?"

"I'll step outside for a moment. Why don't you change?"

Her face still bore the look of bewilderment. She appeared in a few minutes, wearing Goma's dhoti, and said, "I'll go help bhauju."

In the bedroom, Ramchandra changed into dry clothes and sat down on the bed. Goma had removed all the photographs from the walls. He got up and checked the closet: her clothes were gone. He checked under the pillow, where she kept the necklace she'd been given by his family at their wedding for good luck; it was no longer there. Outside, a bicyclist rang his bell, and the sound rumbled in Ramchandra's head. He ran his hand over the clean bedsheet. This is where Goma wanted him to sleep with Malati. He held his head in his hands.

Goma called him, and reluctantly he went to the kitchen, where Malati was scooping rice from the pot onto the plates. She didn't look up when he entered. Goma called the children, but only Rakesh came.

"Where's Sanu?"

"She's doing her homework."

"Well, it's time to eat."

"She says she's not hungry."

"I'll go fetch her," Ramchandra said and went to get his daughter.

Sanu was on the floor in her room, her books spread out before her. The baby was sleeping close by.

"Sanu," Ramchandra said, "why don't you come?"

"I'm not hungry."

"You'll be taking your exams soon. If you don't eat, you'll not do well."

She didn't respond, and he asked, "What's the matter?"

"Nothing."

"Then why is your face like"—he searched for a funny simile—"a piglet's swishing tail?"

"Why is that woman here?"

"She needs a place to stay."

"This is a big city. Why couldn't she go somewhere else?"

Ramchandra braced himself. "Daughter, you shouldn't hold anything against her. The fault is mine, not hers."

"I'm not blaming anyone. If there's anyone to blame, it's me."

"And why is that?"

"I'm just a stupid girl."

He knelt beside her. "No, your father is stupid. You know everything, don't you?"

"I don't want to look at your face."

"You don't have to. Just come and eat. Eventually, you'll forgive me."

"I'll never forgive you. I'll never forgive Mother for allowing her to come into this house."

"Your mother has a kind heart." He touched her shoulder,

but she jerked away. "Okay, I'll bring the food to you," he said.

"I won't eat anything you touch. I want to go back to Pandey Palace."

"This is your home, Sanu."

"What kind of a home is this?" she said. "She's not my sister; she's not my mother; she's not my cousin. So why is she here?" Now she turned to face him, and anger burned in her eyes. "And you're not my father. Why don't you two go live someplace else?"

Ramchandra shrank back from his daughter's anger. "Please, Sanu, please find it in your heart to forgive your father."

"Never."

In the kitchen, they talked about mundane things. Actually, it was Goma who talked; Ramchandra and Malati mostly listened. Goma had taken Sanu's dinner to her room, though Ramchandra was sure she'd leave it untouched. In the middle of the dinner, Rachana began to cry, and Malati went to her.

"I am not sleeping with her in this house," Ramchandra said.

"And why not?"

"With the children? Are you crazy? Have you lost your mind, Goma?"

"It's funny that you're the one asking me that question."

"This is insane."

"It's an insane world. It's better this way."

"Goma, please don't do this."

Rakesh turned his head back and forth like a pendulum, watching his parents.

"We've had this conversation before," Goma said. "And I thought we agreed."

Ramchandra could no longer eat. "I'm going to be sick."

"You asked for help, and this is the only way I know to give it to you."

Malati came back. Sanu hadn't eaten, she said softly, and hadn't responded when Malati talked to her.

"Why is she so upset?" Rakesh asked.

"She'll be fine."

After dinner, Malati helped Goma with the dishes while Ramchandra looked after Rachana. Both children had gone to bed. When Malati discovered that she was to sleep with Ramchandra in the bedroom, she was shocked. "Bhauju, what are you doing?" she cried.

"I'll sleep with the children," Goma said.

"I can't do this. Why are you punishing me?"

"This is not a punishment. I am allowing you two to be together."

"Please don't do this to me."

Goma led her to the bedroom. "What I am doing is right. Please trust me."

Malati kept trying to dissuade her, but Goma didn't budge. Once they were inside the bedroom, with Rachana sleeping on a mat in a corner, she shut the door behind her. Ramchandra and Malati looked at each other. "I can't sleep with you here, sir," Malati said. "I simply can't. Not with bhauju next door. I won't be able to sleep."

Ramchandra checked the closet and found a bedsheet, which he spread on the floor. "Why don't you sleep here with Rachana?"

"But there's only one blanket."

"I won't need one."

"Of course you will. It's cold."

Ramchandra ignored her, handed her the blanket, then lay down on the bed.

For a long time he couldn't sleep, wondering what was going to happen to him and Goma. Malati also tossed and turned.

He woke to the sound of the baby crying, and Malati got

up to breast-feed her. In the dark, he shivered, and watched the outline of the mother and the baby.

"Is she eating?" he whispered.

Malati said yes. Once Rachana went back to sleep, he heard Malati say, "I can't sleep."

"Neither can I. But we will, eventually."

Malati said, "Sir, I can see that you are shivering. Why don't you come down?"

It took him only a moment to make the decision. Her warm body felt good, and soon his hands were roaming over her chest. "Not now, not tonight," she said, but feebly, and suddenly they were kissing and he was fumbling with the strings of her petticoat, and he thought, This is crazy, this is crazy, and he thought he heard Goma laughing in the next room.

8
· · · · · · ·

OVER THE NEXT FEW WEEKS, the apartment took on an air of ordinariness that stunned Ramchandra. Goma acted as if nothing were amiss, as if Malati were her younger sister. Rakesh began referring to Malati as "Malu Didi," and displayed great fondness for Rachana. "My little sister," he cooed to the baby, who smiled at him, her minuscule index finger reaching out to touch his nose. He kissed the baby often and shared his toys with her, something he'd never done with Sanu. Part of this affection, Ramchandra gathered, grew from the boy's pleasure at no longer being the youngest in the household. Sanu, however, remained unhappy. She barely spoke to her father, and with Goma she remained sullen. She never met Malati's eyes. As for the baby, Sanu ignored her in company, but Ramchandra spotted her patting Rachana and whispering to her when she thought no one was looking.

It was Goma, however, who most perplexed Ramchandra. Much of the sadness had disappeared from her face. She'd begun to laugh, and he heard no hint of muted pain in the laughter. In unexpected moments, alone in the kitchen or on the landing, she smiled as if to assure him that everything was proceeding according to plan, and he was bewildered. Once, he caught her in the kitchen by herself and asked, "And, so . . . ?" But he was unable to articulate his thoughts. She pretended that he was speaking about lunch, and, looking straight at him, said the meal would be ready in a few minutes. When she was not in the kitchen, she spent time in the children's room. One morning he discovered her there reading the Mahabharata, an old edition he'd received as a wedding gift from an uncle. It had been in a corner collecting dust. Goma was sitting on the floor, the book in front of her, her lips shaping the words on the page. When she sensed him standing in the doorway, she looked up and asked, "You never read this, did you?" He thought he detected a hint of sarcasm in her voice, as if, had he read the Mahabharata and heeded Lord Krishna's advice to Arjun about what was important in life, their lives wouldn't have turned out this way.

The hope grew in Ramchandra that one morning something would click inside Goma and she'd walk into the bedroom, where Ramchandra and Malati would be entangled in each other's arms, and tell them that she had changed her mind, that Malati could no longer live there. Every morning Ramchandra hoped this would happen; he even pictured Goma trying to separate the two of them with her hands. Or dragging Malati by her hair down the staircase and slamming the door in her face.

Winter intensified in Kathmandu. In the morning it was so cold that Ramchandra didn't feel like leaving his sirak and Malati's warm body next to him. But the exams were only a few weeks away, so they forced themselves to rise and, warming their hands by making fists and blowing into them, sat on the floor for their session. Goma would bring them tea, then shut the door quietly. Rakesh was instructed not to make any noise. By the time Ashok arrived, both Malati and Ramchandra were tired. Ashok, who'd been surprised to see Malati living in the house, was now distracted by the coming exams, and he no longer cracked jokes about Malati. "My father has become a dictator," he said to Ramchandra. "Hitler, sir; he's a real Hitler. He's threatened to disown me if I don't pass."

At school, Ramchandra encountered whispers, glances, and subdued laughter. Bandana Miss was tight-lipped in front of him, and the other teachers maintained a politeness he knew was unnatural. No one asked him what was happening at home. During tea break one afternoon in the staff room, someone mentioned a former colleague who'd taken in a second wife because his first wife couldn't bear children. Everyone glanced at Ramchandra. "It happens with much more frequency than we think," Bandana Miss said. "Lack of children is one thing, but people do it for all kinds of reasons. The old thinking still persists."

One teacher joked that Bandana Miss was speaking from personal experience. Everyone knew Bandana Miss's husband had left her soon after their son was born, although no one was certain it was for another woman. Bandana Miss glared at that teacher, who smiled apologetically.

"Ramchandra-ji, do you know anyone who's ushered in a second wife?" That was Shailendra. A smile hovered on his lips. A few weeks ago Namita's parents had taken her out of school without much fanfare. She'd simply stopped coming. Shailendra had been unhappy since then, and he probably saw this as payback.

"No, I don't know anyone," Ramchandra said.

"No one in your neighborhood? It's an old neighborhood, Jaisideval. Many people with old-type thinking there."

"Which world are you living in, Shailendra Sir?" Ramchandra said. "Perhaps your neighborhood is old."

"No young flesh you yourself have brought?"

Ramchandra was about to say something sharp when Bandana Miss interrupted. "We need to discuss whether we'll have debating teams next year. The school is closing again in a week for winter, so let's decide this right now."

Ramchandra swallowed his anger and shame and feigned interest in the debating teams and the other extracurricular activities Bandana Miss was considering.

One morning, after spending two hours going over several math problems with Malati, Ramchandra went to take his bath downstairs and ran into Mr. Sharma. So far, Ramchandra had orchestrated his bath time so that he'd enter the courtyard just as Mr. Sharma was leaving. But today Mr. Sharma was late.

"How are you, Ramchandra-ji?" Mr. Sharma said, a bit too jovially.

Ramchandra said he was fine, that he had too much going on at school.

"Of course," Mr. Sharma said. "And things are busy at home too, I see."

Ramchandra knelt and poured the water over his body.

Mr. Sharma, who was soaping himself, said, "It's the same girl, isn't it? Very attractive. I've seen her in the morning sometimes. Have felt like talking to her." Malati was the first one to use the tap in the morning. She always wriggled out of Ramchandra's arms before the sun rose.

Ramchandra recalled Sanu's complaint about Mr. Sharma, but he held back his angry words. Hands all over his body, Mr. Sharma was soaping himself. "Lovely, lovely," he said, giving the impression that he was complimenting his own physique. The silence extended; then Mr. Sharma blurted out, "So, you've taken her in, have you?"

"A guest," Ramchandra said. "She'll move out soon." Although he hadn't washed all the soap off his body, he reached for the towel.

"Where does she sleep? Is there enough room up there?"

"Enough room for everyone. This is a big universe, Mr. Sharma; you know that. It's your god, after all, who provides."

Oblivious of the barb, Mr. Sharma said, "So, you no longer complain of the apartment, eh? That's good. We all must learn to be satisfied with our lives. Where is her husband?"

"I don't know." Ramchandra finished rubbing his body with the towel.

"Do you mind if I ask you a question?"

"Depends on the nature of the question, Mr. Sharma. A wise man like you would never ask an objectionable question."

Mr. Sharma laughed sheepishly. "You are a wiser man than I am. I was just wondering, you know. I have that room that's not being used. If your apartment is congested, I could easily take in—"

"This kind of talk doesn't suit you, Mr. Sharma. You're too old. Besides, she wouldn't want to live with a stranger."

"I am only offering out of the kindness of my heart."

"I know," Ramchandra said. Stop staring at my daughter, he wanted to say, or I'll hurt you.

Talk of the strange arrangement in Ramchandra's apartment spread across the city with the urgency of a thousand bees. Neither the Pandeys nor Nalini and Harish came over, and Ramchandra wondered what crazy thoughts were buzzing through their heads. Goma hardly mentioned them these days. When Ramchandra ran into relatives in the streets, they appeared to have forgotten how to make natural conversation. Some tried to pry things out of him by asking pointed questions about the size of his apartment.

One day the shopkeeper with the phone shouted Goma's name from the courtyard, saying that her mother was on the line. Goma left, and came back in a short while. Judging from the expression on her face, Ramchandra knew they had argued. When he asked her what had happened, Goma said, not meeting his eyes, "She wanted to know why I was destroying my house. She wanted to know why I was destroying the family name."

The next morning, before anyone was out of bed, a loud rap sounded downstairs, and Malati shot up in bed, saying it must be Malekha Didi. Who else would be here this early? So it was she who went down to open the door, in her petticoat, and soon Mrs. Pandey was on the landing, her eyes exploring the apartment. Malati was cowering in a corner, a terrified look on her face.

"Where's Goma?" Mrs. Pandey asked in an imperious tone.

Goma came out of the children's room. Ramchandra wondered whether he should join her, but he decided to stay in bed and let Goma handle her mother.

"What's going on here?" Mrs. Pandey said. "Who is this girl?" she asked, jabbing a finger near Malati's face, though she surely knew perfectly well who she was.

"This is Malati, Mother."

Malati did a namaste, and Mrs. Pandey narrowed her eyes.

"Mother, why don't you go in there?" Goma pointed to the children's room. "I'll make some tea."

"I didn't come here to drink your tea." She looked at Ramchandra through the door. "Do you know what people are saying? All over the city? Where is she sleeping?" She pointed contemptuously toward Malati.

"What are people saying, Mother?"

Rakesh appeared, looking bewildered, sleep marking his face. He opened his mouth to say something to his grandmother, then swallowed some air.

"With young children at home, you commit such an outrage," Mrs. Pandey said. Her lips were quivering.

"Mother, why are you so angry? I am doing what is necessary for my life."

"This is necessary? You bring your husband's randi, his whore, into your house, and that's necessary?"

Malati gasped. Rakesh seemed to be mouthing the word *whore* as if it were a piece of chocolate. Goma signaled to Malati and Rakesh to go inside. In her confusion, Malati went into the bedroom and shut the door. She and Ramchandra heard Mrs. Pandey fume about Malati's going there. Goma must have taken her mother to the kitchen and shut the door, because the voices became faint. Malati leaned against the wall and closed her eyes. Ramchandra went over and put his arm around her shoulder. She shifted away. "A whore."

"She's a lunatic," Ramchandra said. "Her words mean nothing."

"But she's right. I am a whore. I have broken up your family."

"Goma doesn't think so, and she's the one who counts."

Mrs. Pandey's voice grew louder. There was a bang. Pots clattered to the floor. Ramchandra rushed into the kitchen. Mrs. Pandey was on the floor, holding her head, crying. Goma, her lips pursed, was standing near her. Two pots lay next to her mother, and it wasn't clear who had thrown them.

Mrs. Pandey saw Ramchandra. "You've turned my daughter into a madwoman," she said. "All these years of suffering, and now she's gone insane. What woman in her right mind would invite her husband's mistress into her house?"

Ramchandra helped her up. "Stop using that word," he said.

"What should I call her?" She continued to rant. Goma calmly made tea, and Mrs. Pandey drank it while protesting that she hadn't come to drink tea. Before she left, she said to her daughter, in a sobbing voice, "The whole world knows, Goma. I can't show my face anywhere. Please do something."

Goma said, "We'll see you again, Mother," and escorted her downstairs.

They were in the kitchen. Malati was cutting mustard greens, the children were playing in the courtyard, and the baby was sleeping.

"I was thinking of visiting the Dakshinkali goddess," Goma said. This was the right time to visit the temple, she said, to ask the goddess to bless Malati on her exams, now only a few days away.

Ramchandra didn't believe that she wanted to offer a sacrifice only for Malati. Ever since her mother's visit, she had acted as if she were struggling with herself, as if she'd absorbed her mother's feelings and now doubted that Malati should be living with them.

Ramchandra said, "But we'd have to sacrifice something to the goddess, and where will the money come from?" The household expenses had nearly doubled, something Goma had neglected to consider when she proposed that Malati move in with them. Ramchandra had already transferred five thousand rupees from their savings to their checking account. And once the S.L.C. was over, Ashok would stop coming. Until the time of next year's exams, there would be no tutees. The financial situation had become nearly hopeless.

"I'll take care of it," Goma said. "Besides, we didn't slaughter a goat or a hen for Dashain."

"Bhauju, there's no need to go to the goddess," Malati said. "I think I'll pass."

"Still, a blessing from the goddess would ensure success. She is powerful."

"Maybe we can go there but not sacrifice anything," Ramchandra said.

Goma said that it was impossible to go empty-handed to the goddess. "It's useless," she repeated. "The goddess will listen only if there's a sacrifice."

A short time later, when Malati went to check on the baby, Ramchandra whispered angrily to Goma, "And how are we going to pay for it? Does money grow on trees?"

Goma shrugged. "The girl needs to pass. Of course I have money. My parents are rich. Did you forget?"

"Did you borrow money from them?"

Goma shook her head and sat down to dice potatoes. "Father opened a bank account for me when you and I got married. I've never taken anything from it."

Ramchandra stared at her. "How come I never knew about this?" How could she hide such a thing, when all this time he'd been battling headaches about money. He wondered how much she had, but thought it better not to ask.

"I wanted it to be used only in case of an emergency or for the children. Had I told you before, you'd have asked me to spend it on a plot for the house."

"A house? Forget about the house; forget about land. This," he said, sweeping the air with his hands, "is our glorious destiny."

"I never asked for a house. It was you."

"It was your parents."

"Let's not get into that now. Besides, they're not thinking about that right now, are they?"

"What else do I not know about you, Goma? Tell me."

"You know everything," she said. Her face was sad.

On Saturday they got up before daybreak to prepare for the trip to Dakshinkali. Goma had bought a baby goat, which stood at the head of the stairs, bleating, in a pile of pebble-like droppings around its feet. Ramchandra had assumed that Goma would bring home a chicken and was surprised to see the black goat, which he figured must have cost at least three hundred rupees. And then there was the matter of transportation to the temple. Ramchandra thought that, despite the recent tension, Goma would borrow a car from the Pandeys or from Harish and Nalini. Rakesh was excited at the thought of riding in his aunt's car, a Pajero, an excitement Goma had doused instantly. "How about Grandfather's car then?" he'd asked, somewhat disappointed but still with hope, because he liked the Pandeys' driver. Goma said they were not going to borrow anyone's car, that she'd already arranged for a taxi to take them there and bring them back. Another four hundred rupees, Ramchandra calculated.

Sure enough, under the dim light of the streetlamp, the taxi was waiting for them, a middle-aged man at the wheel. He leaped out of his vehicle as soon as he saw them and helped them load the baby goat into the trunk, making sure he left a small opening so that it could breathe. Ramchandra worried about the goat's hurtling out during the winding trip to the goddess, but the driver assured him that goats were timid animals, too scared to do such a thing. "Bhakta dai," Goma called to the driver, and explained to the others that in his younger days he had worked at Pandey Palace.

Bhakta drove with admirable skill through the narrow streets of Kathmandu, toward Kalimati, honking at the slower cars, swerving past pedestrians and bicyclists, plunging fearlessly into the morning fog. Houses dotted the sides of the street, and bones of new houses under construction were visible everywhere. It had been quite a while since Ramchandra had been in this part of the city, and he was amazed at how quickly the population had soared. Once they left Kalimati, however, the traffic thinned out, and the air became clearer.

Goma, Sanu, and Malati sat in the back, Rachana on her mother's lap; Rakesh sat on his father's lap in the front. An air of festivity filled the taxi, and, despite his earlier doubts, Ramchandra began to anticipate, with pleasure, the act of paying homage to the goddess. The last time they'd gone to Dakshinkali was years ago, probably right after Rakesh was born, when the baby's chest troubles had bothered Goma so much that she'd suggested going to the goddess. Rakesh's chest congestion hadn't gone away completely, but it had subsided almost immediately after the visit, and Ramchandra had begun to believe that Dakshinkali was indeed powerful, and that if she were pleased, she would cast her benevolence on her devotees.

Ramchandra noticed that the driver kept checking the rearview mirror, even when no traffic was behind them, and after a while he realized that Bhakta was observing Malati. This irritated Ramchandra, and he wanted to tell the man to keep his eyes on the road. But Malati did look attractive in her red salwar kameez, and the driver was closer to her age than Ramchandra was. He felt painfully inadequate.

Malati, who held Rachana in her lap, appeared contented. Last night he'd asked her, after their lovemaking, "Are you happy?" and she'd said, "Bhauju has become a goddess for me." She'd said nothing about him, and he felt that he was being taken for granted. Then, as if to make up for what she had not said, she'd clasped his hand in the darkness and asked, "Do you think we're going to live like this forever?"

"How would I know?"

"What about you? Are you happy?"

He laughed softly. "No, I am not happy."

"You're not happy to be with me?"

He didn't know the answer to that. Goma was drifting away from him, and Sanu still didn't speak to him properly. The intensity of passion he'd felt for Malati before she came to the house had subsided, surely, but he couldn't conjecture how he'd feel if she weren't around. Only that his body would miss her.

"I still love you," he said.

"But you're not happy I'm here."

He acknowledged that was so. "How do you expect me to be? It was better when you were living in your house, and we were seeing each other that way."

In the morning, as they got dressed for the trip, she was silent, and she brightened only when she saw Goma.

The Temple of Dakshinkali, goddess of the south, sat in a bowl surrounded by hills, and they had to descend a long stretch of stairs to reach the shrine. They waited in a line of devotees, the baby goat in tow. At the temple entrance they took off their shoes. The floor of the small courtyard with the shrine was sticky with blood. A priest, his shirt drenched with blood, was cutting the throats of chickens and goats. Their bare feet were icy on the cold floor, and they had to jostle other devotees to reach the statue, where Goma performed some puja and signaled Malati to pray to the goddess. Malati knelt down, and Goma beckoned to Ramchandra to kneel beside her, as if she were marrying them. His shoulder touched Malati's as they sat on their haunches, touching the goddess's feet. When Ramchandra looked up at the goddess, he became briefly disoriented; what he saw there was Goma's face, smiling. The vision unnerved him, and he quickly rose to his feet.

The priest sprinkled red powder on the goat's forehead and sliced its throat with his knife; the goat screamed. Sanu covered her eyes. The priest kept the severed head, along with the forty rupees that Goma handed him, and they all left the temple, Ramchandra dragging the animal's body. His legs were shaky, and the sun bore down on him.

Nearby, some men were boiling water in an enormous black vat and skinning the headless goats. Ramchandra handed his to the butchers and waited.

"Where are we going to have our picnic?" Rakesh asked.

"We'll have to find a place," Goma said. "Maybe your father can find one for us."

Ramchandra had sat down on the front steps of a shop. "I'm not feeling well."

Malati came over and placed her hand on his forehead. "You're burning." She sat down next to him. "Do you want to drink some water?"

He shook his head.

He expected Goma to come over too, to place her hand on his forehead, to ask if there was anything she could do. But she didn't move; there was a puzzled expression on her face, as if she didn't know where she was. She said to him, "Just rest for a while. I think it's the crowd." Quickly, she turned to the butchers.

Malati took his hand, and Ramchandra looked up to see Sanu holding Rachana, wiping dirt from her nose, and a voice in his mind asked his daughter, What? Are you becoming used to this too? He clasped Malati's hand. His head hurt, and his eyes felt like embers. "I think I should lie down," he said, and stretched out on the steps with his head in her lap. She ran her hand through his hair and told him to close his eyes; everything would be fine. In his mind he pictured Goma, first as a bride, her face merely an outline under the bridal veil, her lips quivering under his gaze. Then as an angry goddess, like Kali, squashing heads under her feet. That image intensified, and he cried out, and somewhere in the cavern of his mind he heard Malati calling Goma—and then he plummeted into a darkness that was strangely comforting.

He woke up to Malati's face. "What happened?" he murmured. A cold cloth was on his forehead.

"You passed out," she said. "And then you woke up and began babbling." She smiled. "But everything is fine now. You have a slight fever, and the taxi driver helped to carry you up."

Ramchandra looked around. Trees surrounded him, and he was lying on the grass. There were sounds in the distance: people talking, goats bleating, the clang of temple bells. Nearby, Rachana chewed on a frayed doll. Bhakta and Goma worked at a stove, while Sanu chopped onions. Rakesh was throwing pebbles up at some branches. "Ba is awake," Sanu called to her mother, and Goma came over. "You're getting old," she said to him plainly. "Shall I get you something to drink? I can make some lemon water."

He shook his head. "I'm fine now."

"Let me know if you feel that way again," and as she walked toward Bhakta, she said, "Now, you two relax, enjoy the day."

Malati said, "Bhauju is incredible, isn't she?"

"Yes, she is."

It was clear that the seeming normality of their lives had affected Malati. She didn't recognize the oddness in what Goma had just said. It was Goma who was Ramchandra's wife, not Malati. Goma was his children's mother, not Malati. But Ramchandra looked at the beautiful face in front of him, the finely shaped nose with a small glittering nose ring, the soft, silky hair.

Deep affection welled up in him. He reached out and smoothed a strand of hair on her forehead, and she said softly, "The children are here. Later, maybe we can go for a walk?" Perhaps the natural surroundings had brought out the romantic in her. Had she been to places like this with Rachana's father?

He fell asleep and, when he woke, felt better. The food was ready. Goma and Bhakta had prepared rice pulau, goat curry, cauliflower, and an achar of grated cucumber. They sat on a mat and ate. Ramchandra was swept by an immense hunger, and he started devouring the food with quick movements of his hands. The others laughed. He continued eating even when everyone was finished, and he asked for more. But Goma said, "Don't eat too much; you'll be sick."

They sat down to play cards, but Ramchandra excused himself, saying he was sleepy again. "Why don't we go for a walk?" Malati suggested. "That way your mind will clear." Goma agreed, and even though Ramchandra didn't want his children to see him walking off into the woods with Malati, he didn't have the strength to resist. He and Malati headed toward the clearing that led to the dense forest.

Once they were out of the view of the others, Malati took his hand, and said, "I feel very good today, very optimistic. I know I will pass the exam. More than the goddess, bhauju's blessing will carry me through."

But you don't know what Goma is feeling, he thought.

He put his arm around her shoulders, and they walked up the incline, listening to the occasional howl of a jungle cat, the rustling of the leaves. They walked until they could see, from between the trees, the spot where the others were sitting. Rakesh's laughter shot up in the air. Malati shouted at them, "Hey, we are here," and waited for the others to look up from the card game. But they didn't.

They trudged farther up, and Ramchandra's legs became

pleasantly numb. His hand, entangled with Malati's, was sweating, but he was reluctant to let go. Occasionally, he had to help her up a steep step, and once, she tumbled into him, and her breasts brushed against his arm. He looked at this girl, at the happiness in her face, and he knew that she would not be able to live apart from them. This knowledge was like a blow, and he felt like crying, but the presence of her body so close to his, and their being alone in these pristine surroundings, free to do with each other what they wanted, also aroused in him a sensation of soaring, of power.

In Jaisideval, people had congregated in small groups in front of shops and newspaper vendors. As the others walked up to the apartment, Ramchandra ambled over to the tea shop, where a few people, holding the day's newspapers, were speaking in excited voices. Ramchandra read, over the shoulder of one man, the big news of the day. The leaders of the different political parties had finally reached an agreement, after three days of discussion at the residence of old Nepali Congress leader Ganesh Man Singh, and had released a statement. It specified the day, February 18—the very day four decades earlier when the Ranas had been ousted from their autocratic throne, now celebrated as Democracy Day—as the day when the parties would start a rebellion against the Panchayat system and would reinstate the multiparty system. That these people had specified the date showed how serious they were. "This is amazing," someone said. "The government did nothing while these leaders gathered in Ganesh Man's house? Is the government scared?"

"The government scared?" said another. "It's just waiting for the right moment. It's like a cat playing with a mouse. Wait and see."

"What do you think will happen?" Ramchandra asked the man whose newspaper he had been reading.

"How do I know?" the man said testily. "Am I God? All I'm worried about is that the schools are going to close, and my son will lose another year. These bastards."

"Such a momentous thing happening in our country," another man said, "and you're worried about your son? What about the rest of the janata who are suffering?"

The two of them started arguing, their voices lashing out at each other, and the cold evening air became charged.

Ramchandra walked into the house, wondering whether the country was indeed plunging into a revolution, or whether it would whimper and die down when faced with the government's wrath. What did Mr. Pandey make of this latest development? He must be fuming, Ramchandra thought with some relish.

9
· · · · · · ·

THE FIRST MORNING of the S.L.C. exams,
which ran for ten days this year, was so cold
that Ramchandra walked around the house wrapped in a bulky
sirak. Goma put some tika on Malati's forehead and prayed
to the small statue of Lord Ganesh in the kitchen. "No need
to worry," she told Malati. "You've worked hard for this, and
you'll succeed." Besides, the first exam was on Nepali, in which
Malati excelled.

Before they left, Malati touched Ramchandra's feet and
said, "I need my guru's blessings." Ramchandra helped her up,
kissed her on the forehead. Malati had said that she would go
alone to the testing site in Patan, but Goma wouldn't hear of
it. At least on the first day, she should be accompanied. Goma
looked questioningly at Ramchandra, who agreed to take her.

They caught a crowded bus in Ratnapark, and it lurched toward its destination. The bus was filled with other S.L.C. candi-
dates, all nervously talking about the exams. Malati, too, talked

to some of them, and Ramchandra recalled his own S.L.C. days, when he'd stay up late at night, studying by candlelight because they couldn't afford to use the electricity too long. Sometimes his mother would get up and coax him to go to sleep, or she'd make him some tea. The nervous excitement of the exams, he and his friends testing one another's knowledge before the exam, then quizzing each other afterward to see which answers were correct—Ramchandra recalled it vividly.

They got off in Pulchowk and walked toward a high school near a dirty pond. Malati chatted with her newfound friends while they walked, and when they reached the gate, she turned to Ramchandra and smiled. "You can go now. You have to go to school."

He put his hand on her head to bless her and walked away. This is it, he thought. All these months of work, and in ten days, it will be over. He felt as if he were already losing her.

When she came home later that morning, Malati said, with a laugh, "It was so easy." He congratulated her, and then reminded her that for her math exam, to be given in three days, they needed to go over some of the main points. This was especially necessary in algebra, where she was most weak. "It might confuse me more," she responded. "I think I'm fine now."

Although he wanted to tell her that he didn't share her confidence, he was afraid to rattle her, so he kept quiet.

That evening, as they were eating dinner, they heard quiet footsteps on the stairs. Panic covered Malati's face, and Goma quickly got to her feet and went to the door. "It's only Nalini," she called. Goma invited her sister to dinner, but she declined, saying she'd already eaten. She glanced at Malati and said to Goma, "No phone call, no visit. Have you forgotten about us completely?"

"Well, after Mother's visit, I didn't know what to think."

"I don't know what's happening, Goma Didi. What's going on in this house?"

"Whatever is happening, it's better for everyone."

"It's hard to live with all the rumors. People are mocking us."

Goma took Nalini to the children's room while the others ate. Malati finished her dinner and helped Rakesh wash his hands and mouth. When she began to do the dishes, Sanu helped her. "Don't you need to study for tomorrow's exam?" Ramchandra asked Malati. He told her to let Sanu finish the dishes, but she continued, saying she'd be done soon.

Goma and Nalini appeared, and Nalini quietly left the house.

"What did you say to her?" Ramchandra asked.

"She was upset, but I explained everything."

Ramchandra didn't ask her what "everything" was.

That night, while Malati studied for her second exam, which was on English, Ramchandra listened to the BBC on the radio. The news was mostly about the threat of the uprising. It was said that those in power were preparing to crack down on any sign of rebellion. Occasionally Malati would ask him a question: Was this a proper grammatical construction? Was this the correct interpretation of the passage? And he would try to answer as best he could. He'd seen her writing in English, and knew she'd pass that exam.

All this while, he could hear the faint murmur of Goma's voice. She must have been talking to Sanu, for Rakesh had gone to sleep right after dinner. Her voice was a steady hum, rising or lowering in intonation. A question? An answer? He could imagine the attentive expression on Sanu's face, the faint knot that formed between her eyebrows as she processed what the world presented to her. She was no fool. She knew how to think for herself. Even as a baby, she had been quick, her sharp black eyes judging and comprehending her world instantly, much to the amazement of those around her, especially the Pandeys, who had once commented that baby girls usually weren't as smart as baby boys. Ramchandra recalled the day she was born, the anxiety he'd felt, waiting for the nurse to come from the delivery room at the Prasuti Griha—heightened by the maddening chatter of Mrs. Pandey, who was sitting beside him on the rickety bench. He'd felt like shouting at her, but after the nurse summoned him into the room where Goma lay, and handed him little Sanu, he'd looked into those piercing eyes, and his entire body was filled with feathery lightness. He'd cooed to his new daughter, held her for a long time, comparing her features to Goma's and coming to the conclusion that she resembled him more than she did her mother, especially with that pointed nose.

These memories made Ramchandra want to see Sanu right now, and, telling Malati that he'd be back soon, he left the bedroom, shut the door, and knocked lightly on the children's door. The murmuring stopped. "Come in," Goma said. Ramchandra opened the door and stood there. "Why aren't you sleeping?" he whispered.

"We're talking about old times."

He entered and sat on the floor with them. "What old times?"

"When Sanu was younger. How you two used to romp around the room, how you'd make faces at her and she'd start laughing aloud."

"I too was thinking about the past. That's why I came here."

Sanu was watching him intently, but when their eyes met, she looked away, as if embarrassed. After a while she said, "Ba, do you remember when you brought me my first painting kit?"

Ramchandra remembered. He'd been impressed by the little drawings Sanu made when she was in second grade, the confident lines, the attention to detail. Once, she'd drawn a postman, with a large head, and a bag that had POST OFFICE written on it. He'd taken it to the school where he was teaching and shown it proudly to his colleagues. And that afternoon, he'd gone to the market and bought an expensive painting kit, made in Hong Kong. "It's the best in the market," the shopkeeper said. "All the foreigners buy it for their children." Goma had scolded him for spending so much money, nearly thirty rupees, for what she'd called a luxury, and he'd said, "My daughter is an artist. Don't stand in her way."

"Where is it now?" Ramchandra asked.

"It's still here," Goma said, "in that cupboard."

"You were such a good painter."

"I never showed one painting I made, though," Sanu said.

"Why didn't you?"

"I didn't think it was good."

"Impossible. I don't believe it." She'd stopped painting when she went on to fourth grade, and he'd been disappointed. He'd encouraged her to continue, but she'd concentrated on reading, and since that too was "an intellectual endeavor," as he'd told Goma, he'd been pleased.

"Do you want to see it?" Sanu asked.

"You saved it?"

"Somehow, it was the only painting I saved."

She got up, rummaged in the cupboard, and pulled out a large sheet of paper, the corners curling, and handed it to Ramchandra. The drawing was of a large mansion, and the caption, at the bottom, read PANDEY PALACE. The two people standing above the house were labeled Grandfather and Grandmother. Their faces were clearly unhappy; drooping curves were drawn as their lips. Above Grandfather's head she'd written, "The

Guru of Money." Alongside the mansion was a smaller house, with broken windows (Sanu had neatly cut the windows in half, with jagged lines showing their panes), and a door that seemed to hang on the hinges. Underneath was written "The Acharya Hut." The four people above the hut, who reflected her own family, had smiling faces, and above Ramchandra's head was written, "The Guru of Love."

Ramchandra laughed, and so did Goma. "This is very good," he said. "When did you draw this?"

"When she was about nine," Goma said.

"So you knew about this?"

Goma nodded. "At first I was angry, but then I thought it was funny."

Their talking had awakened Rakesh, who looked at them with sleepy eyes.

"Why didn't you show it to me?" Ramchandra asked Sanu.

"I don't know."

"It's fitting, don't you think?" Goma asked. "The Guru of Love."

Ramchandra said nothing but reached out and hugged his daughter. Then, embarrassed, he said, "Okay, okay. Do you want to listen to that story I never finished?"

Both children nodded.

"Do you remember where we left off?"

"On the day of the wedding, something surprising happened," Rakesh said.

"At the very moment the merchant was about to put the garland around the girl's neck," said Ramchandra, taking care not the mention the girl's name, "a loud voice was heard from the entrance of the tent. Everyone looked, and there was a young man on a horse, his back straight, dressed in very fine clothes. The man came into the tent with his horse and said, 'This marriage cannot take place.'

"People began to whisper, and the merchant said, 'And who are you to stop it?'

"'I am her father,' the man said, pointing toward the girl.

"Everyone gasped. The merchant signaled to his cronies to take the man away, but when they stepped up, the man got off his horse and drew his sword, which was nearly as big as he was, and with such a shine on its blade that people had to shield their eyes. The cronies became afraid, and the man said, 'Take everything and leave! If I see any of you again, I'll chop off your heads.' The cronies ran away, and the merchant, mumbling obscenities, also took off.

"The girl looked at the man and said, 'Father?'

"The man laughed. 'No, I was just trying to show some authority. I am a prince from far away. I have come to marry you.'"

Sanu groaned. "That sounds unbelievable."

"It's a story," Ramchandra said. "Stories are supposed to be unbelievable."

"What happened next?" Rakesh asked.

"What do you think happened?"

"They married and lived happily ever after?"

"Of course they did. Even the mother was happy, because now she was the mother-in-law of a prince instead of a merchant."

"Idiotic story," Sanu said, and they all laughed.

Ramchandra wanted to stay in the room, in the glow of their laughing faces. But Malati was probably wondering why he was gone for so long. He got up and from the doorway asked, "It was a fun story, wasn't it?"

The children nodded and became solemn, and he went next door.

"What was all that about?" Malati asked

"Nothing. I wanted to talk to them."

She left her books and joined him in bed. "I couldn't concentrate."

"Why?"

"I thought maybe you were talking about me."

"We weren't talking about you."

"So, what did you talk about?"

"Nothing. Just this and that."

"You don't want to tell me." She turned her face away.

"It was nothing, really. Sanu showed me something she'd painted a long time ago."

"I thought I heard laughter."

"I told them a funny story."

She sulked for a while, then said, "I wonder how Malekha Didi is doing these days."

"Do you want to visit her?"

"After what she did to me?"

"She must at least miss Rachana."

"I'm sure she does, but it serves her right. Crazy woman." Then she said, "When the exams are over, can you and I go to the Manakamana Temple?" The Manakamana Temple was at least a two-day trip, with a hike up steep hills that took hours. The temple was located between Kathmandu and Pokhara, and the goddess, as her name reflected, was considered powerful in granting people's wishes.

"Maybe we can plan for all of us to go," he said.

"But I want it to be just the two of us."

"The others might feel hurt."

"I already talked to bhauju. She said it would be easier if just the two of us went."

Ramchandra knew that if the children heard about it, they'd certainly want to go. The last time they'd been there, about three years ago, Rakesh had thoroughly enjoyed the trip. He'd climbed up the hills tirelessly, coaxing others to climb faster.

"We'll talk about this once the exams are over, okay? As it is, things in this country look dangerous right now."

"It seems you don't want to go with me alone."

"It's not that. We have to consider everything. We'll definitely do something."

It took him a while to appease her, which he did by touching her, first her face, then her bosom, then her belly, until she started to squirm and clasped him tightly.

During dinner on the evening before the math exam, a boy who was a neighbor rapped on the door and said someone wanted to see Malati. The man wouldn't give his name, the boy said, sounding breathless, itching to get back to whatever game he'd been playing. "He's waiting in the tea shop," the boy said and ran away. "Let me go with you," Ramchandra said. Someone sent by Malekha Didi, he thought, and the same thought seemed to register on the other faces in the room. But Malati stopped him. "No need to disturb your dinner. I'll go by myself. Must be someone who didn't realize I'd moved here."

She washed her hands and face and disappeared.

Malati didn't return even after they finished eating, even after they congregated in the children's room and, on Rakesh's insistence, played a game of carom. At one point, Ramchandra went to the bedroom window that afforded a partial view of the tea shop. If she was in the shop, she must have been farther inside, because he couldn't spot her. Darkness had fallen. Why was she taking so long?

"Why don't you go downstairs and check?" Goma suggested. But Rakesh, who was his partner in the game, wouldn't let him. "We haven't played in so long, and now you want to spoil it," he cried. So Ramchandra stayed. When one round was over, he got up and said, "I'd better see what's going on," and went downstairs. In the dark, Malati bumped into him under the arch that opened to the street. "You took so long. I was worried," he said.

"Nothing to worry about," she said.

"Who was he?"

"A relative. He wanted to know what I was doing." Her voice was heavy, as if she'd been crying.

"What's wrong?"

She walked toward the door. "Old memories."

Upstairs, she gave the same story to Goma, who exchanged a look with Ramchandra. Goma heated her food, and they sat with her while she tried to eat. But she played with the food and said she'd lost her appetite. "I'll eat it tomorrow, bhauju," she said. Her eyelids were slightly puffy. "I don't want this food to go to waste."

In the bedroom, Ramchandra wanted to review some material for the next day's exam, but Malati said she was exhausted, that she couldn't concentrate, and that she already knew enough to pass the exam.

"But there are some areas—"

"Please, sir," she said, then cradled Rachana and went to bed.

He woke in the middle of the night to feel her shifting beside him. He said, "What's happening with you? Are you scared about the exam?"

"Yes."

"You'll do fine," he said.

But her apprehension had aroused his anxiety. He imagined her in the exam room, holding her pen, paralyzed, unable to write the proper answers. The picture played over and over in his mind until he shut his eyes tightly and willed his pleasant scenes into view.

In the morning, Goma performed another puja in front of Ganesh, and although Ramchandra offered to accompany

Malati to the exam center for moral support, she declined the offer. "It's probably better for me to go alone," she said, "so that I can clear my head."

"At least let me walk you to the bus stop," he said.

She seemed reluctant even about this, but he insisted.

She walked quickly, although there was plenty of time for her to get there. Ramchandra reminded her of this, and she slowed down. He noticed that she kept looking back, as if she thought someone was following her. He teased her about her nervousness, saying she was anxious but was too embarrassed to show it, and she smiled at him sheepishly. At the bus stop, he squeezed her hand before she boarded.

He walked home slowly, enjoying the crisp morning air, the way it cleared his nostrils. On New Road, he listened to the crowd gathered under the peepul tree. The government had arrested the top leaders of certain political parties: one communist, one Congressi, and a well-known chairwoman of United Left Front. In Janakpur, a southern city bordering India, a pro-government rally was disrupted by young men waving black flags and chanting for the death of the Panchayat system. Ramchandra lingered by the crowd, listening to the opinions and analyses. This is real, he thought, and a tremor of antici-pation ran through him. A police van went by slowly, the cops scanning the crowd. The voices died down, and the people dis-persed.

As Ramchandra was waiting at the curb to cross the street, a car stopped beside him, and he recognized Harish. Ramchan-dra did a namaste, and Harish rolled down the window and offered him a ride. Ramchandra declined. "You're probably late for an appointment," he said. "Besides, Jaisideval is only a stone's throw away." But Harish got out of the car. He was wearing a suit and a tie, and Ramchandra couldn't help comparing his outfit with his own frayed shirt, trousers with stains near the pockets, and discolored shoes. The two men stood there awkwardly.

"I hope things are fine at home?" Harish finally said.

Ramchandra said they were.

"How is Goma Didi?"

"She's fine. The children are fine." This entire universe is fine, he wanted to say.

"And your . . ." Harish's pale face turned crimson. "And your guest?"

Ramchandra couldn't help laughing. "She's fine too. In fact, I just saw her off at the bus stop. Today is her big math exam." And he found himself becoming garrulous. He explained to Harish how she'd first come to him, and how he'd devised all the strategies that he hoped would help her. After he finished, he was embarrassed, but he also felt good, as if he'd needed to tell someone how Malati had become part of his life. Harish, having listened attentively, said, "Remarkable. I'm sure she'll be fine." Then he added, "As long as Goma Didi is fine."

"Your Goma Didi is fine with this," Ramchandra said. "Maybe too fine."

Harish looked at him quizzically, but Ramchandra didn't elaborate. Right then a policeman came by and said Harish was illegally parked and proceeded to write him a ticket. "We were about to leave," Harish said, and handed the man a twenty-rupee note, which he pocketed and left.

"I can go by myself, Harish babu," Ramchandra said. "Give my regards to Nalini."

"Let me know how I can help," Harish said.

"I think I'll pass," Malati said. "I think I did well."

Ramchandra looked at the question sheet. She'd done some

calculations on it, and they were wrong. "Let's go over this and see what you wrote down," he suggested.

"Do I have to? I've been through this so many times." A hint of irritation appeared on her face.

"Did you discuss your answers with others?"

"Let it go," Goma said to Ramchandra. "She must be tired. It's been a long haul for her."

That night in bed she seemed preoccupied. She'd smile for no reason, then suddenly frown. A few times she looked at Rachana and stroked her lovingly. He asked her what she was thinking.

"I'll be so happy once the results are in. Then I can really start thinking about getting a job and going to college at night."

"What kind of job are you thinking about?"

"I don't know. A secretary, maybe. I can take a typing course."

"And what will you study in college?" He found it remarkable that he'd never asked her that before.

"What do you think I should study? Math?" She laughed softly.

"You could," he said, "although that'll take a lot of effort."

"I'm thinking about economics or maybe even commerce."

"Both of those involve math."

She laughed. "There's no way out for me."

Later, when he tried to touch her face, she turned away, saying she was tired. She'd never done this; usually she needed only a touch to respond to him. "What's on your mind?" he asked.

"Nothing. I am tired. Can't a person be tired sometimes?"

When he woke the next morning, she was getting dressed. "I'm going out for a short while," she said.

"Where?"

She was putting on a bright sari. "A friend has invited me for tea this morning."

"What about Rachana?"

"I'm taking her with me." Rachana was chewing the end of a pencil. Malati had dressed her in a colorful frock, put kohl around her eyes, and even pasted a red dot on her forehead. She looked adorable.

"Which friend?" He didn't like the strident tone of his voice, but she was holding something back.

"You don't know her. I met her at the exams."

She talked to Goma in the kitchen before leaving, and later Goma said to him, "What's the matter? Why is your face like this?"

"Like what?"

"Like"—she searched her mind—"like a goat whose head is about to be chopped off."

Ramchandra laughed. "It's nothing like that."

"She's been acting strange the past few days," Goma said. "Something's on her mind. Do you know what?"

"Why would she tell me?" Goma said. "You'd be the first to know."

"She talks to you more than she talks to me." As he said this, he understood that he'd felt it many times.

"I'm sure you know things about her I'll never know," Goma said, and when he looked at her, he saw a hint of something. Sadness? Loss? But she'd already turned her face away.

"Well, what shall we do today?" he asked. It was Saturday. "Let's do something."

"Let's see what the children want to do."

The children wanted to go on a trip. Rakesh suggested Balaju, with its garden and gushing stone spouts. Sanu wanted to go to Swayambhu and admire Buddha's eyes on the stupa that cast a kindly gaze over the city. After much wrangling, Rakesh won, and they settled on Balaju. They decided to go after the morning meal, after Malati returned.

But she didn't return. They ate and waited. Rakesh was getting impatient, so they decided to leave without her.

"Should we take a taxi?" Ramchandra asked.

"What for? It's only a few kilometers."

They made their way through the crowded streets. They climbed the small hill of Chhauni and walked past the museum, while the sun, hot for February, bore down on them. Rakesh complained, Sanu lagged behind, and Ramchandra wondered where Malati was.

By the time they passed the Swayambhunath Temple, they were tired. "Let's just go to Swayambhu today," Ramchandra suggested. "We can go to Balaju some other time." But Rakesh started arguing, so they pressed on. They walked the Ring Road that circled the city. Runners passed them, in their jogging outfits, woolen caps on their heads. "Why couldn't we have at least taken the bus?" Sanu complained, and Ramchandra lay the blame on Goma, who finally agreed that perhaps walking wasn't such a great idea.

Outside the gate of the Balaju gardens, they went to a restaurant and relaxed, sipping hot tea. "The money for tea could easily have covered a taxi," Sanu complained to her mother.

"Okay, okay, shut up now," Goma said. "Walking is good for your health."

They entered the gardens and headed toward the water spouts. Men in underwear soaped themselves under the streams flowing from the spouts. Women washed clothes and banged them rhythmically against the stones. They sat on a grassy area nearby and watched. Rakesh said he too wanted to take a bath, but Goma told him that he'd catch a cold in such icy water.

Ramchandra had to urinate; excusing himself, he wandered around, hoping to find a bush behind which he could perform the job. He hated doing this here, but the lack of public bathrooms in the city was a serious problem. In Balaju, the only urinals were inside the swimming pool complex, and he'd have to pay an entrance fee to get in.

About two hundred yards away, he found a bush that would hide him. He looked around and opened his zipper. As he was urinating, he heard laughter that made him suck in his breath. Then a voice drifted toward him and rang in his ears. Malati's. He peered around the bush and saw, a few yards away, a couple sitting on a mat spread on the grass under a patch of sunlight beneath the trees. Malati's back was to him, but he recognized the bright sari. Rachana was playing on the grass nearby. The man sitting in front of Malati was young, Ramchandra could tell, even though he couldn't see his face clearly. He had a mustache, and he was saying something that made Malati laugh. The man glanced up, saw Ramchandra, and stopped talking. Malati turned around, but Ramchandra hid behind the bush again. He zipped up his trousers and hastened back to Goma and the children.

They spent the day at the gardens, walking around, eating some bhujiyas Goma bought, and Ramchandra kept trying to doubt what he'd seen. By the time they were ready to go home, he had come to the conclusion that he'd been mistaken, that his anxiety about Malati that morning had blurred his vision.

The family caught a bus, which dropped them off at Shahid Gate, and they walked home.

Malati came to the landing as they climbed the stairs. "Where did you go? I've been waiting all day for you."

"When did you get back?" Ramchandra asked.

"Around eleven. You must have left just before that."

Goma told her about the trip to Balaju.

"You went to Balaju?" Her face turned crimson.

Ramchandra couldn't help saying, "Why? Were you there too?"

"No, no," she said. "I told you. I was back here at eleven."

Goma and Malati went to the kitchen to cook dinner, and Ramchandra sat down with the children to play carom.

Throughout dinner, he searched Malati's face for hints of guilt. But why did he expect her to feel guilty? After all, what relationship really bound them together?

Later, after she changed into her sleepwear and slipped into the bed, he felt a strange dislike for her. Why had she lied to him? Why couldn't she come right out and tell him—and Goma—where she'd been and whom she'd been with? And this resentment prompted him to say what he'd held back until now. "You really didn't go to your friend's place, did you?"

"What makes you say that? Why would I lie to you?"

"Somehow I know. But I don't understand why you haven't been honest."

"The exams are on my mind; that's all." Her science exam was the next morning.

"If you're worried about your exams, why haven't you been home studying?"

She was about to turn off the lights but stopped. "What's happened to you? Why are you speaking to me in that voice?"

"I don't understand why you're not focusing on your exams. Why the need to go all over the city?"

"I wasn't all over the city. I was at a friend's house, drinking tea, discussing the exams."

"Yes, yes."

"Where do you think I was?"

"Do I have to tell you?"

So far their voices had been quiet, murmurs, but now hers took on a hard edge. "Can't I have a moment of peace in this house? Do I have to be watched all the time? By everyone?"

The strident tone surprised him; then it angered him. "You ungrateful woman," he said. "Even our Sanu has better sense than you do."

"Of course your daughter has better sense. She's blood, after all. What relation am I to you?"

"None," he said. "I was foolish enough to think there was something between us. There's nothing anymore."

His words seemed to cut her; she got up from the bed and knelt on the floor and said, loudly, "God, what have I done?"

"Stop that, Malati. You'll wake everybody up."

But she remained where she was, her back to him. In the next room, the bed creaked, and Ramchandra knew that Goma must have heard their raised voices.

"Come back here," he said, gently now, and this time she obliged.

"I was with him," she said.

"Who?" By now he knew what the answer would be, and he dreaded it.

"Rachana's father."

"After all this time?"

"He's left his wife."

"And earlier, he left you."

"He says he thinks about our daughter all the time."

"Do you believe him?"

She nodded. "That's why I agreed to see him again."

He wanted to tell her that she was foolish to believe him, but he remembered how young she was.

She said he'd found out about her from Bhakta, the taxi driver who had taken them to Dakshinkali, and he claimed his heart was cut to pieces when he heard that his daughter and the mother of his daughter had been kicked out of the house and were living with strangers. That's why he wanted to see her, wanted to see his baby, who, he said, looked just like her.

"And what has he been doing all this time? Where has he been?"

He had a small trading business in Birgunj, she said, but right now the business was slow, and he'd come back to Kathmandu and was driving a taxi. He was sorry for what he'd done to Malati, and he wanted to make it up to her.

"What's his name?"

"Amrit," she said. "I'm not going to see him anymore, but today I felt sorry for him. He wanted so badly to hold Rachana."

"Where does he live?"

"He has a room near Ranjana Cinema Hall."

Ramchandra lay on the bed, his hands folded across his chest, breathing slowly.

"I shouldn't have fought with you," she said, and placed her hand on his belly.

When he didn't respond, she moved her hand farther down, and at first he ignored her, his mind on her laughter in Balaju. But her hand was persistent, and he became aroused.

In the midst of their lovemaking, he whispered, "Will you promise not to see him again?"

She promised.

"What was all that about?" Goma asked Ramchandra the next morning when they were alone.

He considered telling her about the taxi driver, but decided there was no need for her to know. "We had a small argument."

"About what? Were you scolding her again for not study-ing?"

"No, I told her to let us know of her whereabouts so that we wouldn't worry."

"You mean about yesterday? God, she was with her friends. Why do you have to be so strict? She's not your daughter."

"I'm not strict with my daughter."

Goma said her parents had invited them to dinner that eve-ning.

"So, they've come around?"

"I don't know. I think Mother misses me and the children."

"She doesn't miss me," he said with a chuckle.

"So do you want to go?"

"What about Malati?"

"Malati and Rachana will go with us."

"It'll be uncomfortable."

"That's their problem. I'm not uncomfortable with it," she said challengingly. "Are you?"

"I don't know, Goma. I don't know you anymore."

"I don't know myself anymore."

He didn't know how to handle her sadness, so he said, "We can ask Malati what she wants to do."

Malati said she didn't want to go, that she couldn't face the Pandeys' hatred, but Goma insisted. She pointed out that Malati was very much a part of the family now, and that her parents would accept her. Malati looked at Ramchandra, but he had no advice for her. Finally, she said, "I'll think about it after my exam today. I have too much on my mind right now."

In the evening, she appeared subdued, and when Goma brought up the subject, she acquiesced, seemingly too tired to protest. When they were in the bedroom getting dressed for the dinner, he asked whether she thought she'd done badly on the exam that day. She didn't respond, and he asked again. In a quiet voice she said that Amrit had appeared at the exam center, saying he wanted to see her and his daughter.

"What did you tell him?"

"I told him I couldn't. That he was the one who'd ended it, and that was that."

She didn't seem to trust her own voice.

Outside Pandey Palace, Malati was awestruck by its grandeur. "They must be very rich." Then she became frightened. "What will I say to them? I have nothing to say."

"You don't have to say anything. Just enjoy the food." Goma was holding Rachana, who clung to her as if she were her mother.

They walked in through the gate, but no one came to receive them on the porch. In fact, the place was so quiet that it seemed to be abandoned. No sound came from the servants' quarters. A heavy smell of incense in the house made Ramchandra uncomfortable. Goma pushed open the door and went inside, and it was she who found Mrs. Pandey seated on a step at the top of the staircase. "Where is everybody? Why are you here like this?"

"Everyone is gone," Mrs. Pandey said.

"Where?"

"They're all gone, Goma."

Ramchandra and Goma exchanged glances. Later, Ramchandra recognized that this kind of understanding came from their years of living together, knowing what each other thought without having to say it. The same dread had entered their minds simultaneously. Something had happened to Goma's father.

"Father?" Goma asked.

"He's gone. He's inside."

Goma sat down beside her mother. She let out a sob. "He's gone?"

"Gone."

"When did this happen?"

"A few minutes ago. He lay down to sleep, and then he went."

"Did he say anything?"

"Nothing. He just went."

"Did you give him water?"

Wide-eyed, Mrs. Pandey looked at Goma. "Water? What for? I burned incense."

"Are you sure he's gone? Maybe he's sleeping." Goma looked at Ramchandra. "Will you check?"

Ramchandra hesitated. But Goma looked at him pleadingly, so he went into the Pandeys' bedroom. The old man lay on the bed, his face peaceful. Ramchandra put his fingers below the old man's nostrils and didn't feel anything. Then he put his ear to his chest, and there was no movement. The window was open, and a gust of wind blew in, ballooning the curtains. Ramchandra closed the window and looked outside. The sky was covered with gray clouds. The old man would no longer cast critical glances at him. But Ramchandra didn't feel relieved, as he'd thought he might. In the past, in moments of extreme misery, he had imagined Goma's parents dead and his feeling of satisfaction. But where was that feeling now? Ramchandra went to the landing and said, "He's gone."

Goma began to cry, and then they all were crying, even Malati.

"We should move him downstairs," Ramchandra said. "Where are the servants?"

Mrs. Pandey said the servants had gone to the market earlier to buy food for dinner.

"Then I'll carry him downstairs. Rakesh, you'll help me."

Rakesh clung to his mother, afraid. "How can he help? He's a child," Goma said. Ramchandra went back into the room and, with some difficulty, placed the old man's arm around his shoulders. Any moment he'll wake up and pat me on the shoulder, Ramchandra thought, and wanted to laugh at his own stupidity. Mr. Pandey's hand was cold. The dead man's feet dragged as Ramchandra pulled him to the landing. Goma rushed downstairs to place a mat on the floor for the body.

Once they'd placed him on the mat, the women began to cry again.

Then Mrs. Pandey noticed Malati. "What is she doing here?" Malati backed away toward the wall.

"What's that woman, this whore, doing here?" Mrs. Pandey said to Goma.

"Mother, this is not the right time," Goma said.

"Of course this is the right time," Mrs. Pandey said. "My beloved husband is dead, and that filthy woman's in my house. I don't want to see her."

Goma looked at Ramchandra, who signaled to Malati to follow him outside.

"I think just for today, it's better if you leave," he whispered to her on the porch.

"I knew I shouldn't have come," Malati said. She set Rachana on the floor, sat down, and covered her eyes. "I can't take it anymore. I've been reduced to a whore by everyone, and I've done nothing."

"She's like that always," Ramchandra said, trying to calm her. "Pay her no attention."

"Why did you bring me here?"

"You mustn't think about yourself," he said. "We don't want to upset Mrs. Pandey more." He sat with Malati, mollifying her by saying that the old woman was in shock and was uttering nonsense. He gave her some money for a three-wheeler, patted Rachana's head, stood up, and turned to go back inside. Malati threw the money on the porch and walked away, and didn't look back when he called.

Goma was holding her mother, who had begun to wail, rocking back and forth beside her husband's body.

10

·······

MR. PANDEY'S BODY was cremated on the
banks of the Bagmati River. As he had no
sons, his closest nephew, a man Goma and Nalini barely knew,
performed the rites. He lit the fire that quickly engulfed Mr.
Pandey's body on the funeral pyre, made of fresh wood. Ramchandra watched the smoke drift up to the cloudy Kathmandu
sky, and tried to formulate some wisdom about the nature of
death, but the words became entangled with the memories of
how Mr. Pandey had treated him. He looked at the windblown
face of his wife, and he tried to gauge her feelings. He'd never
heard Goma speak fondly of her father, although there was no
question that she respected him, perhaps was even in awe of
him. Did she love her father? Was it a dutiful love rather than
a genuine one? But — and here Ramchandra's heart sank — did
Sanu feel the same way about him? His daughter, standing near
him, appeared to have grown into a woman in the past few

weeks, a wise young woman with a sad understanding of how the world worked. Sanu caught his eyes and smiled faintly, and Ramchandra's doubts vanished, just as Mr. Pandey's body was turning into ashes at the bottom of the pyre.

Goma and Nalini had insisted on attending the funeral, even though women traditionally were not allowed to. "He had no sons, so we are his sons," Goma said when Mrs. Pandey objected. "And who has the right to tell us that we can't see our father off?" In the end, Mrs. Pandey herself came to the banks of the Bagmati, drawing criticism from the relatives, who said that such behavior would displease the gods, that perhaps the old man's spirit would find no peace. Mrs. Pandey merely pointed to her daughters and said, "I tried to convince them, but this is what they want."

Ramchandra had had to shave his head, as had the other male members of the family. At first he'd resented this intrusion on his body from a man who had not shown him one iota of respect while he lived, but within hours he got used to it and took pleasure in running his fingers over his smooth scalp. His ears caught the wind easily now, and sometimes they tickled for no reason. Mrs. Pandey had said that he had to wear white clothes, but Goma intervened and said it was not necessary for a son-in-law to be dressed completely in white; only one article of clothing had to be white. So Ramchandra wore a white cap.

The mourning period lasted for several days. The children returned to Pandey Palace with Goma. Malati was on the last leg of her exams. She seemed to have lost all interest in studying; she didn't even look at the books anymore. Often she'd be in the kitchen, cooking and singing. She had a sweet voice, Ramchandra discovered when he first heard her. He stood in the doorway, holding Rachana, listening. "Where are all these songs coming from?" he asked. Since he now went to Pandey

Palace right after he'd finished teaching, and returned to the apartment only late at night, he felt that he'd lost touch with Malati. He felt awkward with her. She hadn't mentioned Amrit again, but he suspected that when he was at Pandey Palace in the evenings, she went to see him. The day Mr. Pandey died, he'd been at Pandey Palace all day, making the funeral arrangements, notifying relatives, and in the evening he'd called the shopkeeper with the telephone and asked him to fetch Malati. But the man came back shortly to say that no one had answered the knock on the door. When Ramchandra later asked her where she'd been that evening, she'd replied testily, "What does it matter where I was? I was kicked out of someone's house, wasn't I? It's my fate to be kicked out of everyone's house. Who knows when I'll get kicked out of this one." Her face changed when she said such things, when anger made her words acidic.

In bed, she didn't respond to his touch as eagerly as she had, and he saw her eyes become glazed when he entered her. One time, when he started caressing her, she turned away and said, "I'm tired," and he was left with his hand on her hip.

On the morning of her last exam, he told her that he'd take her to a restaurant later to celebrate. He wasn't supposed to do this during the mourning period—eat food with salt, let alone have meat. But he was tired of the restrictions, and he figured no one would know. When she asked him where they'd go, he said, "There's a restaurant with umbrellas in Ranipokhari. Three stories high. A rooftop." He liked the way the word sounded; he'd heard people call it that. He'd often seen the restaurant when he walked by Ranipokhari, and he used to speculate about the people who ate there. When he'd looked up, he'd seen the heads of people, talking and enjoying the scenery below, as if they were the lords of the city.

"Have you been there before?" she asked.

"Never. That's why it'll be a good place to go."

"It must be expensive."

"For today, we'll not worry about that."

Ever since Malati had entered his life, he'd been saying variations of this. The meal at the restaurant would probably cost around eighty rupees, and with no tutoring fees for the next few months, that was a large sum of money. But they had to celebrate, he rationalized, and perhaps this moment of rejoicing would once again bring him close to Malati.

"Aren't you supposed to go to Pandey Palace?" she asked with a smile, as if she already knew the answer.

"I'll make up an excuse," he said, also smiling. He liked the idea of their having a secret.

The excuse that he came up with, when he called Goma from the school, was that he needed to go to the school to work out some details about extracurricular activities for the next academic season, which would start soon. Goma seemed to have forgotten that it was the day of Malati's last exam, because she didn't mention it; she talked only about how her father had apparently left her mother with more debts than they'd thought he had. "Now the creditors are already banging at the door. Can you imagine that?" she said. "In a matter of days. These people have no morals."

He asked to talk to the children, told Rakesh not to give his mother any trouble, and asked Sanu how she'd done in the school spelling contest. "I came in first," she said nonchalantly, and he laughed with pleasure.

Actually, he did have to go to the school that afternoon. Bandana Miss had called in a panic, saying that Khanal Sir had become gravely ill and would not return next year, so they had to discuss how to cover his classes until they found a replacement.

Ramchandra found that the death of his father-in-law had served to lessen his colleagues' disapproval. They sympathized with him, even though some knew that Mr. Pandey had treated Ramchandra badly. Only once during the meeting in the staff room did Shailendra make a reference to second wives, but he got no encouragement from the others, so he kept quiet for a while. Bandana Miss was making preparations for her son to go to America, and between their discussion of the classes and the budget for the coming year, she talked about him at every chance she got. "You should think of sending your children to America, Ramchandra-ji," she said, and Ramchandra merely smiled and said, "America is a distant dream for most of us, Bandana Miss."

"That's precisely the sort of attitude," Bandana Miss said, "that makes Nepalis so hopeless. They never learn to dream."

"We dream of feeding our family and sending our children to a school, any school," someone said.

"Unless you dream of something higher, you'll never move toward it," Bandana Miss said.

"So, what's your dream?" Shailendra asked Ramchandra.

Ramchandra was daydreaming about Malati, about the evening on the rooftop, and he replied, "I dream of a house of my own in Kathmandu."

"And who will occupy that house? All your family members?" Shailendra said, emphasizing *all*.

"Yes, all my family members," Ramchandra said. "You don't expect me to ask you to occupy the house, do you?"

Everyone laughed, and Shailendra became quiet again.

Malati wasn't there when Ramchandra got home that evening. He made himself a cup of tea and waited by the window. It began to drizzle, the cold rain of winter, and he worried about having to spend more money on the three-wheeler they'd need to go to the rooftop restaurant. He finished his tea, went to the bathroom in the courtyard, then came up to sit by the window again. It was nearly six-thirty. The rain was falling harder. The tea shopkeeper had no customers and was standing in the door-way, watching the rain. A crow landed on an electric wire right in front of Ramchandra and started making its raucous noise. Ramchandra shooed it away. The shopkeeper looked up, and, after making some small comments about the rain, said, "She went in a taxi. Around three o'clock." Ramchandra pretended he didn't hear, and the shopkeeper stood there, smiling.

Not long after that, a taxi pulled up, and Malati got out from the front seat, holding Rachana. She rushed to the entrance of the courtyard and stood there, waving to the taxi driver. Ramchandra strained his neck trying to see the man, but his view was obstructed. He moved away from the window and picked up one of his school textbooks from the floor. When she stood in the doorway, he pretended not to see her.

"Is it too late for us to go to that restaurant?" she asked.

"It's raining."

"I am sorry. I had to visit someone."

"You don't need to be sorry. No one should be sorry in this world."

"We could take a taxi."

"I can't spend money like that all the time."

"I have some money."

"How?"

"An old friend gave it to me."

Ramchandra felt his chest twist, but he forced himself to say, "Do you need to change?"

She said she was fine.

By the time they reached the street, the rain was letting up, and they decided to walk. All the way to the restaurant, Ramchandra's chest remained constricted. They walked through Basantapur, into Indrachowk, where the evening shoppers clogged the streets. They stepped into puddles and got their feet wet. In Asan, a bull came charging at Malati, and with a loud "Ama," she dashed to the side, clutching Rachana tightly. Ramchandra bravely waved his arm to shoo the bull away. Some pedestrians laughed.

Once at the restaurant, Ramchandra and Malati climbed the narrow staircase to the third floor, where the city opened out to them. Below was the Ranipokhari Pond, with the small white Temple of Shiva in the middle. On the horizon they could see the tip of the Dharahara tower, pink in the light of the setting sun. A steady cacophony of traffic noise rose from the crowded street. Ramchandra and Malati stood in front of the counter, expecting the man behind it to guide them to a table. But he gestured, without looking, and said, "Sit anywhere you want." They chose a table that gave them a good view of the pond. A waiter approached with a menu. The prices were high, higher than Ramchandra had expected.

"What would you like?" he asked Malati.

"I'm not all that hungry," she said. "Maybe I'll have tea."

"I plan this big dinner for you, and you're not hungry?"

"My stomach's been upset since this morning."

He ordered chicken chili for himself, and Malati, probably aware of his disappointment, asked for a plate of samosas, which she shared with Rachana. An uneasy truce hovered between them. Ramchandra tried to make small talk, and Malati said that her last exam, an optional one on history, had gone well. Now there would be the long wait for the results, which sometimes took six months or more. She said that she'd run into Malekha Didi in the market the other day, and her stepmother ignored her and talked only to Rachana, who became frightened and cried. Ramchandra talked briefly about what was happening at Pandey Palace. Then there was a lull in the conversation, and they looked at the street, now glistening with lights from the shops.

"What's that?" Malati said, pointing to the horizon.

In the dark, it was hard to tell, but it turned out to be a crowd heading toward Ranipokhari. As the crowd came closer, they could hear a soft chant, although Ramchandra couldn't make out the words.

"There are police vans," Ramchandra said, pointing immediately below them.

When the throng reached the mouth of Kamalacchi, men got out of the vans and merged with the crowd. Ramchandra heard some shouts that sounded almost like shouts of joy, and for a moment it seemed as if the policemen were dancing with the people. "What's happening?" others on the rooftop whispered. And then the shouts turned into cries of pain, and Ramchandra saw people being hauled into the vans. As abruptly as the crowd had appeared, it disappeared, and the next moment, the police vans took off. Within a few minutes, it was as if nothing had happened.

The customers in the restaurant talked about what had happened. "The government's going to squelch this even before it begins," someone said.

"I don't know," one waiter said. "There'll be a bloodbath tomorrow, Democracy Day."

The chanting of the protesters echoed in Ramchandra's head as he paid the bill and they headed down.

This time they avoided the alleys and took the main street of Ranipokhari. As they were walking past Bir Hospital, it started to rain again, hard, and they ran for cover under the awning of a shop. It was the first floor of Mahankal Temple, right across from the military hospital.

The rain clattered loudly on the awning, accompanied by

thunder and lightning that ripped open the sky. Other pedestrians squeezed against them, seeking shelter, and Ramchandra's body pressed against Malati's. The sensation didn't give him the pleasure it used to, although his heart still raced and he could still smell the mustard oil in her hair. Soon Rachana began to squirm in Malati's arms, then started crying, which brought disapproving looks from the others. "So much noise in here," said a woman wearing expensive-looking clothes.

A taxi stopped on the street before them, and the woman rushed over to it, but the driver didn't let her in, and there was an argument. Malati's face brightened, and Ramchandra immediately knew who the driver was. By then, he'd also recognized the taxi, with its sharp streak of silver on the side where the paint had peeled off.

"Shall we go?" she said.

"You go. I'll wait for the rain to die down."

Rachana, impatient, was trying to wiggle out of Malati's arms. "Please. She's becoming difficult."

"You don't need me. Why do you need me?"

"But you're stuck in the rain here."

The others were listening intently to their conversation. The woman had come back and was muttering curses under her breath. Malati insisted, and Ramchandra said no and looked at the sky, which was getting darker now that night was falling. Finally he thought, What do I have to lose?

They rushed to the taxi and got in, and the driver said, "Why did you take so long?" He said this to Malati, but it seemed directed at Ramchandra. He was a strikingly handsome man, Ramchandra had to admit, like a movie star, and Ramchandra suddenly felt ugly. Malati didn't introduce him, and the driver pretended that nothing was unusual. He didn't speak during the short drive, although Ramchandra caught the driver appraising him in the rearview mirror.

In Jaisideval, Amrit said to Ramchandra, "That'll be twenty rupees." And he laughed.

Ramchandra took out a twenty-rupee note, threw it at him, and got out. Amrit protested, saying he was joking about the fare.

Ramchandra climbed the stairs in front of Malati, too angry to speak to her. In the bedroom, after she'd set down Rachana (who had quieted down in the taxi and was now asleep), Malati said, "Why are you like this?"

"Don't talk to me," he said.

"I don't understand," she said. "He was only giving us a ride. Was that so bad?"

He looked at her as if she were crazy. "He treated you like an animal. And you take him back as though he'd done nothing."

"He didn't treat me like an animal."

"He lied to you and left you pregnant. That's your story, not mine."

"But he's changed. He regrets what he did."

"He regrets. And that's enough for you?"

"What do you want me to do?"

"Nothing." He went to stand by the window. Darkness had taken over the street, and the lights had gone on in the shops. A bicyclist pedaled his way through the dark, weaving in and out of traffic.

"Do you think I'm happy here?"

Her words stung him, and he turned around and glared at her. "What? You're not happy? Can you imagine anything better for you than what you have right now? You sleep with a woman's husband, and she takes you in and treats you as if you were her sister."

"I never wanted pity from you, and I don't want it now."

"No one's pitying you. You're an ungrateful little wench, that's all." He regretted his words even as he spoke them.

"Go ahead. Why don't you call me names too, the way everyone in this city does." She picked up Rachana, who squirmed but went right back to sleep in her mother's arms. When she made a move to leave the room, he said, "What? Is your lover waiting for you outside? To take you away with a wedding band?" At that thought, he strode over to the window. The car was still there, in the shadows, the silhouette of a man leaning against it, smoking a cigarette. "You made plans with him, didn't you? That's why you picked a fight with me."

"I made no plans with anyone," she said. And as though the whole thing had exhausted her, she sat down near the door, holding her head.

"I don't know what to do with you," he said, his arms crossed over his chest.

"Please, just leave me alone for a while."

"Are you going to see him now?"

"Leave me alone, please. I'm not going anywhere."

He walked down the stairs, into the courtyard, and out to the street. The driver was still leaning against his taxi, the cigarette glowing. Ramchandra moved toward him, thinking he'd say something, although he wasn't sure what. But as he neared the man, he saw that it wasn't Amrit. And feeling foolish, he walked past.

For some time he roamed the streets, where pockets of people were discussing what would happen in the country tomorrow. Pressure was building in Ramchandra's chest, as though he were about to break out in a sob. In Indrachowk, he spotted a bhatti, with a couple of customers inside, drinking the local liquor. He entered and asked for a glass of raksi. The drink went easily down his throat, and he asked for another. After three drinks, his mind seemed to clear, and he began chatting with the shopkeeper, who sat behind the counter under a poster of a heroine from an Indian film. The conversation was light, with much laughter, but the shopkeeper soon went to join some customers who were talking about the arrests in Kirtipur. Moments ago the police had raided the houses of student activists and taken hundreds of them off to jail. Ramchandra listened to the talk about the incident. He felt like telling them that his father-in-law, who had disapproved of him, had recently died. And that Mr. Pandey's soul must be happy at those arrests, because he believed that those in power must hold on to their power. If I have another drink, Ramchandra thought, I'll really start blabbering and making a fool of myself. He left the bhatti.

At home, Malati was already in bed, and he changed and slipped in beside her.

"You've been drinking," she said.

"Just a bit," he said.

"I don't like the smell."

"You don't like anything about me anymore."

"That's not true," she said. She ran her hand through his hair. After a while she said, "He wants to marry me."

"Your taxi driver?"

"Amrit. He told me that today."

"And what do you want to do?"

"I don't want to marry him."

"Why?"

"I don't trust him."

"That's right," he said. The alcohol had taken hold of him now. When he opened his eyes, the room spun, so he kept them buried in her armpit. The room was dark, and he was more comfortable this way.

"But Rachana does need her father," she said. "When she grows up, people will mock her, say she's a bastard."

"I'll adopt her as my daughter."

"You're not serious."

"She's already a part of the family, isn't she? I can formalize the adoption." In his drunkenness, the idea appealed to him even as he said it. He could lay claim to another daughter. Both Sanu and Rakesh adored Rachana, and Rachana loved Goma as if she were her mother. Why not?

"What will bhauju think?"

"She won't mind. Remember, your living here was her idea."

Malati was quiet, and he listened to his own breathing, the slight gurgling sound in his nostrils. The alcohol floating inside his head was like a sweet syrup.

"But you're not her real father," she said. "And that's what she needs."

He sat up. "What real? How real was he when he left you pregnant? When he didn't seek out Rachana after she was born?"

"He had a wife. He had his own difficulties."

It occurred to him that she was using him as a sounding board, arguing with him to clarify her own thinking about Amrit. Or perhaps to convince herself about what she wanted to believe. Somehow, in the dark, he found her face and slapped her.

Her silence told him she'd expected this. He'd never lay a hand on Goma or on his children, but that he'd slapped Malati about a taxi driver was a sign to him that something had gone terribly wrong, that something was terribly wrong with him.

"I shouldn't have done that," he said immediately. "I am sorry." But he didn't reach out to touch her.

"I make many people angry."

He didn't want to listen to her self-pity, so he said, "The fault is not yours. People who become angry become angry for their own reasons, not because of you." His voice had become distant, remote. "You do what you need to do in life. I shouldn't stand in your way."

Dawn was a few hours away, but neither of them slept. He could see that her eyes were open and she was staring at the ceiling. Once the effect of the liquor wore off, he became lucid, wide-awake, with only a tinge of a hangover. He suddenly recalled from his childhood a boy, slightly older than he was, coaxing him to spit at the sky. He did, and the spit landed right back on his face, and people laughed, strangers. He remembered a small girl who made necklaces for him, and his mother teasing him, saying the girl wanted to marry him. The memories emerged and disappeared, and he found solace in them, and gradually he drifted to sleep.

He woke just as light made the room visible. Malati had already packed her belongings. "I'm leaving now," she said.

He nodded.

"Please tell bhauju I'm sorry. I'd like to see her, but I don't want to go there."

"I'll tell her."

He got up and embraced her, kissed Rachana on the cheek. He thought of giving her some money, but decided that would be in bad taste. He did ask whether she had enough money for a three-wheeler, and she said yes.

He walked her down the stairs, carrying her suitcase. Mr. Sharma was at his window, brushing his teeth, and he waved his hand with the brush. Ramchandra waved back.

Outside, they had to wait before an empty three-wheeler came their way.

"I'll keep an eye out on the S.L.C. results. I have your exam number." He helped her into the cab, and as it took off, she said, "Please tell everyone I was thinking of them."

He climbed up the stairs and sat on the bed. The house was empty without her and the sweet noises Rachana made.

An hour later he left the house and walked toward Pandey Palace. Democracy Day was a holiday, so he didn't have to go to school. The sky was filled with gray clouds, like an omen of the trouble that would start today. All the way to Bhatbhateni, Ramchandra saw people standing outside their houses or in tea shops, talking about what was to happen.

At Pandey Palace he found Goma alone in the kitchen and told her that Malati had left.

"But where did she go?" Goma appeared alarmed. "Back to her stepmother?"

He told her about the taxi driver.

"What do you think of this?" Goma asked, watching him carefully.

He shrugged. "It's her decision. She has to do what's good for her."

"You mean you don't care?"

"I care," he said. He really wasn't sure what he felt. There was a sense of relief, as though an elephant had stopped pressing on his chest, but he was anxious, and his throat was parched by some craving he couldn't identify. It wasn't associated with Malati; he didn't ache for her body as he used to.

After eating his morning meal, he fell asleep on the living room couch, and when he woke his heart was hammering. His throat was so dry that it hurt to swallow. He went to the kitchen and drank some water, but the anxiety remained. He went upstairs, where Goma was sitting with her mother, and said that he was going out for a walk.

"But where? There's going to be trouble today."

"I'll just walk around the neighborhood," he said. "Nothing will happen here."

"Come back soon," Goma called out as he headed for the door. "Otherwise I'll worry."

On the lawn, Sanu and Rakesh were looking at the flowers and chatting with the gardener; he went past them silently.

Malati had mentioned that Amrit lived near Ranjana Cinema Hall, so he headed toward New Road. How would he find Amrit's house? And what would he say to Malati? He had no answers, but the only way he could lessen his anxiety was to see where she was, how she was going to live from now on.

On the way he saw police vans patrolling the streets. Many shopkeepers had closed their shutters in fear of riots. In Asan and Indrachowk, people walked around aimlessly, waiting for something to happen. When Ramchandra reached the statue of Juddha Shumshere on New Road, he saw a large group of people rushing toward him from the east, holding red flags and shouting accusations against the government. Ramchandra needed to turn left at a particular alley, but got pushed to the opposite side of the street, under the famous peepul tree. The protesters ran toward Indrachowk, their antigovernment chants floating in the air. "The Panchayat rally is coming any minute," someone said. "That'll be fun." People had wild expectation on their faces. Then someone called out, "They're coming! They're coming!" From the far end of the street, near the New Road Gate, a procession headed in their direction. They could hear the faint chants: "Long live King Birendra," "Panchayat system jindabad." As the parade came closer, the bystanders could see a large poster picturing King Tribhuvan, the present king's grandfather, who had liberated the country from Rana dictators. Government ministers in official dress appeared first, led by the prime minister.

Ramchandra's attention was drawn elsewhere. Across the street, at the mouth of the alley leading to the cinema hall, he saw Malati, with Rachana on her hip, standing next to Amrit. Why were they here with the baby? He shouted, waved his hand, but their eyes were on the parade. Ramchandra was thinking about crossing the street, telling them to take the child away from this mob of people, when a commotion broke out behind Amrit and Malati, near the cinema. A handful of men rushed into New Road, carrying the flag of the Congress Party. The next moment, seemingly at the wave of a scepter from one of the two million gods above, men and women appeared from all the New Road side streets, carrying Congressi flags and banners. Strident voices broke the air: "Down with the fascist Panchayat system!" The men and women headed straight toward the crowd, where the prime minister now stood still. Ramchandra's eyes were on Malati, who was trying to push through the crowd toward the cinema. Amrit was trying to clear the way for her, but he was stopped by the mass that surged forward. Ramchandra saw Rachana fall from Malati's arms and disappear into the rush of arms and legs around them.

Ramchandra experienced a twisted knot of panic; he was only dimly aware that the government procession near him had broken into chaos. The prime minister and the other ministers were running back toward the New Road Gate. Someone shouted, "They have their tails between their legs," and people laughed. The men in the government parade scrambled to get away from the angry men and women bearing down on them from all the side streets. Some of the onlookers under the peepul tree got caught up in the frenzy. Now the crowd was rushing in every direction. Some ran to Indrachowk; others took off in the opposite direction, to Dharahara.

Sweating, Ramchandra shoved his way through the crowd. At first he didn't see them; then Amrit's taxi inched its way past, and Ramchandra saw Malati holding Rachana in her lap. The child's head was bloody. He shouted Malati's name, and she looked up, her eyes filled with tears, but she didn't seem to recognize him. The taxi honked, lurched forward, took a sharp left turn, and disappeared toward the New Road Gate. They were headed for the hospital.

Ramchandra lingered for a while. The action had already moved toward Tundikhel. He wanted to go to Bir Hospital, where he was sure Amrit had taken his daughter, but as the crowd around him swirled and voices of excitement rose to the sky, he let this impulse pass. All he could do was pray that the little girl had not been badly hurt.

To avoid getting caught up in the confrontations around him, he took a circuitous route. In spots, small groups of people broke out into chants that decried the government repression and demanded multiparty democracy. In Naxal he found an open tea shop and sat down to rest. People inside said that the protesters had called for a nationwide strike the next day. All schools, shops, and traffic would be shut down.

At Goma's insistence, he slept at Pandey Palace that night, in a small room next to the one she shared with her mother. The children slept in another room near the staircase. Because he didn't want Goma to worry, he said nothing about Rachana's injury. When Goma had asked why he'd been away so long, he told her he'd run into a colleague from school and had ended up going to the man's house for tea and conversation.

That night, about two hours after he'd gone to bed, he was awakened by an incessant cawing outside his window. As his eyes grew accustomed to the darkness, he saw a crow, poking its head in the air and creating a ruckus. He opened the window and shooed it away, and by that time he was wide-awake.

He decided to walk in the garden to calm his mind. It had

been a long time since he'd slept at Pandey Palace, but he knew the house well, having been here so often for meals and festivals. Before, the house had evoked in him a feeling of dread; its corridors reeked of wealth he wasn't born to, couldn't dream of amassing in his life, let alone passing on to his children. When he ate in the big kitchen, with its shiny tiles and sparkling cutlery, with the three servants who tiptoed around deferentially and created near-perfect dishes, the food refused to go down his stomach, especially when Harish was present and Mrs. Pandey's hands flew near him to serve him. Now, after Mr. Pandey's death, the house had become transformed; it was almost as if the big mansion was his to do with as he wanted. Ramchandra scolded himself. What kind of a man was he, fantasizing about owning someone else's house; not just any anyone's but his own in-laws'? If people knew what he thought, they'd laugh at him. And that led to another thought, one that made him cringe. What would happen if Mrs. Pandey were to die tomorrow? Who would take over the mansion? Harish and Nalini? But they were rich already. What would they do with a big house like this? Is it possible, Ramchandra wondered, that Goma would inherit the house?

In the garden, Ramchandra tried not to think about this possibility, but his imagination took off, and he pictured himself living here as the owner. He visualized himself walking through its corridors, opening doors to take peeks at his children sleeping in their separate bedrooms. Or climbing down the stairs, his hand caressing the smooth balustrade. Or inspecting the garden on a bright spring day, giving instructions to the gardener. Or having workers install a Western-style commode bathroom on each floor of the house, which now had only a squatting-style bathroom. He saw the servants, quiet, courteous, and wearing freshly washed clothes, asking what he'd like for his evening meal.

But how would he retain the servants with his schoolteacher's salary? How would he install those expensive commodes? Even if Pandey Palace were bequeathed to Goma, and thereby to him, there wasn't any way he could maintain it. Or would Mrs. Pandey leave behind a large sum of money for Goma? That thought made Ramchandra crazy, and he muttered to himself, "Stop, stop."

He was about to head back when he looked up and saw the outline of a figure upstairs. It was Goma. Was she looking at him? He wanted to say something to her about himself and Malati. Or about her. But the words became jumbled with other words in his mind. She was watching him, and he was watching her watch him, and when he saw himself through her perspective, he came upon a stranger. Goma, he said in his mind. What is to become of us, now that Malati is gone?

11
· · · · · · ·

THE CITY CONTINUED to explode into riots. Angry citizens taking to the streets were tear-gassed or fired on by the police. Men and women died. A student's death in Jhapa, a district bordering India to the east, infuriated college students across the country, and the campuses in Kathmandu became battlegrounds for the police and the students. Nor did Ramchandra's school remain untouched. His students, especially those in the upper grades, didn't want to study. They came to school and then left to join the demonstrations. With the image of Rachana's bloody head still vivid in his mind, Ramchandra tried to dissuade the students, but they wouldn't listen. Instead, they chastised him for not sympathizing with those who were giving their lives for freedom. One student even accused him of being a government crony, and Ramchandra said, bitterly, "Yes, you're right. I have a lot to gain by seeing that those in power remain in power. That's why I'm stuck in this miserable job, teaching you miserable students, clinging to my miserable salary."

The student's accusation annoyed him, and he muttered to himself, "Do what you want. What do I care? I am just here to teach." But he did worry about the students, and in bed he had nightmares about their young bodies lying in gutters as their mothers pounded on Ramchandra's door.

Most of the teachers supported the protesters, but a few came to the regime's defense. "These people want nothing but trouble," Bandana Miss said one morning, after the older students had left to support the antigovernment demonstrators and the younger ones had gone home. Her brother occupied a high position in the tourism department. "This will lead our country nowhere."

"You mean you don't want democracy?" Shailendra asked with a smirk.

"We need control," Bandana Miss said. "Otherwise we'll end up like America, where people shoot each other on the streets."

"I thought you liked America," someone said. "Didn't you send your son there?"

For a moment Bandana Miss was stumped. Then she said, "Sending your son to America for education is one thing. Agreeing with its philosophy is another."

"I've heard you sing praises of America," Ramchandra said.

Bandana Miss became defensive. "That's an entirely different thing. We can't let this country fall to anarchy."

"What's your take on this, Ramchandra-ji?" Gokul asked. "You haven't offered us your opinion."

"I have none. Revolutions come and go. I still don't have a house of my own in this city."

That made everyone laugh, and even Bandana Miss found a

way to save face. "So true, so true, Ramchandra-ji," she said, placing her hand on his arm.

"So, Ramchandra-ji," Shailendra said, "you mean to say that your personal problems are more important than the country's problems?"

"My personal problems are my country's problems," Ramchandra replied. "My history is this forsaken country's history."

"Not to worry," someone said. "Democracy will make us all prosperous. We'll get rid of all those corrupt politicians, and you'll be able to build a house in Kathmandu, Ramchandra-ji."

"You mean Bandana Miss will raise our salaries? Will you, Bandana Miss?" Shailendra asked.

"Where will the money come from?"

"From Mr. Democracy. He has a vault with millions of rupees."

That brought forth more laughter; then the bell rang in the empty school.

The mourning period for Mr. Pandey ended about two weeks later, and Goma and the children returned to Jaisideval. Spring, with its painted blue skies and brisk sunshine, began to adorn the streets of Kathmandu. Gone were the sweaters, the rubbing of cold palms early in the morning, the families gathered around the single heater in the house. Even though the mornings and nights were chilly, at noon the sun enveloped the city, and people mopped their brows and complained of the heat.

Soon after moving back to Jaisideval, Ramchandra got into the habit of rising early in the morning, bathing at the tap before Mr. Sharma did, and doing push-ups and breathing exercises in the bedroom. "I have to do something constructive," he told Goma. "Otherwise my mind will go dull." Goma nodded. "That's an excellent idea," she said. "You'll become healthier as you age." She was still sleeping with the children, and although Ramchandra hinted a couple of times that she might move back to her bedroom, she ignored him. She didn't mention Malati, but sometimes when they were eating, in the children's presence, she seemed to be thinking of her.

And he did feel energetic every morning after he finished the exercises and drank his first cup of tea. He would take a walk in the neighborhood, stopping briefly to chat with shopkeepers and acquaintances. In the evening, he read while the children played hide-and-seek in the courtyard or carom and cards in the bedroom. Sometimes his thoughts turned to Malati; then he became uneasy and couldn't concentrate on the book he held.

One day, while Sanu and Rakesh were wrestling on the floor over a brand-new pack of cards that Ramchandra had bought them, the shoulder strap of Sanu's frock slipped, and Ramchandra caught a glimpse of her breasts, now like those of a young woman. She caught his gaze and quickly covered herself up and left the room.

"San-di became naked," Rakesh said.

Ramchandra scolded him, saying he shouldn't talk like that about his sister.

He asked Goma whether she had bought Sanu a bra.

"Yes, but she complains that it constricts her, and she can't breathe."

"She's growing. She should wear one." He thought of Mr. Sharma watching his daughter.

"You know how she is."

Maybe he should talk to Sanu, but she'd probably be uncomfortable, talking about such things to her father.

During this time Ramchandra and Goma often went to Pandey Palace, because Mrs. Pandey was having health problems.

Her hands swelled, and she had difficulty walking up and down the stairs. Often in the middle of a family conversation she'd become quiet, and when Goma asked her what was wrong, she said that she was lonely in the house by herself, that the walls were chasing her. She said that at night she heard the voice of her husband. She complained that someone tapped on the floor at dawn, urging her to wake up.

"Why don't you have one of the servants sleep in the house instead of the servants' quarters?" Ramchandra suggested.

"They'd rob me blind at night," she said, and despite assurances from Goma and Ramchandra that they'd been devoted servants for years, Mrs. Pandey was adamant.

Within a few days of this discussion, Mrs. Pandey's health grew worse; it declined so rapidly that people wondered whether Mr. Pandey's soul had indeed been tapping on the floor, claiming his wife. She fainted a few times, which fueled further speculation. Mr. Pandey's sister, a stout woman with deep religious convictions, told Goma that Mr. Pandey's soul had come to her and whispered that he wasn't happy. Goma was upset by this kind of talk. "She's already paranoid," she told her aunt. "And you want to make her more afraid?"

And then one morning they received a phone call from a servant. Mrs. Pandey had collapsed in the garden and was lying there, clutching her heart. Goma urged him to call an ambulance immediately, even though she knew it wouldn't arrive in time. Ramchandra suggested that they call Nalini, but she had accompanied Harish on a business trip to Bangkok. So Ramchandra and Goma rushed to Pandey Palace, where Mrs. Pandey was sitting in her bedroom, her face ashen. As soon as she saw Goma, she began to cry, "Don't leave me alone, please, Mother. Don't leave me alone." Goma held her tightly, as if she were indeed Mrs. Pandey's mother.

That day all the city hospitals had declared a strike, protesting the imprisonment of some doctors and medical students. They did get her to the Teaching Hospital in Maharajgunj, where doctors were examining patients in the open air. Mrs. Pandey was asked to lie on a table, and a doctor, after examining her, said it was most likely that much of Mrs. Pandey's affliction was psychological, although there were signs that she also suffered from diabetes. "She needs to be around her family at this time," the doctor said. "That'll take away some of the paranoia."

Suspicious, because he thought the doctor had arrived at the diagnosis too quickly, Ramchandra said, "Maybe she needs a more thorough checkup?" But the doctor had already moved on to another patient.

Mrs. Pandey clung to Goma as they left the hospital, and when they were back in Pandey Palace, Goma told Ramchandra that they'd all have to move there.

"What are you talking about?" Ramchandra said. "I can't live here."

"And why is that?"

"You know very well why."

"No, I don't," Goma said tersely. "My mother is very ill. She needs me, and you can't take care of the children by yourself. There's no point in paying rent to live in that crummy apartment while this big house is empty."

"Goma."

"Look," Goma said, "this is about my mother. I made a large concession to you not long ago. Have you forgotten?"

"But you know that—"

"Fine, if that's the way you feel, then the children will live here with me, and you can live in the apartment by yourself."

"She's not going to get better any time soon."

"Then she won't. But I'll stay with my mother until . . ." And her voice broke.

He got up and held her, and she leaned against him. "Please. Don't you see? It'll help me if you're here."

"Yes," he said and kissed her on the lips. It was the first time since he'd confessed to her about Malati that he'd held her like this, and he embraced her until she broke away from him, saying that she had to make soup for her mother.

Ramchandra hoped that the one moment of physical proximity would restore their intimacy, but he was wrong. Goma maintained her distance, as if she could smell Malati on him, as if her initial reaction to his confession remained inside her, muted but strong.

Two days later they moved from Jaisideval to Pandey Palace, but not before they had a raucous fight with their landlord, who demanded that they pay a month's rent because they'd not given him advance notice. "This is not a hotel," the landlord said. The shouting match took place in the courtyard, with the neighbors watching from their windows.

"This is an emergency situation," Ramchandra said. "It's one thing that you never took care of the apartment while we lived here. Now the least you can do is let us go in peace."

"What about my peace, then? How am I going to find someone on such short notice?"

"Plenty of people in this damned city are looking for shelter."

They finally reached a compromise. The landlord would let them go if they paid half the next month's rent. The idea was Goma's, who had been sitting on the doorstep, listening to them argue.

"Only because of you am I making this concession," the landlord said to her.

Harish had sent a truck from his company for the move, along with a couple of young men to help, and by evening they'd emptied the apartment. On the final trip, Ramchandra sat in the front of the truck with Sanu, who'd been quiet since she was told that they were going to live in Pandey Palace.

"So, what do you think?" Ramchandra asked her now. These days he talked to her as if she were a grown woman.

"Think about what?"

"About us living in Pandey Palace."

"Since when did my opinion matter?"

"You don't approve?" He noticed a hint of rouge on her cheeks.

"I prefer to live in Jaisideval. I have friends here."

"But you understand your grandmother's problem, don't you?"

Silent, she looked out the window; then she said, "I don't know what to think. They've always made so much about our not having a house of our own, and now we're moving into their house."

"You should feel some pity for your grandmother. She's not what she used to be."

"What do you feel about this?"

The way she asked him, her head slightly tilted, reminded him of Goma. "I am following your mother's wishes. She wants to take care of your grandmother."

Sanu said, "I hope it's not a permanent move."

"I don't think it will be. Once your grandmother gets better, we'll find a place of our own." But he knew his words were unconvincing.

He kept hoping he'd run into Malati in the street, but when he didn't, he wondered whether something bad had indeed happened to Rachana. Sometimes on a rainy day he'd stand by the main door of Pandey Palace, looking at the garden, hoping that the next time the phone rang, it would be Malati. He once ran into Ashok in Ratna Park, and the boy asked him about Malati. Ramchandra had nothing to say. Ashok was waiting impatiently for the exam results, and when Ramchandra told him the results might not be issued for months, maybe even a year, given the political mess, Ashok said, "I don't know what my father will do to me if I fail." Gone were Ashok's mocking smile and small witticisms. He even had a couple of white strands in his hair. The only thing Ramchandra could do was pat him on the back and assure him that he'd pass.

The next afternoon Ramchandra went to Goma, who sat in the living room, darning one of Rakesh's sweaters. Mrs. Pandey was sitting on a sofa nearby, her head resting at an awkward angle against the back, her mouth open. Her health had deteriorated, but her paranoia had diminished. Now, unless she was moved, she sat in one place, mumbling. Her face showed signs of human expression only with Goma; with others, she remained silent, or looked at them quizzically, as if trying to figure out who they were. How quickly things change, Ramchandra thought.

He started to speak to Goma, then changed his mind. Then changed his mind again. He told her that he'd lied to her about that day when he'd gone to New Road to find Malati.

"Why did you lie?"

He couldn't answer, and she didn't press further. She resumed her darning, and after a while said, "So, did you see her?"

He told her that he'd seen Rachana get injured in the stampede.

Goma's hands became still. "How is she now?"

He said he didn't know, that he'd not gone back to find Amrit's house, that he was worried.

"I hope nothing has happened to the child. How could you not tell me?"

"I didn't want you to worry."

"I want to know what's happened to that little girl," Goma said.

"Why don't you go, then?"

"But I can't leave Mother," Goma said. "Any moment something could . . ." She stroked her mother's cheek. "Why don't you go? You were planning to go anyway." Mrs. Pandey tilted her head toward her daughter.

As Ramchandra got up to leave, Goma said, "If Rachana is fine, ask Malati to come for a visit. I want to see the two of them."

She told him to take the car, but he said he'd rather walk. He still didn't feel comfortable in the Pandeys' Honda. The driver was a bit of a snob, and Ramchandra smelled Mr. Pandey inside the Honda.

On the way, he was again beset by anxiety. What would he say to her? Goma wanted to know how her daughter was doing; that's how he'd start the conversation. Then he remembered that he didn't know the exact location of Amrit's house; there were so many houses lining the alley in front of the cinema hall.

Near Tangal, Ramchandra, on impulse, took the lane that led toward Sunrise Boarding School.

At first he didn't recognize Malekha Didi's house. The yard was a mess, filled with garbage and old, cracked furniture. The chicken shed had been demolished and was lying in a heap. On the front porch, two stray dogs were keeping guard over a bone, and Ramchandra had to shoo them away to knock on the door. There was no sound, and he was about to leave. Then he heard Malekha Didi's tired voice ask who was there.

When Ramchandra identified himself, she opened the door. "What do you want, professor?"

She wore a dirty dhoti, and her hair was in filthy clumps.

Even from behind the screen, he smelled rotting food. "Do you know where Malati lives?"

"That whore?" Malekha Didi said. "She left me in this state."

Ramchandra was about to remind her that she'd thrown Malati out. Instead, he asked what happened, waving his hand to encompass the yard, the chicken shed.

Malekha Didi opened the screen door and stepped out. "Everything's gone. Some motherfucker fed poison to my chickens one night, and the next morning they were all dead."

"Who was it?"

"Who knows? Many didn't like my prosperity. And there are lunatics in this city who only need an excuse to loot."

"Where is Malati?"

"She's living in front of Ranjana Cinema Hall with that taxi driver." She described the house.

When he asked whether she was going to get the chicken business going again, she asked whether he would extract some money from his ass to give to her.

He said goodbye to her and walked away as she shouted, "So she left you, a professor, for a taxi driver, eh?" Her vulgar laugh rang inside his head.

Once he reached New Road, however, instead of trying to find Malati's house right away, Ramchandra walked into Ranjana Cinema Hall. He stood in the middle of the compound and turned around casually to face the row of houses across the alley. Malekha Didi had said that Malati's building housed a tailor shop on the first floor. But he didn't see such a sign. He did remember that one of the shops at the bottom was a famous samosa restaurant he'd frequented when he was young. Ramchandra saw the sign: HERO RESTAURANT. Yes, that was the name.

He walked out of the cinema hall and into the restaurant,

where he immediately recognized the proprietor, a dark man with pockmarks. Ramchandra identified himself, and it took a while for the man to remember him, but when he did, he offered Ramchandra tea and samosas, and they chatted about some of the people they used to know. Finally, Ramchandra got around to inquiring about Malati, and the proprietor instantly knew whom he was talking about. "You've come to the right place," he said. "She lives on the top floor of this house. The entrance is through the side door. A pretty girl, but that man of hers is not right."

"Why?"

"I've seen him sit here and eye the girls who enter the cinema hall. Sometimes he walks in there," the proprietor said, pointing toward the hall, "and tries to strike up a conversation. A real Romeo, that guy."

"Are they married?"

"Yes, they got married a few days ago in a temple ceremony."

"Are they up there now?"

"The husband leaves with his taxi early in the morning, but she may be there. Do you know her?"

Ramchandra told him that she was his student. This was a good opportunity to talk to her, but he realized, with a jolt, that it'd soon get dark—and dangerous.

As he was leaving the shop, Malati stepped out the side door, wearing a red dhoti, which connoted her recent marriage. The part in her hair was streaked with vermilion powder. Ramchandra held his breath and stopped. She didn't see him and went down the alley that led to Indrachowk. Ramchandra followed a few yards behind. In Indrachowk she bought some vegetables while Ramchandra maintained his distance. Sometimes he caught her profile, and was disappointed that he saw no trace of sadness on her face or of dissatisfaction with her husband. She was lively and bright, bargaining and chatting with the vendors. When she was finished shopping, she walked back, Ramchandra still following her. He saw that Rachana wasn't with her. Had something happened to the girl? But if it had, wouldn't Malati's grief have kept her from marrying Amrit?

A few minutes after she walked up to her apartment, he climbed the narrow staircase and knocked on the door. A woman opened it, and just as he was asking for Malati, she appeared, with Rachana straddling her hip. Rachana gave out a squeal and babbled something, and a wave of relief washed over Ramchandra.

"Sir," Malati said softly, "did you forget your way?"

He didn't know what to say, so he remarked that Rachana had grown.

Malati wiped her daughter's nose with her hand and said, "She often gets sick these days. I think it's the pollution in the city. Too many three-wheelers and old vehicles."

Ramchandra felt awkward, standing on the landing. "Aren't you going to invite me in?"

The woman told Malati she was leaving, and headed down. "My husband's sister," Malati explained. "She looks after Rachana sometimes."

The apartment had one room and a kitchen, and they sat on the bed. The place was congested but neat. Ramchandra smelled cigarette smoke.

"Tea, sir?"

He shook his head and asked her, indicating Rachana, "You married her father?"

"Yes," she said with a laugh. "Amazing, isn't it? We had a small temple ceremony."

"Are you happy?"

"I am very happy," she said, meeting his eyes as if in challenge.

He asked her about Malekha Didi.

"Oh, she's come around," Malati said. "You know, full moon, no moon. She found out where I live and she came and held Rachana in her arms. She says she misses us. But that's only because her business has collapsed." She paused and then said, "It's hard for her now. But my husband gives her some money every month. He really cares about her."

Ramchandra pitied Malekha Didi. Earlier, she couldn't admit that Malati was helping her.

Malati asked about his family, and he told her everyone was fine except Goma's mother. "Where's your husband?" he asked. "Ajit, is that his name?" Pretending that he didn't recall the name made him feel less vulnerable.

"His name is Amrit. He comes home around this time, to drink tea, and then goes out again. Sometimes he drives the whole night."

Ramchandra noticed a small scar on Rachana's left cheek. "What happened?" he asked.

"An accident," Malati said. "You know how frisky she is."

"Goma would like to see you," he said.

Malati wiped Rachana's cheeks and forehead before saying, "It's probably better if I don't enter your lives again."

He understood and he agreed.

A few minutes later, he said goodbye and went down to the street. In all the noise and the swarms of moviegoers walking toward the cinema hall, he heard someone shout, "Professor saheb! Professor saheb!" In the dusk, it took him a moment to recognize Amrit, with his curly hair and long mustache, at the other side of the alley, trying to get to him through the crowd.

Ramchandra merely waved and walked on, but Amrit pushed people aside and caught up with him.

"How are you, professor?"

"I am not a professor," Ramchandra said mildly. "I am only a schoolteacher."

"What difference does it make? Where are you going?"

"I just finished watching the cinema."

"Oh, we live right here," Amrit said. "Why don't you come for tea?"

"It's getting dark."

Amrit grabbed his arm. Ramchandra noticed the cigarette between his fingers. "Come on, professor saheb. Just for a few minutes. Malati will be very pleased. She keeps talking about you."

What had Malati told her husband about him? Ramchandra wondered. Obviously not everything, or Amrit wouldn't have invited him to visit.

Right near them, in the famous soda shop of New Road, bottles were opened with a pop and the carbonated lemon water sizzled in glasses. The shopkeeper urged Ramchandra and Amrit to move on, because they were blocking his customers.

"How is Malati?" Ramchandra asked as they headed back toward the apartment. He hoped that Malati wouldn't let on that he'd already been there.

"She's fine. The baby is a little sick."

They climbed the stairs, the cigarette smoke drifting down to Ramchandra as he followed Amrit.

"Look who's here, Malati," Amrit said when they walked into the room. "Your professor."

Ramchandra looked at Malati apologetically, and Malati said, "Sir, it's been a long time. Everything well?"

"Everything is fine," he answered.

Smiling, Malati went to the kitchen to make tea, and Ramchandra and Amrit, who was now holding the baby and talking to her in baby talk, sat on the bed. Ramchandra asked Amrit about his driving schedule, about how much he made during a day. Amrit was friendly, talkative.

Malati brought tea, and for a while they sipped in silence. Ramchandra said to Malati, "The results will be out in a few months. Are you still planning to go to college?"

"If I pass," Malati said. "I'm stupid in math, remember? I'm a math monkey."

Ramchandra was embarrassed by the reference.

"Passing the S.L.C. is no good these days," Amrit said. "Even people with college degrees are driving taxis."

"She might find a job as a secretary."

"Who'll take care of the baby?" Amrit said in a friendly tone. "As it is, I drive the taxi from morning to night."

It was dark outside, but neither Malati nor Amrit got up to turn on the light.

Ramchandra said to Amrit, "You should turn on the light. It's hard to see in here."

"No," Amrit said. "Let it be dark. It's the blackout night; haven't you heard? At seven everyone's to turn off the lights, so we may as well wait."

Ramchandra did remember now. The Nepali Congress and the communist parties had called for a ten-minute blackout this evening to protest government killings. Ramchandra peered at his watch. Only a few minutes more, and the entire nation would plunge into darkness.

He was close to the window and could see that some people were burning a tire near the cinema hall. Soon, a strong whiff of scorched rubber floated up. At seven o'clock, darkness enveloped the neighborhood, and whistles were heard. Someone nearby turned up the volume of a cassette player, and a popular

Nepali song blared into the air. Ramchandra, feeling drowsy, wanted to lie down right there on the bed, but he knew he should get going, darkness or not. He forced himself to sit up. "I'd better leave now," he said.

"It's too dark. Why don't you wait for ten minutes? I'll turn on the lights then."

They sat still, and in a few minutes Amrit turned on the light.

"You'll come to visit us again, sir?" Malati asked.

"Of course I will," he said, knowing he wouldn't. "When I have time."

"Give my regards to bhauju and the children."

"Of course."

"My regards too," Amrit said, laughing, "even though I haven't met them."

"Come and see me if you need anything," Ramchandra said. They nodded.

Outside, a procession on the street was chanting, *"Hatyara sarkar murdabad."* Death to the killer government.

A group of policemen stood under a streetlight a few yards away, but they only watched. Ramchandra let the procession pass, then headed home.

"God has protected that little girl," Goma said when Ramchandra told her that Rachana was fine. He mentioned Malati's marriage to Amrit, but didn't say that he'd spied on her before going to visit.

"Will she visit us?" Goma asked.

Ramchandra shook his head, and Goma nodded in understanding.

That night the image of Malati bargaining with the vendors, a smile on her lips, kept returning, and he felt cheated. He imagined her as perfectly contented with her new life—a husband to take care of her and her baby, a husband who had once abandoned her, and who now, in all probability, slept with other women. Her naïveté annoyed him, and he wanted to go back to that house and give her a piece of his mind.

After everyone had gone to bed, he strolled in the garden, trying to calm himself. Despite everything, he loved the garden at Pandey Palace. It was large, with a fountain in the middle and beds of daisies, roses, and sunflowers lining the periphery and filling small plots throughout. A garden table with a bright umbrella sat in a corner; sometimes the family gathered there on Saturday afternoon, and Ramchandra watched contentedly as Sanu and Rakesh ran around nearby. The servants brought glasses of juice or tea and deep-fried snacks, and the afternoon stretched out before them like a pleasant dream.

But it was a mirage, a fantasy, Ramchandra reminded himself. This was not his house, and he felt shame at enjoying its privileges. Mrs. Pandey's health was better, although she still occasionally became agitated when she saw ghosts or heard voices. Her body was weak, and sometimes at the dinner table she'd throw up without warning. One day, at a relaxed moment under the garden umbrella, Ramchandra had broached the topic of finding an apartment of their own, but Goma had refused. "I won't move until she's completely better."

"Maybe Nalini can take care of her for a while," Ramchandra said.

"Nalini can't take care of her. She doesn't know how."

Ramchandra suspected that Nalini and Harish were glad they'd been in Bangkok when Mrs. Pandey collapsed. Nalini did visit almost every day, but she stood at a distance. She never slept over, not even when, one evening, Mrs. Pandey was so weak and paranoid that she was literally frothing at the mouth, and Goma had developed a migraine that, she said, was "splitting her head in two with an ax." Everyone seemed to assume that only Goma was capable of caring for Mrs. Pandey. When Ramchandra tried to do something for his mother-in-law, she pushed his hand away; sometimes she asked Goma who he was. And then there was Harish, who rarely came, and, when he did, was ill at ease, like a nervous schoolboy.

12
. . . .

S
EVERAL DAYS LATER, a son of a bureaucrat
came to Pandey Palace for assistance with his
S.L.C. exams. When Ramchandra told him that it was somewhat early to be studying for the next year's exams, the boy said
that he wanted to pass in the first division, because he had plans
to go abroad for further studies.

For Ramchandra, it felt odd to be tutoring the student in
Pandey Palace, with its enormous rooms and spacious air.
Strangely, part of him longed for the cramped quarters in
Jaisideval, with the deafening traffic and the leaky ceiling.
Now he tutored the student in the large living room, where
his voice disappeared in the expansive space, and he caught
himself speaking too loud. The student, who was smart, understood the problems and their solutions quickly. Ramchandra compared him to Malati, who used to chew on her pencil's
eraser and nod vigorously even when she had no clue about

how to solve a problem. The memory made him smile. Then he remembered, too, the happiness on her face in the market, and he frowned.

Two mornings after he'd begun tutoring, he came down to the living room and found Sanu talking to the student. She was smiling, looking down at her feet and then up at the boy as he talked about his recent trip to Bombay. Neither of them noticed Ramchandra, until he said, "Sanu, don't you need to finish your homework?" Startled, she quickly left the room, but not before flashing another smile at the boy.

In the garden that evening Goma joined him, and they walked around quietly. When they stopped to admire a blooming fuchsia, Ramchandra placed his hand on her back and said, "How long will you remain like this?"

She pretended not to hear him and pulled out some weeds.

"Goma."

"I've done nothing," she said.

"Can you not forgive me?"

"You did what you needed to do. This isn't a matter of accusing and forgiving."

"Then why do you stay so removed from me?"

She turned toward him. "There's a hardening in my heart. I can't help myself."

"Please don't be like this."

"I can't help myself," she repeated.

He cringed a little and then said, "Everyone can be forgiven. Please." He wanted to talk to her about Sanu, to say he was troubled by what he'd seen that morning, that their daughter was growing up too quickly, that he needed Goma to make sense of it for him. But all of that retreated to the background now. Did Goma think that he still longed for Malati? Did he? He couldn't tell. He did know he wanted to see her again, talk to her, ask her once more whether she was happy, and to demand the absolute truth.

That night he dreamed that Sanu, her belly swollen with child, was wandering the streets of Kathmandu, digging into garbage.

People continued to march in the streets, unfurling banners against autocracy, some even with words condemning the king, which left many people aghast. Processions, rallies, and riots became daily events in the city, and police trucks, crammed with helmeted men, hurtled through the streets. People talked in whispers that the king would soon declare military rule. "The army worships the king," people said. "They won't hesitate to massacre the people."

Sanu had started to wear makeup.

"What's wrong with her?" he asked Goma.

"She's growing up. It's natural."

Ramchandra suspected that Sanu was spending time with the bureaucrat's son, Kamal — outside the house. He'd reconciled himself to the fact that Sanu lingered in the living room while he tutored Kamal. But Sanu began to vanish from Pandey Palace for long stretches of time after school in the evening, and when she returned, her face was flushed. The bureaucrat's son lived only a couple of blocks away, which strengthened Ramchandra's suspicions. Sanu had also started sketching images from American comic books that showed two young lips kissing, with hearts floating above them. He showed these to Goma, who simply laughed. When he mentioned his suspicion about Sanu meeting the boy outside, she said, "It's her age. What do you expect her to do?"

Goma's casual attitude baffled him. She acted as if she

herself had been through this; that she understood what her daughter felt. Once again doubt about Goma's past bothered him. Again he wondered why the Pandeys had married her off to him. These days he found himself looking at Sanu sternly whenever she passed by, and she, aware of his critical expression, kept her head down and barely spoke to him. When he was tutoring Kamal, Ramchandra sometimes scolded the boy for minor errors, even though he solved most of the math problems with careless ease.

"If no one controls her, what will happen if something goes wrong with her and the boy?" Ramchandra said to Goma.

"You don't trust your daughter?"

"It's not a question of trust. It's her age. I've seen how she looks at him. Can you guarantee that she'll control herself?"

"Guarantee," Goma said. "I couldn't guarantee that you'd control yourself, and you're an adult."

The next day he discovered in Sanu's schoolbag a letter addressed to Kamal. He hadn't meant to pry, but that evening, after Kamal had left, he was calculating the month's household budget and lost track of the numbers and fumbled around for a pen. When he couldn't find one, he noticed her bag in the corner and looked inside. The letter, written in Sanu's clear handwriting, proclaimed infinite love for Kamal, reminded him of some promises he'd made, then went on about the happy family they would have. It also proclaimed that neither would ever cheat on the other. Ramchandra was stung by the way Sanu had processed his relations with Malati.

When Sanu came home later that evening, he accosted her in the hallway and showed her the letter. If he'd expected her to cower, to make apologies, to run away crying, he was wrong. The skin on Sanu's forehead became tight in anger. She snatched away the letter and said, "I didn't think anyone would have the nerve to go through my belongings without my permission."

"I'm your father."

"Being a father doesn't give you that right," Sanu screamed. "If you were a good father—" She caught herself, then stormed upstairs and slammed her door. Goma came down the stairs and, her hand on the railing at the bottom, said, "Why did you go through her bag?"

"I needed a pen," he said. His knees were wobbly.

"Use your brain, will you?" she said. "You don't go poking around in a young girl's private things. Embarrassing for you, embarrassing for her."

He told her what he'd found.

"You still don't understand. I don't care. Let her do what she wants. She's a good girl." Yes, he thought, but you didn't say that when she didn't like your parents.

After that he stopped talking to Sanu. Actually, it was she who no longer spoke to him. During dinner or when passing each other in the hallway, she turned away, and a couple of times when he started to speak to her, she left the room.

The growing unrest in the city rarely reached Pandey Palace. Busy taking care of her mother, Goma didn't even glance at the newspapers Ramchandra brought into the house. One day, after reading about skirmishes in different parts of the country, Ramchandra asked what she thought, and she said, "I have no time to think about those things."

She wiped the drool off her mother's face. These days, whenever Goma touched her, Mrs. Pandey clasped her daughter's arm so tight that her knuckles turned white.

Perhaps to alleviate the pain of Goma's disenchantment with him, Ramchandra found himself taking a keen interest in what was happening in the country. At school, it was he who now initiated political discussions, often holding a newspaper article in his hand.

"So you've come around, eh, Ramchandra-ji?" Shailendra said. "So now you think if we have democracy, you'll be able to build a house in the city?"

Ramchandra said, "Well, whether I have a house or not, things in this country must improve."

"Dream on," said Bandana Miss.

Mrs. Pandey was rushed to the hospital again because of heart palpitations, and this time the doctors said that her condition was serious and that she'd have to stay for at least a few days. This meant that Goma had to stay with her, and suddenly Ramchandra found himself in charge of the household, a task he didn't relish. The house was too big. Added to it was Sanu's insolence. Rakesh, too, frequently defied his father and got into arguments over petty things. He clearly resented his sister's new lack of interest in playing with him, and he called her names every chance he got. Each morning the servants took Goma's food to the hospital, and each evening Ramchandra went there, carrying her dinner. When Sanu and Rakesh accompanied him, they fought in the car. At the hospital, their faces brightened when they saw their mother, who embraced them and asked questions. Often, Ramchandra excused himself and walked the corridors of the hospital, sometimes stepping out into the cold to smoke a cigarette, a recent habit; he did make sure not to light up in front of the children. The cigarette warmed him, softening the urgency of his thoughts.

Mrs. Pandey was brought home, but her condition was worse. Now she had trouble sitting up. Sometimes Goma had to force open her mother's mouth to spoon in some soup, which dribbled down her chin. Her eyelids had turned blue; she didn't recognize even Goma. Nalini came by occasionally to help, but the strain of the situation appeared to be too much for her, and soon she conjured up excuses for not visiting.

Sanu and Kamal began to see each other in public. People said that they were "holding hands in broad daylight." Rakesh became more and more belligerent, and frequently got into fights with boys in the neighborhood. One day Ramchandra discovered a long chain in his son's room, and when he questioned Rakesh about it, the boy snatched it from his father and walked out of the room. Later Ramchandra learned that the ragtag group he hung out with liked to call itself the Chain Gang.

Goma brooded in the evenings, and the children clung to her, offering her assurance. Ramchandra looked on.

One Saturday afternoon, an argument erupted. Earlier that morning, Ramchandra, on his way to the market to fetch the day's newspapers, spotted Sanu with Kamal in a nearby tea shop, sitting close to each other, their hands entwined. Apart from the brazen defiance of social decency, it was the glaring lipstick Sanu was wearing that infuriated Ramchandra. His impulse was to go into the shop and pull her out by her ear, but he controlled himself.

That afternoon, after a late lunch, the four were sitting under the garden umbrella. Rakesh and Sanu were talking about an immensely popular Hindi actress when Ramchandra, without lifting his head from the newspaper he was reading, said, "She looks like a prostitute. That's why she's popular. That's what makes young girls like you imitate her."

Sanu jumped up from her chair and said to her mother, "Ba called me a prostitute."

Goma's face changed. "What has come over you?"

"You do nothing to control her," Ramchandra said.

"I'm not going to be in anyone's control," Sanu said.

"Whatever the case, you must not call her that," Goma said angrily.

Mrs. Pandey, who had been dozing, raised her head, spittle running down her chin.

It was Rakesh who came to his father's support. "Ba's saying the truth. San-di has changed. She's always with that donkey."

Sanu raised her arm to hit her brother, but Ramchandra grabbed it. "She was with him this morning," he said to Goma.

"Yes, I was," Sanu said. "So what?"

"You let her be," Goma said to Ramchandra. "I don't need this tension."

"Ba, don't make Mother tense," Rakesh said. "Otherwise . . ."

The threatening tone of his voice was like that of a man. "No one needs me in this house anymore," Ramchandra said. "I don't know why I live here." And he walked away, through the gate, and out to the street.

The sounds of the traffic and of children playing in the neighborhood washed over him. He felt as though someone had just died. He'd started all of this. He'd made this web. He'd created this world of alienation, and now it had trapped him.

He walked until his feet could no longer carry him. Inside Jai Nepal Cinema Hall, he sat on the wall that surrounded the compound. A large poster caught his eye: the hero's face close to the buxom heroine's chest, the heroine's mouth open, as if she were singing. From a nearby shop, a radio blared a tune about true lovers separated by this cruel world.

A teenager came over to him and asked, "Need tickets?" He shook his head. Ramchandra watched the moviegoers buying fritters and drinks from the stands. A woman wearing heavy makeup, her sari tied around her waist in such a way as to bare her midriff, eyed him from a few feet away, smiling. He smiled back, only because he had nothing to lose. As if waiting for this cue, she came toward him. "It's not a good film," she said, and leaned against the wall next to him.

For a moment he ignored her, but her presence was forceful, pungent. "What's not good about it?" he asked.

"The dances are horrible."

Beneath the makeup, her skin was filled with pockmarks.

"They all dance the same way," he said. "The same gyration of the hips, the same twitching of lips. What about the plot?"

"It's okay," she said, scrunching her face. "Too much action." She said *action* in English, and seemed to relish saying it.

"What's your name?"

"Rumila." She moved closer. "What's dai's name?"

He hesitated, then said, "Shrinath." He knew no one of that name.

"Are you looking for some action?" she said. This time she turned toward him fully so that her breasts nearly rubbed his hand on the wall top.

"How much?" he asked.

"Depends on what you want," she said. "A hundred rupees for regular. But that depends on what I do." A man wearing tight trousers approached them. She gestured to him, and he walked away. "You look lonely," she told Ramchandra.

Ramchandra looked at the poster, at a young girl sucking on an ice bar nearby, at an old crouching man, his hands behind his back, whistling through his toothless gums.

"I can make you feel better," she said.

"A drink," he said. "That's what I need."

"You don't need me?"

He wasn't aroused by her, but he didn't want to let her go. He imagined she lived in a dark, dingy place, somewhere he could curl up and lose consciousness. "Why don't we drink in your place?" he said. Then he thought better of it and quickly said, "Forget it," and walked away. In Naxal, he found a bar and sat there all afternoon, drinking. The alcohol numbed his thoughts, and by the time he left, he felt as if he'd been anesthetized.

At Pandey Palace, dinner had already started, and everyone became quiet when he sat down at the table.

"Where were you all day?" Goma asked. The smell of alcohol must have hit her; she said, "Drinking during the day? What's come over you?"

He ate without talking. Rakesh stared at him, and Sanu kept her head down. When he was done, he went to his room and lay down. The radio in the kitchen was turned on loud, and the voice of the evening newscaster floated through the house.

All night, he drifted in and out of sleep. Toward morning he woke; his throat hurt. In the bathroom, he vomited into the sink and then lowered himself to the floor. Grabbing the cold porcelain of the sink, he cried for help, but no one heard him. After some time, he came to and dragged himself back to his room. He lay on the bed for a while and got up and knocked on the door to Goma's room. When she appeared, wide-awake, he said he needed to talk to her.

Downstairs, in the living room, he explained that he needed to move out of Pandey Palace.

"Where will you go?"

"I'll find a small room somewhere."

She didn't ask him why he wanted to move, yet he felt compelled to offer an explanation, "Living in this house is doing something to me; I think I'm losing my mind."

"Whatever you wish."

"Don't you care whether I am near you or far away?" he asked in a weepy voice.

"I do, but you have a will of your own. And if that's what'll make you feel better, do it. Preferable to your constant arguments with the children."

They sat quietly. Ramchandra rolled his tongue around his mouth to drive away the taste of vomit.

"I think Mother is going to leave us soon," Goma said.

Ramchandra nodded.

"I don't know what I'll do then."

"We have our own family."

"I mean about the house."

He didn't want to ask to whom the house would go. He knew that the Pandeys had an impressive amount of money in the bank, plus a large chunk of land in the outskirts of Kathmandu. He wanted nothing to do with all this wealth falling into Goma's lap. "I'm going to find a place this morning." She said nothing; she seemed to be already in mourning for her mother.

The entire day Ramchandra scoured the city for a decent room at a reasonable price. He was astounded by the increase in rents over the past few years. Rooms that had no windows or rooms that looked over garbage dumps cost six hundred rupees per month. In one place, near Baghbazaar, he thought he'd found a room that was not exorbitantly priced until he saw, through a half-open door, the other tenants in the house: two hoodlums who were drinking and gambling. He thought of Sanu coming here and immediately crossed the place off his list.

Toward evening, just to delay going back to Pandey Palace, he went to Jaisideval and ended up chatting with the owner of the tea shop. "Something incredible is going on," Ramchandra said. He'd read about how even some government employees were joining the movement. The engineers of Royal Nepal Airlines had stopped working for several hours. Earlier that morning a "pen down" strike had encouraged government workers across the nation to put down their pens and refuse to work. "Government workers going against the government?" the shopkeeper said. "That is remarkable."

Suddenly, Mr. Sharma was at the door, and, in an exaggerated gesture of friendship, embraced him. "We miss you here, Ramchandra-ji," he said. Ramchandra invited him to join him for tea, and they talked.

In the midst of their conversation about the people's anger at the government, Ramchandra confessed to Mr. Sharma that things were not going well for him, and that he had to move out of Pandey Palace into a place of his own. Mr. Sharma took this news calmly, as if he'd known all along what was happening to Ramchandra.

"You should talk to our landlord," Mr. Sharma said. "He's having trouble finding a tenant to replace you."

"When so many people are coming to the city?"

"He's asking such a high price for that dump. What do you expect?"

"I can't pay what I used to. I won't even be using the children's room."

"Talk to him," Mr. Sharma said. "He was telling me he realized now what a good tenant you were. I'm sure he'll be glad to have you back."

"It may only be temporary."

"Don't tell him that."

Ramchandra found the landlord in his house, a block away, watering the tomato patch in his garden. He came over when he saw Ramchandra at the gate.

"Everything all right, Ramchandra-ji? What a pleasure to see you."

Ramchandra asked about the apartment, and the landlord expressed his dismay at not finding a tenant. "Why? Are you planning to come back?"

"Only me. But I can't pay what I used to."

The landlord thought for a moment. "How about if you rent just one room? I'll cut the price in half. But if I find a tenant for the other room, you'll have to share the kitchen and everything."

Ramchandra didn't like the idea of living with a stranger, but he had no choice.

The landlord shook his hand with enthusiasm. "I'm glad you're coming back."

He moved the following day. Since he had to transport only his belongings, and some pots and pans, he did it in one trip in the Pandey car. No one but Rakesh seemed troubled by his departure, and even he tried not to show it. "When will you come to visit?" he asked defiantly.

"It's not as if I'm moving to another city," Ramchandra said. He reached out to pat his son's head, but the boy ducked and moved away. "I'll come by every few days. How about you coming to see your old friends at Jaisideval?"

"Why should I? They probably don't remember me."

"Of course they do. You had good friends. Bastola, Gainey."

Rakesh looked wistful, but only for a moment. Sanu didn't even come down to the driveway.

"Make sure you eat at home," Goma said. "Don't eat in restaurants. You'll get sick." The same servant who had cooked for him before would come by in the morning to prepare his meals.

Back in the noisy apartment in Jaisideval, Ramchandra felt disoriented, as if he'd never lived here before. Yet, at the same time, everything was familiar: the crack in the wall that resembled a lizard, the loose hinge in the kitchen window, the creak of the floor as he walked from room to room. He peeked into what had been the children's room, and wondered how it would feel to wake in the morning and find someone else living there.

Since the servant wasn't coming today, he opened his bag and took out the packets of rice and dal that Goma had packed and took them into the kitchen. He looked out the window to the courtyard, and there was Mr. Sharma, elbows on his windowsill. When Ramchandra's meal was ready, he took his plate to the window overlooking the street. The food tasted good, and he ate slowly, watching the activity on the street. The tea shopkeeper stepped out briefly to stretch, looked up at Ramchandra, and waved. Ramchandra smiled with his mouth full. For now, he didn't want to think about anything, about Goma or the children, about Malati, about what was happening in the city. He wanted to sit right there, enjoying the view of the people on the street. This was home.

But his newfound serenity was shattered a couple of hours later, when the shopkeeper knocked on the door, saying that Goma was on phone, calling about an urgent matter.

When Ramchandra reached Pandey Palace, tension hung in the air. Mrs. Pandey was gasping for breath through lips that had turned blue. She'd been brought down to the first floor, where she lay on a cot, her lips moving as if in prayer. She had refused to be taken to the hospital. "Now it's time for me to go to heaven, to reunite with my Lord," she'd said in a faltering voice. Whether Mrs. Pandey meant God or her departed husband wasn't clear.

Goma held her hand. Mrs. Pandey's eyes fell on Ramchandra, and she raised a trembling hand. He knelt beside her and took her hand. Her eyes rested on his face and then turned toward Goma. Holding their hands, Mrs. Pandey died moments later.

Over the next few days, after Mrs. Pandey had been cremated and the mourning period was under way, friends and relatives came to offer their condolences. Ramchandra held Goma's hand, and she reciprocated with a squeeze, until some word triggered a memory, and she'd disengage her fingers. Ramchandra moved back to the apartment, and Goma and the children stayed at Pandey Palace. At times, he wanted to tell her, "The reason we moved here no longer exists, so why not come back to Jaisideval?" But something about her face told him that he would be rebuked for that suggestion.

The days went by in a haze. Government officials were fired for expressing support for the pro-democracy movement. The king announced the dismissal of the government and nominated a prime minister who had a reputation for being softer. That did not prevent the massacre that took place in front of the palace one day. Antigovernment demonstrators had marched from the city grounds toward the palace, clapping hands in unison above their heads. The police fired tear gas. People ran into the Tri Chandra campus and battered the police with bricks. A few hundred feet in front of the palace, agitators vented their wrath on the statue of King Mahendra. They hung a garland of shoes around its neck, broke its crown. The police fired. People collapsed to the ground. In the stampede, those trying to escape left their shoes and sandals behind, so the road looked like a flea market for used footwear.

One morning Ramchandra woke to loud voices in the courtyard. Bleary-eyed, he went to the kitchen window. Below, some young men were shouting obscenities and punching and kicking Mr. Sharma, who, wearing only his dhoti, was trying to ward off their blows and was crying for help. A small crowd had gathered to the side. Ramchandra rushed down the stairs in his pajamas. In the middle of the staircase, the loose board gave way, and he hurtled down, his head crashing on the floor at the bottom. But it was the pain in his right ankle that made him sob. It was twisted badly and already turning blue. But there was Mr. Sharma, so Ramchandra forced himself to stand, his hand on the wall for support, and hobbled outside.

One of the young men was holding Mr. Sharma from behind while others pummeled him. The man's face was bloody. "Call the police," Ramchandra shouted at the crowd and tried to pry off the arms of the man who was holding Mr. Sharma, even as his own leg was burning with pain. "Why are you beating this old man? Don't you have any shame?"

"This old man, this baje, touched our sister," one young man said. "We'll kill him."

The man holding Mr. Sharma let him go, and he collapsed to the ground. "Save me, Ramchandra-ji! Please save me from them!"

Ramchandra knelt beside him, wincing as the pain shot from his leg to his hip. He looked up at the young men. "What happened?"

One of the men's younger sister, barely fifteen, had come to fetch water at the tap early this morning, thinking there wouldn't be a line. Mr. Sharma had come down and yelled at her, then pushed her to the garden, where he touched her breasts and tried to kiss her. The man got angrier as he related this to Ramchandra, and his feet flew up and landed on Mr. Sharma's face. Mr. Sharma fell to the ground, clutching his face, howling.

"Enough, enough! You can't beat someone like this," Ramchandra said.

"What? And he can go around molesting little girls? Are you like him? Is that why you're defending him?"

"Enough," Ramchandra said. "If he did it, he's learned his lesson." It took a while for him to placate the men, but he finally did, and they left, though not before threatening Mr. Sharma that they'd gouge his eyes out if he even looked at their sister again.

Holding Mr. Sharma's arm, Ramchandra limped up the stairs to his room, where he applied some iodine to the cuts on Mr. Sharma's face.

"I think my nose is broken," Mr. Sharma said. "And something is wrong in here." He pointed to his stomach. "It hurts so much."

Ramchandra wet a towel and began cleaning the man's face. "I'd better take you to the hospital."

"No, no," Mr. Sharma said. "What will I tell the doctors?"

Ramchandra looked at his own ankle. It was swollen. "Why didn't you think of that when you took the girl to the garden?" His voice was cold.

Mr. Sharma looked up at him. "Ramchandra-ji, I . . ." And he began to weep.

"Control yourself," Ramchandra said.

Mr. Sharma kept weeping.

Later, Ramchandra enlisted the help of the shopkeeper to take both of them to the hospital in a taxi. They sat in the emergency room until a nurse took Mr. Sharma away. It was another half-hour before Ramchandra was called. The doctor who examined his ankle said that he'd need an X-ray before he could tell whether it was broken or sprained. Ramchandra had to limp all the way to the other end of the hospital to get an X-ray and had to wait almost two hours before he was given the folder. Then he spent another hour on a rickety bench outside the doctor's office. The swelling didn't appear to be getting bigger, and he found some consolation in this.

The doctor examined the X-ray and said the ankle was only sprained. A cloth cast was wrapped around it, and a strange feeling came over Ramchandra as he limped out of the hospital. "This is good," he found himself saying. "I needed this."

He didn't go to Pandey Palace for a couple of days. He called, but said nothing about his ankle. He hobbled around the city, sometimes even after the curfew, as if he dared the police to do anything to him. And then, back in the apartment, he'd scold himself for being so foolish. What was he trying to prove? At night, when he couldn't sleep, he'd walk around the flat, his ankle numbed by the painkiller the doctor had prescribed. Sometimes he'd stand by the kitchen window and look across the courtyard, half-expecting to see Mr. Sharma at his window, chanting. But Mr. Sharma had gone into hiding, probably too ashamed to show his face in the neighborhood.

Ramchandra sat by the window in his room and watched the street. Often he saw drunks, zigzagging across the night, humming to themselves. Sometimes he saw prostitutes, back from their nightly duties, perhaps hurrying to their children at home. At times, a gang of orphaned children walked by, making a ruckus, banging on old pots or singing loudly the latest cinema song. Ramchandra was filled with a longing that he couldn't describe, nor did he feel the need to. It swirled inside his head, and he recalled some of the intense pleasure he'd experienced when he'd first been with Malati. Then his memories went back even further, to the early days of his marriage, when the mere brush of Goma's finger against his in a public place would make him dizzy. Goma was the most beautiful woman for miles around, Ramchandra was convinced, and he'd watch her until she said, "What are you staring at? Haven't you seen me before?" And he'd say, "Not really."

Ramchandra began to miss his children and Goma and Malati and even his mother. He remembered the hardships she and he had endured during their first few years in the city, and how close he'd felt to her then. He remembered the joy Goma had brought into his life, despite the criticism from her parents, and how happy he'd been when both Sanu and Rakesh were born, their tiny faces shining at him.

He got up and dressed. The night was cool. He walked, with a limp, toward Pandey Palace, even though he knew it'd take him at least an hour to reach it. There was no taxi to be found. The streets were deserted. One policeman approached him in Naxal and asked who he was and where he was going. Ramchandra said he was going home after spending some time with friends. The policeman eyed him suspiciously but let him go.

The dog barked and ran toward Ramchandra as he opened the gate and walked in. He patted the dog and was about to go inside when he saw Goma's figure in the garden, sitting under the umbrella. He walked toward her.

"Somehow I knew you'd come tonight," she said.

"How?"

"Just a gut feeling." She noticed how he grimaced when he sat down. "What happened?"

He told her, but didn't say that he'd been running down the stairs to help Mr. Sharma.

She reached down and checked his ankle. "You should have been careful. I'll go fetch some ointment."

He stopped her. "That can wait." He asked her to sit on the adjacent chair, took her hand, and said, "Listen, you don't have to answer this, but it's been bothering me all the time we've been married. Tell me, why did your parents marry you so late, and to me?"

She laughed softly. "You walked all the way from Jaisideval, with that ankle, at this time of the night, to ask me that?"

"Please, give me an answer."

"What good would that do?"

"It'll satisfy my curiosity."

Under the light from the naked bulb on the side of the house, she twirled the end of her dhoti. "It's really simple. I'd said no to everyone they proposed."

"Why?"

"I didn't like their names or their faces in the photographs I was shown."

"You based your decision on that?"

"Yes. I've always trusted my feelings. And I knew there was someone out there in this wide world for me."

"And that was me? How did I get your approval?"

She smiled. "I fell in love with you when you came here to tutor Nalini. The first day, the moment I saw you sitting on the living room carpet with my sister. There was something about your face—your belief in the world, as if you viewed it with an innocence that would drown all sorrows. At the same time, you looked tired, almost wise beyond your years. I was smitten. I used to walk past the living room just to see your face. I knew you didn't notice me, and that was fine. I had no intention of revealing my feelings. After you left, I'd lie on my bed and fantasize about you. I'd repeat your name. In my dreams you came and held my hand, smiled at me. I fantasized that you'd take me away from Pandey Palace, that we'd elope to India and live in a small hut, and that we'd be constantly in love. But even then I knew that my fantasies would be shattered, that I'd be married to someone of my parents' choosing."

She went on to tell him of the day when a lami woman came

to Pandey Palace and showed her parents a picture of a doctor, a successful heart specialist in the city. From behind the living room door, she heard her parents say yes, even though the doctor was a widower and was nearly forty. But Goma was getting old, and her parents were desperate. "What if she says no to this one too?" her mother said after the lami woman left.

"This has gone on too long," her father said. "We won't get a better offer. I don't want to have a daughter who'll spoil our name by being an old maid."

That night Goma didn't sleep. She was wracked by nightmares about the doctor. In one of them, he opened her belly and left a surgical instrument there. The next morning her mother came to her room and showed her the doctor's picture. "Please say yes, Goma. Please. We've already said yes."

That's when Goma told her that if she married anyone, it would be the math teacher.

"Who? That Ramchandra?"

When her mother realized that Goma was serious, she put her head in her hands. "My God, I can't imagine what your father will say."

"Father can say whatever he wants," Goma said, "but that's my decision. You either negotiate with him, or I'll remain unmarried for the rest of my life."

Her mother left the room, and a few moments later her father barged in, made Goma stand up, and slapped her. "So far I've tolerated everything, all your drama about I won't marry this one, I won't marry that one. But I will not tolerate this. I don't want to spend the rest of my life seeing you work as a servant. That puny tutor. Did he make moves on you?"

Goma held her cheek and said that the tutor didn't know anything about her feelings.

She stopped eating.

Days later, her parents gave in. Well, her mother gave in, and persuaded her husband to save their daughter, who, she said, would waste away and die, and no one married a dead woman.

Ramchandra sat still, hardly breathing. Then he slid off the chair and knelt in front of Goma. He held her hand, and a great sob escaped from him. She reached out and tousled his hair, then drew him close to her breast.

"I am nothing compared to you, Goma," he said.

"Shhhh."

"I don't deserve you."

"I've never idealized you. I just knew what I wanted."

"And I betrayed you."

She held him, and he remained kneeling before her, his face buried in her chest. A breeze circled around them.

13
· · · · · · ·

TWO DAYS LATER a communiqué from the king's press secretary declared that the king had dismantled the one-party Panchayat system; there would now be a multiparty democratic system in the country. The swiftness of this change surprised many. "You mean it's over?" people asked one another. In Pandey Palace, everyone stared in disbelief at the television set.

"What does it mean for us, Ba?" Rakesh asked. Perhaps because of the softness of his mother's expression when his father was there, he'd become polite toward Ramchandra.

"I don't know," Ramchandra said. "More freedom, I suppose."

"Can we have a house of our own now?" Rakesh asked.

"You think the new prime minister will buy you a house?" Sanu said. "Is that what you think? You're so stupid." She often used the English word *stupid* these days, sometimes to refer to herself. She no longer spent time with Kamal; Ramchandra had seen the sadness on her face when she came home after seeing the boy for the last time. But he was certain there would soon be another boy in the picture. Then he would again have to struggle with his overprotective attitude. For now, there was an unspoken truce between him and Sanu. He'd been pleased when, a few days ago, she came to him with a math problem that would be on her forthcoming exam. She didn't make conversation with him as they solved the problem together, but he could sense the change in her feelings about him.

When they heard the shouts of celebration on the street, all of them went down to the gate. People were streaming onto the streets, shouting, "Panchayat system murdabad," "Long live multiparty democracy," "This is the people's victory." They tossed red powder into the air. Lighted candles appeared on the windowsills of the surrounding houses. A procession passed by the gate. People in an open truck shouted their triumph, clapping their hands above their heads. Some people danced in front of the truck, and a hand reached out and grabbed Ramchandra. It took him a moment to recognize the face: Mukesh, the student who'd thrown the dead rat at him. "Sir, sir," he shouted above the noise. "Salaam, sir. I won, you lost. Your Panchayat is gone. The rat is buried." He was laughing, so Ramchandra wasn't sure whether he was serious. Ramchandra said, "Are you going to pass your S.L.C.? Are you going to college?" But Mukesh pulled him over and coaxed him to dance, which he did, much to the amusement of Goma and the children. He soon returned to them, out of breath.

The celebrations continued into the night. Sometimes they heard fireworks; at other times, shouts of victory.

That night in bed Ramchandra watched Goma figure out, on a piece of paper, the household budget. Warm glasses of milk sat on the bedside table. Ramchandra's nightly banana, which he claimed he took for its potassium, lay close by.

"We can't stay here forever, Goma," he said. "This is not our house."

Since that night in the garden, he'd slept here with Goma. Every night he told himself, and Goma, that he'd walk over to Jaisideval, because the rent was going to waste. But every night after dinner he wanted to sleep with Goma.

"What will I do with this big house?" Goma said. The Pandeys had bequeathed the house to her, leaving their land to Nalini.

"I hate it," Ramchandra said. "I've always hated it."

She stopped her calculations and looked at him. He'd half expected her to get angry, as though he'd violated the memory of her parents. "But I have to deal with it," she said. "I grew up here, and my parents lived here."

"We should move," Ramchandra said.

"Where?"

"Back to Jaisideval. Where we're paying rent."

"And what will I do with the house?"

"Sell it; put the money in the children's name, for their college."

"Can Sanu and Rakesh adjust to living in that cramped flat again? With no servants?"

"It'll be hard, but that's the way they've lived most of their childhood."

"All that noise. Mr. Sharma's chanting."

He hadn't yet told her about what had happened to Mr. Sharma; he didn't know why. "Think of it as a temporary shelter. We'll be building a house. Soon."

"The same talk again. Where's the money coming from?"

"I'll take on extra tutees. I'll teach part-time in the evenings. Whatever it takes. Even if we can lay only the foundation of a house, that's a start. Things are changing in this country; there'll be more opportunities."

"You know how lazy you've become since we moved here?" she said. "I can't see you working harder as you get older. So forget about a house. A cramped flat is our destiny. We may as well accept it."

He sprang to his feet. "Are you calling me lazy? I'm not lazy. Look." And he started doing some sit-ups right there. First, she smiled. Then she laughed at the sight of the muscles on his scrawny legs puffing under the strain. "You're such a joker," she said softly, and he thought of their wedding night, when he'd shoved the banana into her mouth.

Now, he looked at the banana on the bedside table. Goma looked at it, too. And they smiled at each other, wondering who was going to make the first move.

EPILOGUE

. . . .

ELEVEN YEARS LATER, during the tense days when the Maoists looted, terrorized, and killed people across the country, and a month before the crown prince obliterated most of the royal family, Ramchandra, his hair turning gray, went on his morning walk to the local market in Kirtipur. He walked regularly now, usually in the morning. A few years ago, he and Goma had built their house in Kirtipur. Goma had sold Pandey Palace to a wealthy Marwari businessman, whose extended family lived there.

The house, built on an incline, was small, with only two bedrooms, so Sanu and Rakesh still shared a room. But it was enough for them, and the air here was cleaner than in Jaisideval. The house also afforded a pleasant view of the surrounding hills, and every morning Ramchandra took his tea to the veranda and enjoyed the scenery before starting his walk.

Soon after the declaration of democracy, Ramchandra had

taken on several tutees, often two or three in both the morning and the evening. Goma finally got her sewing business going. While they were still living in Jaisideval, she set up her Singer machine in the kitchen and began to turn out petticoats, vests, blouses, and lahangas for women in the neighborhood. She'd get up early in the morning, and the steady *chuck-chuck-chuck* of the machine could be heard from behind the closed door. Ramchandra was deeply impressed by her diligence. This was a woman who'd spent the first half of her life with servants who catered to her every wish, yet here she was, in the cold, damp kitchen, bent over her sewing as if hard work was an inbred quality.

It was Goma's income that had made the house possible. And as soon as they moved into it, she'd set up her sewing machine in a room adjacent to the kitchen and gone to work. These days she received orders from a well-known tailoring house in the city, and when she did, she would sew night and day, drinking cups and cups of tea, pushing herself to meet the deadline.

Two years ago, Ramchandra had managed to find a job at a private boarding school, one for children from rich homes. His salary had doubled, but then, so had the price of everything in the city. In the morning when he walked, he noticed the changes taking place all over. Houses had cropped up everywhere; traffic, even in the outskirts, clogged the streets; smoke lingered in the air.

Sanu attended Padma Kanya College, where she was studying Nepali literature. She had become active in some local women's groups, and often marched along the streets, demanding economic and social equality for women. When Ramchandra once saw a newspaper photo of Sanu leading a march, he immediately called his colleagues and friends to let them know of Sanu's growing prominence. What pleased him even more was that after Kamal, she'd shown no romantic interest in men, although quite a few of her friends were boys. Her involvement in women's issues was direct and sincere, and over the years had brought Ramchandra much pride. He acknowledged to himself the subtle astonishment he'd experienced at his daughter's sense of purpose. He was already receiving calls for her hand in marriage, some from quite prominent families. Several of those, however, had been withdrawn when the families learned of her passion for alleviating women's suffering. Sometimes Goma was upset at the withdrawals, especially those from well-known families. But Ramchandra always dismissed them. "Who cares if they don't want my daughter? My daughter doesn't want them. Can you imagine Sanu with a sari covering her forehead like this?" Ramchandra put his right palm above his head and his left palm on his chin, imitating a meek bride, and Goma laughed.

As for Rakesh, he'd barely managed to pass the S.L.C. He hung around the house, listening to Western music, which sounded raucous to Ramchandra. Rakesh had grown into a handsome young man, and he often stayed out late at night with girls, sometimes in the local hotels. Ramchandra couldn't help thinking that had Rakesh passed the entrance exams to get into St. Xavier's School when he was younger, he would be someone else now. But when Rakesh failed a second time, Ramchandra had talked to the Jesuit principal to find out what his son was doing wrong. The principal, a short genial Indian priest wearing what looked like a white robe, had advised him not to be obsessed with this school but to try several other schools in the city that were equally good. Ramchandra had not been convinced, but what else could he do? Rakesh did show a quick understanding of computers; frequently he sat for long hours in front of the one Ramchandra had purchased for him a year ago. Rakesh seemed to understand the machine intuitively, and was often called by friends whose computers weren't functioning well. There's a possibility here, Ramchandra admitted.

Three years ago, Nalini and Harish had divorced, citing mutual incompatibility. Nalini had been tight-lipped about it, even to Goma. Ramchandra thought Goma might try to dissuade her sister from taking that step, but Goma said, "If it's not working for her, who am I to tell her what to do?" The divorce had taken place without rancor, and the couple of times Ramchandra had seen them after the decision, when they were still living together, he'd been struck by how they treated each other as they had before—with formality, with aloofness. Goma was worried that Nalini would not get anything in the settlement, but Harish let her have the house and also settled on her a large sum of money, enough for Nalini to contemplate opening an upscale restaurant in a luxury hotel. Harish moved to Bangalore, where he started a computer software company that, Ramchandra heard, was doing extremely well. Maybe Harish can do something for Rakesh, Ramchandra thought, but he'd have to broach the topic with Goma, and perhaps even with Nalini.

The Kantipur School remained in the same squalid condition, the same puddle-filled courtyard, the same lack of space. A few months ago Ramchandra had dropped by to pay his respects to Bandana Miss, and discovered that she had gone to America to live with her son. Her letters to Gokul Sir, who was now the principal, indicated that she was not happy. Her son had married an American, and, Bandana Miss complained, a black American at that, a habsi, and she wrote that she still wished she had chosen a proper, fair Nepali bride for him. According to her, her son and daughter-in-law were so busy with their work that they didn't have time for her, and she felt lonely and sad. "I'm beginning to think that America is not such a great country, after all," she wrote. As the principal and Ramchandra were talking about Bandana Miss, Shailendra came into the staff room. He greeted Ramchandra warmly and asked about his family without any hint of his previous sarcasm. When Ramchandra asked about his, Shailendra smiled. "You don't know, Ramchandra Sir?" Ramchandra shook his head. "I ended up marrying Namita," he said. Ramchandra congratulated him and asked how she was doing. "We have a small baby girl." He told Ramchandra that Namita had continued to see him even after her parents whisked her out of school, and ultimately her parents had relented. "Of course, our castes didn't match," Shailendra said, "not to mention that I am a mere schoolteacher and her parents are very rich, but they have accepted me, wholeheartedly. In fact, I have a feeling that I'm their favorite son-in-law."

Today was Sanu's birthday, and Ramchandra, who wanted to buy some goat meat, went to his usual butcher. While the butcher was cutting the meat, Ramchandra heard a voice that made him swivel his head. To his left, a few yards away, was a woman inspecting some tomatoes and haggling with the vendor. Although her back was to him, he knew immediately who she was. She turned slightly and he saw her profile. There were new lines under her eyes, her chin was no longer smooth, and she'd put on some weight. The butcher handed him the meat in a plastic bag, and he paid and was about to walk over to greet her, when something held him back. It was the young girl standing beside her. She had the same face, the same slim nose. Rachana noticed him staring; she stared back and then looked away.

Malati finally bought what she wanted, and she and Rachana

moved on. He followed, still thinking he'd say something—call out her name, shout namaste, tell her that he was sorry she hadn't passed her S.L.C. that year. The day the exam results were published, he'd looked for her number in the newspaper. It wasn't there. Ashok's was.

A few yards away, Malati stopped to talk to a woman, who exclaimed that she hadn't seen her in years. Ramchandra, too, stopped. He looked in the window of a sari shop and heard Malati tell the woman that they had moved to Birgunj, where Amrit had started a garment factory. But the factory hadn't done well, and they were back in the city, with Amrit again driving a taxi. "It's difficult," Malati said to the woman, "but we hope to buy the taxi from the owner." They continued chatting, and Ramchandra continued to examine the sari shop until the owner came out and asked him whether he was interested in buying anything.

Malati was still talking to the woman when Ramchandra passed them. He deliberately walked slowly so that she would see him and call out, "Sir, sir," and he would turn around and exclaim his pleasure at seeing them and pat Rachana on the head. But nothing happened. He kept walking, and after about a hundred yards, he turned around. She was no longer there.